OF SIDEARMS AND DINNER JACKETS

OF SIDEARMS AND DINNER JACKETS

A Novel

By
ROBERT DEWAR

Copyright © 2023 Robert Dewar

The moral right of the author has been asserted.

Apart from any fair dealing for the purposes of research or private study, or criticism or review, as permitted under the Copyright, Designs and Patents Act 1988, this publication may only be reproduced, stored or transmitted, in any form or by any means, with the prior permission in writing of the publishers, or in the case of reprographic reproduction in accordance with the terms of licences issued by the Copyright Licensing Agency. Enquiries concerning reproduction outside those terms should be sent to the publishers.

This is a work of fiction. Names, characters, businesses, places, events and incidents are either the products of the author's imagination or used in a fictitious manner. Any resemblance to actual persons, living or dead, or actual events is purely coincidental.

The manufacturer's authorised representative in the EU for product safety is Authorised Rep Compliance Ltd,
71 Lower Baggot Street, Dublin D02 P593 Ireland (www.arccompliance.com)

Matador
Unit E2 Airfield Business Park,
Harrison Road, Market Harborough,
Leicestershire. LE16 7UL
Tel: 0116 2792299
Email: books@troubador.co.uk
Web: www.troubador.co.uk/matador

ISBN 978 1 80514 159 4

British Library Cataloguing in Publication Data.
A catalogue record for this book is available from the British Library.

Printed and bound in Great Britain by CMP UK
Typeset in 11.5pt Adobe Garamond Pro by Troubador Publishing Ltd, Leicester, UK

Matador is an imprint of Troubador Publishing Ltd

In memory of my pioneer great-grandparents,
Robert and Maggie.

PART ONE

Chapter One

During the passage aboard the British India liner through the Red Sea (which saw three nights pass), Michael Hood barely went on deck. When he did, he saw the white paint on the stanchions bubbling in the heat, and due to the extreme humidity and the salt air, he felt almost instantly sticky and moist beneath his white linen tropical suit. During the day, and well into the evening, Michael sought shelter in the dry, cool, air conditioning of the ship's first class lounge, dining saloon, smoking room and bar. But some hours after nightfall (how fast the sun plummeted towards the horizon), having dined below, he might take a cigar and a whiskey out on deck, where he could feel a whisper of air from the movement of the vessel through the water, and the temperature may (he told himself) have been a few degrees cooler.

It was then, as he gazed out at a sea dark and smooth as obsidian, beneath a sky glowing with myriad stars, with only a rare light from a small boat breaking the monotony of the velvety night, and a few tiny pin pricks of light from distant settlements on the Red Sea's western shore (for the ship charted a course well clear of the treacherous shoals of the eastern shore), that Michael contemplated not only the immediate future, and his coming visit to Equatoria to meet up with his friend, Patrick Hepburn, but the past also.

Michael Hood contemplated the past one and a half decades which, while comfortable enough, had seemed for year after year to lack in – in what, exactly? Perhaps "definition" was the word he sought. The past had lacked in definition since the end of the War. The War had been a terrible thing, and it had given rise to nightmares which still sometimes visited him, but oh my gosh, how alive, how vital, how deeply embedded in the warmth of comradeship, he had felt during those war years! Michael had joined the Army aged nineteen in January 1940, as a second lieutenant, and by May 1943, with the final surrender of Axis forces in North Africa, he had achieved the rank of major. Exercising his duties towards his men, making tactical decisions with life or death consequences, carrying the weight of his responsibilities easily, Michael had felt fulfilled as he was never to feel in the years following the War. Or was it simply his youth that Michael was missing? His young manhood had been spent in the company of other soldiers, all working towards the achievement of a single, noble goal, and now, aged forty, he sometimes felt that his life lacked purpose, and what purpose it possessed, was selfish, of little benefit to others.

On the second night in the Red Sea, as Michael stood on the first class promenade deck, they passed another passenger liner (which was as brightly lighted as the SS Uganda itself, aboard which Michael was making his voyage to Port Hardinge on the East African coast). The passing ship was festooned in a blaze of light as it headed north up the Red Sea towards Suez, the Canal, and the Mediterranean. There was something very moving about the sheer brilliance and splendour of this passing ship; such a brave, bold defiance in the vastness of the night.

They exited the Red Sea via the Bab al Mandab (the Gate of Tears), and rounded the Horn of Africa, then the ship began its journey down Africa's east coast. When the ship docked at Port Hardinge, the colony of Equatoria's chief port (and the only one capable of taking large ships), the temperature by noon was over

Chapter One

eighty-nine degrees Fahrenheit, with a humidity of eighty percent. Michael had packed two white linen suits, one of which (along with a Panama hat) he was now wearing. If he had been planning a lengthy stay on the coast, he would, he thought, have needed at least one more linen suit, for the heat and humidity meant they had to be cleaned and pressed frequently. But Michael was going up country. None the less, he enjoyed what he saw of Port Hardinge, gathered beneath the protective loom of Santa Maria, the massive fort built by the Portuguese. Known as Mina' alSalam, the port had for centuries been an Arab entrepôt. The Arab influence was clear; in the architecture, and in the look and the dress of the people. It was January, and the north-east monsoon winds had always brought trading dhows from Oman, the Persian Gulf and even India, to the East African coast in December and January. From the deck Michael could see – even now, in 1960 – a great many trading dhows in the port. He thought the big baghlahs in particular were very beautiful, with their low, raked prows, twin, usually forward-raked masts, and high poops. They were just beginning to be motorised.

Patrick Hepburn, who, like Michael Hood, was unmarried, was waiting for him as he disembarked. A tall, dark haired man, and somewhat larger than Michael remembered him, he was a year older than Michael. They had been at school together in England. With Patrick was a young woman – perhaps twenty-five years old – whom Michael did not know. She was not particularly tall, but she held herself so gracefully, her carriage so erect, and her features were so even, that Michael was taken aback by her beauty.

'Old chap! How good to see you!' Patrick declared. The two men shook hands. Michael was struck by how much weight Patrick had gained. And he could not fail to notice Patrick's florid countenance, and the network of tiny broken veins around and on either side of his nose. His grey eyes seemed to lack some spark which Michael only knew he had been expecting because he could no longer find it. The young woman looked on with a slight smile.

'This is Marjory, one of my Hepburn cousins – of some degree.' Patrick smiled fondly at her. 'Her people have the next farm along from us.'

'How d'ye do,' Michael said, smiling, and shook her hand, which was warm, very slightly moist due to the heat and humidity, and which returned his grip firmly.

'Very well thank you. How was your voyage?'

'Not bad at all.' Michael was still smiling foolishly at her. What a smashing girl! Her hair, gathered in a loose chignon beneath a large sun hat, was a lustrous gold, from what Michael could see of it. She had, Michael thought, a most appealing slim neck. She wore a sleeveless cotton print dress. She was wearing no jewellery, other than a wrist watch; neither engagement nor wedding ring, Michael was quick to notice. Her bare arms, her calves and her face were tanned a golden brown. But Michael could not see her eyes, which were hidden behind dark sun glasses.

Patrick was dressed in a safari tunic, with wide, starched shorts reaching to the knees, and long socks below them. On his feet were country-made suede leather pukka boots, known to the Afrikaner community as *"velskoene."* He wore a slouch hat with a leopard skin hat band.

Once the group had left the customs hall, Michael's luggage being pushed by a porter on a trolley behind them, he saw a tall, middle aged Somali in a white *kanzu*, with thin, Nilotic features, standing a little distance away. With him was a young black man wearing khaki shorts and what may once have been one of Patrick's shirts. Speaking *Kiswahili*, Patrick instructed them to load the *Bwana's* luggage in the *gari nguvu*. This was a short wheelbase, open backed, Series 2 Land Rover, toward which the two black men took Michael's suitcases and steamer trunk. Alongside it was parked an enormous Chevrolet station wagon, imported from the United States, for it had left hand drive.

'I've made a booking at the Imperial,' Patrick told Michael. 'That way we can set off early tomorrow morning and reach Namuri by late afternoon.'

Namuri, the colony's capital, was located about three hundred miles inland, at an altitude of almost six thousand feet above sea level. The road between Port Hardinge and Namuri was surfaced with laterite soil, a surface that the colonists knew as "murram." This surface presented no difficulties unless it rained very heavily, then it became extremely slippery. But the short rains were now over. The road surface should be good for their journey.

Over ice cold Tusker lagers, the glasses beaded with moisture, conversation between the two men consisted for the most part of school days reminiscences. Marjory, who was drinking a shandy, looked on. 'How pretty she looks,' Michael thought.

'We read occasionally in the English papers of the troubles in Equatoria,' Michael said to his friend after a while. 'How bad are they really?'

'*Wanaume wa Chui*,' Patrick replied. 'The Leopard Men. The situation is more serious than it was; the Chinese are beginning to arm them now. There has been an increase in the number of road ambushes, and several more outrages on isolated farms; two old people were murdered on their farm about twenty miles from us. It's peaceful down on the coast, of course, but inland, especially in the Highlands, most of us go around armed. At *Mahali pa Kupumzika* we do feel rather vulnerable, because our land is bounded to the east by the Nyahurari Forest, and the swine have camps in the forest.' Patrick frowned angrily. 'Half our labour force has probably sworn the *kiapo*.'

Michael looked puzzled.

'The *kiapo* – taken the *Wa Chui* oath,' Patrick explained. He gulped at his beer and wiped his mouth with the back of his hand.

Michael lighted a cigarette. 'Has the Emergency begun to affect trade and commerce?'

'Yes it has, dammit! Lorry drivers – they're usually Sikhs in the Colony – wont drive now without a man riding shotgun with them, and this has put up haulage costs. Since the branch line between Jiljil and Jackson Falls was blown up, and a train derailed – you must have read about it, there were two fatalities – an Equatoria Regiment machine gun detachment has always been placed on an open wagon in front of trains travelling on from Namuri, as far as Port Caroline on the Lake.'

'Things seem worse than I had imagined,' Michael commented. 'But the road to Namuri is safe, is it?'

'Oh yes, you need have no worries on that score. But we are armed. There's a rifle in both cars, and both Marjory and I will be wearing our sidearms from Namuri onward.'

Michael smiled at Marjory and changed the subject. 'Do you do mixed farming, like Patrick?' he asked her.

'Yes. We have a large dairy herd, like Patrick, and we grow barley and maize. We also manage to grow some wheat – much of our land lies at a lower altitude than *Mahali pa Kupumzika*.'

Michael had yet to see Marjory smile fully, although he remembered that half smile on her face when he had been introduced to her. Michael would have liked to have heard her laugh.

'So, I gather that you and Patrick were at school together in England,' Marjory continued. Did you serve together during the War?'

'Oh no. I was with a tank regiment. Patrick was with intelligence. The last time I saw Patrick was when the Pencaitlands were on leave in Britain – about five years ago, I think. We met in London.'

Michael turned towards Patrick. 'You were on your way up north, weren't you – to visit family in Scotland?'

'We both have lots of relations in Lothian. It's Hepburn stamping ground,' Marjory volunteered.

Chapter One

Michael smiled at Marjory again. 'Clan territory, eh? Patrick and I hadn't seen each other more than once or twice before that since we were both in North Africa during the War. During the North African campaign we ran into each other in Alex.' Michael looked pensive. 'In fact, if you think about it, we have not seen much of each other since leaving school.'

Patrick's invitation for Michael to visit Equatoria had come as a surprise to him. It was his first visit to Africa – if you discounted North Africa during the War. Michael had recently completed writing another novel when he received Patrick's invitation, and he had felt that a visit to Equatoria would be interesting, especially in light of the stories one read now in the British press about the Emergency. And he looked forward to seeing Patrick again; Patrick, who had been his best friend at school. Michael could have flown to Equatoria, but he had no great liking for air travel, while he experienced a positive delight in ships and boats, so he had made the long, and for the most part, very enjoyable and relaxing voyage from Tilbury Docks to Port Hardinge aboard the British India liner. And he could, from Port Hardinge, have taken the train up country, but Patrick had seemed keen to meet him as he disembarked, so they would be driving up together by car. Now (for Patrick seemed to be louder than he remembered), Michael found himself wondering how much Patrick might have changed, and whether being stuck in a car together for many hours was such a good idea after all. But there was Marjory's presence to make the journey more interesting!

Some distance away, from the Arab quarter, the Muslim call to evening prayer came to Michael's ears. He was reminded of Cairo during the War. The brief equatorial dusk – there seemed to be minutes only between daylight and nightfall – would soon be overtaken by night. Patrick suggested they go in to dinner.

Chapter Two

Patrick did not speed along the untarred road towards Namuri, although the big car could safely have gone much faster. The Land Rover, which Karim, the Somali manservant, drove, fell a long way behind, in order to avoid the dust raised by the Chevrolet. They passed the occasional heavily laden lorry grinding along, laden with produce from the Highlands for export by sea, or transporting imported goods inland, but for the most part, imported goods, and produce for export, was transported by rail. There were very few other cars on the road. Once they had gained in altitude and left the intensively cultivated, well watered coastal belt behind them, there was little to be seen on their journey but wilderness ("Nothing but *bundu*," as Patrick said). It was a terrain of sometimes dense growth, alternating with stands of open grassland, and dotted with acacia trees. However, at one point they came across heaps of elephant dung, of recent origin, for it was not yet broken up by small scavengers.

As they drew nearer to Namuri, having gained the central plateau, *shambas* (small native farms) and communities of mud walled, thatch roofed huts, became more frequently seen. Maize – what the colonists (having borrowed the name from the Afrikaner community) called *"mielies"* – was the dominant crop. They had broken the journey half way to Namuri at the dak bungalow at Sultan Murad, where a dining room for European travellers existed, and here they had eaten lunch.

'You would probably have been more comfortable by train,' Patrick remarked over their chicken curries, 'but the journey would have taken far longer, and I doubt you would have eaten any better. This curry isn't bad, is it?'

Michael, who was enjoying the curry, which was served on a bed of rice, with a variety of condiments, such as fruit chutney, and a number of side dishes (including diced tomato, grated coconut and sliced bananas), agreed. Both men were drinking Tusker lager to help wash down the fierce curry. Marjory was drinking Coca Cola.

Michael saw no evidence of the Emergency in Namuri, which was a busy town, with a great deal of traffic moving on the wide streets. There were surprisingly few black faces to be seen, but a great many Indians. It was a town as yet free of high-rises; few of the buildings were taller than four or five stories high. Most, unless (as was often the case) they were built of cut, dressed stone, were plastered brick painted white. Patrick had made reservations for them at the New Cedric Hotel, and that evening, about an hour after sundown, the three of them were sitting in the restaurant at the Thorn Tree Boma.

'Cheers!' declared Patrick, as he raised an inevitable glass of cold Tusker lager to the other two.

'Cheers, Patrick, cheers Marjory,' answered Michael.

'Cheers,' Marjory responded. She too was drinking a Tusker lager this evening. 'I'm a lucky girl, aren't I – sitting here with two such eligible bachelors at my side.' She smiled broadly, almost a grin. Michael was astonished.

'I'm not sure that I'm very eligible,' he retorted, a smile on his lips. 'I've lived alone so long I've picked up a lot of bad habits.'

'Nothing a good woman couldn't put straight, I'm sure, Michael,' Marjory responded.

What had got into Marjory this evening? She was being positively playful, almost flirtatious, and she had shown no indications of possessing a playful or flirtatious temperament during the long drive up from the coast. Perhaps she had not been feeling well, and she was now beginning to feel better?

Patrick however did not seem very pleased by this latest mood of hers. A frown crossed his face.

'Pat tells me you write historical novels,' Marjory addressed Michael. 'I do not think I have read anything of yours. Name me some titles, if you would.'

'Well . . . uhh . . . *"Fanfares and Drumbeats"* was my first. It was set in Britain and Europe during the Napoleonic Wars. Then there was *"Rajas and Ruffians,"* set in India in the eighteenth century. That gave birth to a trio of adventures set in India, in which I followed the generational story of the British family the reader first met in *"Rajas and Ruffians."*

'I certainly haven't come across them,' Marjory interjected with a laugh. It was a very attractive laugh, Michael thought: light, mirthful, completely unaffected. 'But I like their titles. Do your stories earn you a lot of money, Michael?'

'Really, Marjory!' Patrick exclaimed, the frown back on his face. 'You don't go asking a chap whether he earns a lot of money!'

'Oh, Pat! I'm sure Major Hood knows that it's just my fun.' She smiled broadly again, a smile barely short of a boyish grin. 'You see, I know that you held the rank of major during the War. I wonder, do you also miss the War, like so many men do?'

She was teasing him, Michael thought. Strangely, he was not minding it much. And what a pretty tease she was, her features golden and ruddy, her hair gleaming in the light cast by the oil lanterns on the tables and fixed to the walls. But how had she guessed that he missed the War?

Chapter Two

'I miss the camaraderie of the War years,' Michael answered. 'I miss the friendships. But no one calls me "Major Hood" anymore, I do assure you.'

Marjory's face lost its slightly spiteful look of amused good humour. 'I think I can understand how one might feel nostalgic for one's time in the Army,' she responded. 'I'm sorry, I shouldn't have been teasing you.' (So she had been teasing him!) 'Can you forgive me?' She smiled again – this time, a restrained, rather shy smile.

'There's nothing to forgive, Marjory.' Michael raised his glass. 'Your good health.'

Marjory inclined her head.

'Well, how about we order some supper?' suggested Patrick. He looked around him. An African waiter wearing a snowy white *kanzu*, with a black sash around his waist and a black fez on his head, stood not far away. Raising his voice and clicking his fingers, Patrick called, *'Kuja hapa!'*

The waiter approached their table. *'Ndiyo Bwana?'* he said.

'Leta ya menu,' Patrick demanded. After the waiter had brought them a menu each, the men both ordered large sirloin steaks with potato chips, sautéed green beans and onion rings. Marjory also ordered a sirloin steak, but she had what was listed on the menu as a "lady's helping." The three travellers shared a bottle of South African red wine. Michael followed his steak with a peach melba (the peach was tinned, and came from South Africa), and all three of them then helped themselves to some cheeses from the cheese platter.

'Some of these cheeses come from *Mahali pa Kupumzika*,' Patrick remarked.

'Really?' Michael responded. 'You produce cheeses on the estate?'

'Oh yes, we have a dairyman, he's an old man now – a Native who was trained by an English dairyman when I was a boy – in charge of the operation, and we supply cheeses throughout East Africa,' Patrick elaborated.

The coffee they drank after the meal was excellent. It was grown in the colony, and Michael remarked that he had rarely tasted better coffee. The two Equatorians, like Michael (whose culinary tastes had not matured a great deal since his days at school), had simple tastes, but Michael, unlike most of his compatriots, had a fondness for good coffee, properly prepared. Perhaps this came from living in Soho, where one could obtain good coffee day or night. The three of them sat talking for about forty-five minutes after their meal. Marjory was interested in Michael's life in London. Michael thought his life there was rather dull, but it did not appear to seem so to Marjory. Michael was to realise over time that for many colonists, life in the imperial capital was of huge fascination. Michael had many questions to ask both Patrick and Marjory about the colony, and he had questions for Patrick about *Mahali pa Kupumzika*, its management and economy. Marjory was nursing a brandy; Patrick and Michael were drinking Scotch whiskeys. Each was puffing on a cigar.

The Land Rover driven by Karim, with his young native assistant, set off at dawn the next morning. The Europeans, however, ate a leisurely breakfast, recommencing their journey at about half past eight. Marjory appeared to have reverted to her quiet, somewhat withdrawn mood. Patrick too was somewhat taciturn this morning. Both of them were now wearing holstered revolvers on their hips. A powerful looking rifle lay on the car's back seat, alongside Marjory. The countryside after they had left Namuri behind them, Michael was thinking, became increasingly interesting and attractive the further they drove. Periodically, farms, often with lush, artificially irrigated paddocks in which horses and cattle grazed, and broad, naked fields of red soil which were devoid of crops at this time of year, could be seen in the rolling hills. There were tracts of indigenous forest between the farms. After some time on the road they saw a large body of water to their left – calm, peaceful waters reflecting the deep blue of the sky, in which a spreading blush of pink at one end indicated the presence of flamingos – which Patrick told Michael was named Lake Laivasha. They passed through the tiny settlement of Laivasha. About forty-five minutes later they reached the town of Jiljil, whose main street was tarred, two lanes wide, and on either side were wide dirt verges, used by cattle, mules and horses. The dirt verges were planted with very tall eucalyptus trees, which dropped great long curling strips of pale peeling bark on the ground beneath them. Beyond the trees either side was a pavement, lined with commercial buildings, some built of brick, one or two of the modern ones of ugly concrete, a few so old that they were built of wood, or even of corrugated iron. Those built of brick were often two stories tall. They were usually plastered and painted white, and had painted, corrugated iron roofs shading the pavement below. The most prominent of these brick built buildings was the Jiljil Hotel, whose plastered walls were painted white. It was set back from the pavement, and had a covered veranda running its full length. Michael could see a number of Europeans seated at tables on the veranda. Most of them had tall glasses of beer in front of them.

'Jiljil is our nearest town,' Patrick told Michael. 'There are several Indian *dhukas*.'

'*Dhukas?*' asked Michael.

'Shops,' Patrick responded. 'The shops around here are mostly Indian-owned.'

At Jiljil they left the Namuri – Port Caroline main road, and headed north north-east. European farms, mostly given over to cereal crops and dairy farming, so Patrick told Michael ('But the fields are awaiting ploughing and harrowing, the land is fallow right now,' Patrick commented), dominated the landscape, but stretches of indigenous bush – acacia trees, scrub and grassland, with frequent tracts of dense forest – were commonplace between the farms. The road itself was of red murram dirt, and was heavily rutted in places. Patrick was driving very much slower than he had been doing on the main road. 'During the rains you need a four wheel drive for this road,' he remarked. The road began climbing gradually after a while, and several times, it doubled back suddenly on itself, climbing sharply, before continuing on its way.

'We're leaving the Valley behind,' Patrick remarked.

After following this route for about twenty-five miles (and Michael had a distinct impression of altitude gained), they turned off the road at Ol Kamau (which consisted of nothing but a native trading store and a few shacks), onto a narrow single track road, heading east, and six or seven miles further on, the road still climbing gradually, they came across a painted signpost reading *"Mahali pa Kupumzika"* and continued following the single track dirt road (which was now very well graded) to the east-south-east, heading deeper into the hills, ascending steadily. Striking red flame lilies grew alongside the edge of the road. They passed an old man with a donkey cart coming towards them – *'Jambo! Jambo Bwana!'* – and once in a while they came across a native on foot, usually an old man (sometimes alone, sometimes accompanied by an adolescent boy), who clasped his hands together and bobbed his head at the passing car.

'These are all our people,' Patrick remarked. 'We've been on Hepburn land since we saw our signboard.'

They were driving through uncultivated land, much of it forested. ('Yes, we have a lot of leopards on the estate,' Patrick answered Michael's question. 'The *Kiswahili* for "leopard" is *"chui,"* thus *"Wa Chui"* – the Leopard Men.') But after a while they began to pass bare fields of red soil, awaiting preparation for the planting of maize with the coming of the long rains in March. In due course these bare dirt fields gave way to tracts of bright green, irrigated lucerne, grown for animal feed, and then to large grassy meadows, in which dappled black and white Friesian cows grazed. In the distance, a large house came into view. Nearer the house they drove past extensive paddocks, in which handsome horses grazed. Michael, who had visited the United States a few years earlier, thought that the terrain showed similarities with some of the North American landscape. There was little here that was especially tropical African in feel – other than that the sun was so high in the sky, it cast almost no shadows.

The weather was pleasant; warm but not excessively so. It was of course the altitude which accounted for the clement climate; they were about eight thousand feet above sea level, Patrick had told him. The gardens in front of the house (an enormous, double story building of cut and dressed stone, with tall chimneys, and dormer windows in the shingled roof) were bright with colour. Flame trees – brilliant splashes of scarlet blossom – shaded the well kept lawns. A large, many branched cedar (a true Cedar of Lebanon; *Cedrus Libani*) grew to one side of the house. Banks of blue and purple hydrangeas grew below the veranda in front of the house. Roses – white, yellow, and all the permutations of red – and scarlet cannas, along with gladiolus, begonias, and huge dahlias, filled the flowerbeds, which were bordered with marigolds, petunias, delphiniums, hyacinths, freesias, pansies and irises. At the bottom of the gardens, where the trees became more numerous, grew red, purple, and white azaleas. Growing up the stone pillars supporting the long veranda roof were pink, purple, and mauve bougainvilleas.

'What a beautiful place,' Michael said. 'I never knew how lovely your home was, Patrick.'

'That's thanks to my mother,' Patrick responded. 'She began the gardens as a young bride just after the Great War, which was when my father built the house. But Dad came out here in 1896. This land has belonged to my family since the turn of the century.'

Patrick had halted the car on the gravel drive below a wide

flight of stairs which led to the veranda. The tall Somali in his white *kanzu* came out of the house, and three dogs bounded towards the car – a pair of Rhodesian ridgebacks, and an Alsatian.

'That's good,' Patrick commented. 'I see that Karim has arrived safely.'

A woman, probably in her late sixties, appeared on the veranda. 'Oh Darling,' she declared. 'I am so glad you have made it safely home. One never knows these days.'

Patrick, Marjory and Michael climbed the stairs to the veranda, the dogs sniffing Michael's legs. Patrick kissed his mother on the cheek and said, 'Mother, you remember I often mentioned Michael Hood in my letters from school. Michael, this is my mother, Lady Fiona Pencaitland.'

'How d'ye do, Lady Pencaitland,' Michael greeted her. She smiled and extended her hand, which Michael shook.

'Of course I remember Patrick telling me about you, Michael. You are most welcome.'

Lady Pencaitland (Patrick was himself correctly titled Viscount Winton, for his father was an earl) had her grey hair piled loosely on top of her head, but wisps of hair had escaped the pins and clips which kept it there. She was about five feet tall, rather slim, with patrician features. Michael thought that her face had the sort of bone structure which would remain beautiful no matter how old she grew. She had a slightly distrait air. 'Karim? Where are you?' she said, looking vaguely to either side.

'I am here, *Msaba*,' the Somali answered, and stepped forward.

'Oh there you are. You must show *Bwana* Michael his room.' She turned to Michael again. 'Come back downstairs after you have cleaned up – one gets so grubby on a long journey, don't you think? – and Karim will show you where the dining room is. I think *Mpishi Moja* has something cold laid out for the three of you.'

'You are hungry, aren't you Michael?' Patrick grinned at him.

Chapter Two

It was the first entirely carefree grin Michael had seen from his friend since meeting him at the dockside yesterday. There was no doubt that Patrick felt more relaxed now that he was home again.

'Have you taken *Bwana* Michael's luggage to his room, Karim?' Patrick asked the Somali manservant.

'*Ndiyo, Bwana Kidogo,*' Karim replied.

'Good. I'll show *Bwana* Michael to his room. You go check on the lunch.'

'*Ndiyo Bwana.*'

'Will you be joining us, Mother?' asked Patrick.

'Oh no. There was something I had to do. It will surely come to me in a moment,' Lady Pencaitland replied.

'Right-O. Follow me, Michael.'

Chapter Three

'The dining room is through there, Michael,' Patrick said, pointing at an open door leading off to the left from the panelled hall. 'I'll show you your room.'

At the top of the stairs was a galleried landing which, through twin archways, had a view down into a vast room reaching right through two floors in height, which Michael took, from a quick glance, to be the drawing room, but he followed his friend down a corridor and into a big bedroom which looked across the gardens. His two suitcases and the steamer trunk stood in one corner.

'I can get Karim to give you a hand with your unpacking if you wish,' Patrick said.

'No thanks, Patrick. I can manage.'

'There's a bathroom and a lav a little further down the corridor.'

'Right-O. I'll be down in a few minutes.'

Patrick smiled at him and left the room. Michael found the lavatory, down the corridor and around a corner, and when that was done he washed his face at a basin in one corner of his room. The white porcelain basin was mounted in a built in wash stand unit of teak, with a marble surface either side of the basin, on one of which stood a carafe of drinking water, with a glass. Below the

Chapter Three

basin were cupboards, and above it was a small glass shelf. Above that a mirror was fixed to the wall. To one side of the unit a towel hung on a brass rail.

The face that stared back at Michael from the mirror above the basin was a narrow, fairly good looking, intelligent face, with light brown hair and hazel eyes. It sported a clipped military moustache, and was looking a little weary. Michael wondered when he would meet Lord Pencaitland, Patrick's father. He knew too that there were two teenage girls in the family, the daughters of Patrick's younger brother, who (with their mother) had died in a motor accident some years ago – but they might be at boarding school. He wondered whether Marjory was staying here at the moment, or whether she would be going home.

As Michael made his way down the stairs to the dining room, he met a very old lady dressed in an antiquated fashion, making a resolute ascent of the stairs. He said good afternoon to her.

'Oh! Malcolm!' she exclaimed. 'I have not seen you for a while. Have you been away?' Malcolm was the name of Patrick's deceased younger brother.

'I've just arrived,' responded Michael. The old lady smiled at him and continued her slow ascent of the wide staircase. Michael wondered who she was. He asked Patrick over the cold lunch.

'That's Aunt Catherine. She's my father's sister. She lives with us. She's a bit batty, but perhaps not as much as she likes to pretend.'

Marjory was still with them, Michael was pleased to see. At the end of the meal she said, 'I'm going to have my coffee on the veranda.'

'Good idea,' Patrick responded. 'We'll join you.' He turned to the houseboy standing against the wall. *'Leta kahawa tatu kwa veranda,'* he told him.

'Ndiyo Bwana,' the young houseboy responded, and left the room. Five minutes later he reappeared, bearing a tray on which

were a silver coffee pot, a jug of milk, a sugar basin (both these items were also of silver), and three straight sided cups with saucers. He placed the tray on the table.

Patrick thanked him. '*Asante* Mwara.'

'I shall pour,' said Marjory. Michael took his coffee black, with two teaspoons of sugar. The coffee was superb. The garden, with its plenitude of trees, was full of birdcalls, none of which Michael could recognise. It was not too warm on the shaded veranda, but at this time of day, three o' clock, with the sun still high in the sky, Michael would have needed to wear a hat outdoors. There was neither winter nor summer in Equatoria, just wet seasons and dry seasons. This was a dry season.

'How long do you plan to visit, Michael?' asked Marjory.

Michael drew on his cigar. He enjoyed a cigar after a meal. 'As long as Patrick and his family can tolerate me,' he replied. 'I have no plans, and no pressing need to get back to England.'

'Of course, it's winter time in Britain right now. I haven't been Home for years. The last time we visited Britain, I was still a teenager,' Marjory remarked.

Michael smiled. 'You say "Home." But surely you were born here,' he commented.

Marjory laughed, a pleasant, light laugh. 'I know, it's silly really, but we grow up still thinking of England – or in our case, Scotland – as "Home." And in fact, I would probably hate living there if ever I had to. The cold and wet!'

So much for an Englishman taking Marjory back to England as his wife, thought Michael. But how much longer would the European settlers be able to hang on in Equatoria? Right across Africa, the Empire was divesting itself of its colonies, granting them independence. What Britain would not do, was grant that freedom to territories that were caught in the grip of insurgency. But once the uprising (for that is how Michael saw the Emergency) was put down in Equatoria, then the granting of independence

Chapter Three

would be brought very much closer. And how welcome would the European settler class be in an independent Equatoria? A great many Europeans would then have to go "home," Michael thought, whether they wished to or not.

Later that afternoon, Michael fell into a short doze in a comfortable chair on the veranda. The two Rhodesian ridgebacks lay nearby. He had a copy of Chinua Achebe's novel, *Things Fall Apart*, on his lap. It depicted pre-colonial life in south-eastern Nigeria, and the impact of the European invasion in the late nineteenth century. The novel had taken London's literary world by storm when it was first published in 1958; the first novel written by a black African author to do so.

During teatime soon after Michael's brief doze (a tea which had included warm scones, topped with fresh double cream from the estate's own dairy, and strawberry jam imported from South Africa, and a rich fruit cake – Michael realised that he was not going to starve during his visit), he had at last met Lord Pencaitland, who was in his eighties; he had a heavy build, and although once tall, he now had a slight stoop. He still had all his hair, which was a snowy white. Like Michael, he too wore a clipped, military style moustache.

'So you're the lad Patrick used to write about when he was at school. Your family was always very kind to him. I believe you are a writer. Do you intend writing about Equatoria?'

'I do not plan to, Sir,' responded Michael. 'I'm very much off duty right now.' Michael had met none of Patrick's family before. During the long summer break each year, while the two had been at school together, Patrick had usually returned to Equatoria. The remaining school holidays he had either spent with his Hepburn relations in East Lothian, or with Michael at his family home in Oxfordshire.

'Well, you are welcome at *Mahali pa Kupumzika*,' Lord Pencaitland said. 'Stay as long as you wish.'

'Thank you, Sir.'

Patrick had introduced Michael to his aunt, Lady Catherine Hepburn. 'Yes, we have met before somewhere, is that not so?' the old lady said. Her dress, of black lawn, fell almost to her ankles. She wore a necklace of jet and she smelled of lavender.

Michael smiled. 'That's right – we have. On the staircase, earlier today.'

'I'm sure that was very nice,' Lady Catherine responded, somewhat cryptically. 'I think I shall have some of this fruit cake.'

At six o' clock the sun plummeted fast towards the horizon. One moment (it seemed to Michael) it was daylight; the next, night had descended on the land. Michael went upstairs for a bath and a change of outfit. Dinner that evening was black tie. An occasion was being made of Michael's arrival. Anticipating that he would need it, he had packed his dinner jacket in London. They ate rainbow trout from the fast flowing streams on the side of Mount Kirinjogu (caught that morning, transported to Hari Patel's *dhuka* in Jiljil, placed in his cold room, and delivered to *Mahali pa Kupumzika* that afternoon). The trout had been dredged in cornmeal, fried, and served with tomatoes in tarragon, and were followed by a delicious roasted round from an impala rump (gifted them by Marjory's father, who had brought it to *Mahali pa Kupumzika* that morning), with roasted potatoes, along with peas, carrots and parsnips (all these from *Mahali pa Kupumzika's* kitchen gardens), the latter two vegetables glazed with honey and baked in the roasting tray. A good Hermitage wine from South Africa accompanied this main course. This was followed in turn by a substantial steamed pudding drenched in hot syrup (or by fruit salad for those whose capacity had expired), then by three varieties of cheeses from their own dairy, and some more of the superb coffee of Equatoria. It was a meal perfectly suited to Michael's rather immature culinary tastes. The meal had been served by Karim and his young assistant, Mwara. Both wore a gleaming white *kanzu*, a black sash, and a fez on their

Chapter Three

head. But where Mwara's fez was black, Karim's was red. Mwara was barefoot, but Karim wore sandals.

The presence of the three dogs in the dining room did not so much distract from the meal's sturdy elegance, as complement it.

With the meal's conclusion, the two elderly women present (although Lady Catherine had fifteen years or more on Lady Pencaitland) left the dining room for the drawing room, that huge room overlooked by the staircase gallery. The Alsatian dog accompanied them. Marjory remained with the men, one of whom was a man in his thirties named André Myburgh, the estate manager, who had been invited to the dinner, and they sat at table for another twenty minutes or so, smoking and drinking (Lord Pencaitland, Patrick and Michael drank whiskeys, while Marjory and André Myburgh each nursed a brandy). The estate manager's revolver lay on the table in its holster in front of him, as did Patrick's at his place.

Marjory, who would, Michael learned, be staying at *Mahali pa Kupumzika* tonight and tomorrow night, looked stunning in a lilac silk dress which left her shoulders bare. She wore a string of pearls at her bosom. Her golden hair gleamed in the candle light, and her healthy tan glowed. Patrick paid her much attention during the meal, but she appeared to accept his attentions simply as her due. Instead, she spoke frequently with Michael.

'I know where I've seen you before,' she remarked at one point. 'It was in the pages of *Tattler*. A photograph – you were with some young woman leaving a nightclub in London. Are you famous in London?'

Michael laughed. 'Hardly! But as I recall, the young woman I was with was rather photogenic, wasn't she?'

'You are very modest, Michael,' Marjory smiled. 'Who was she?'

Michael too smiled. 'Her name was Antonia Thrupps, the daughter of Lord Slaughthill.'

'And how did you meet her?'

'She is the youngest sister of a chap Patrick and I went to school with. Do you remember Miles Thrupps, Patrick?'

Patrick removed the frown from his face. 'Yes, I do. He was a year above us, wasn't he? A decent sort of chap.'

'He does something in the City now.' Michael turned back to Marjory. 'I bumped into him and his sister at a party one night. Thereafter I took his sister out a few times. Your *Tattler* must be quite old.'

'I expect it is. They're already a month old by the time they arrive here. And I suppose it had been knocking about in our house for quite a while after that.'

André Myburgh belonged to the community of Afrikaners which had taken root in the colony in the early years of the century. (His grandparents had trekked north from the Transvaal, following the defeat of the Boers by the British, and had settled in Equatoria). He had little to say either during or after dinner, and what little he had to say was directed at Lord Pencaitland and Patrick, and concerned estate matters. Michael did not see himself becoming bosom chums with the estate manager, who was a dour, charmless man.

In due course the four men, along with Marjory and the two Rhodesian ridgebacks, joined the two elderly ladies and the Alsatian in the huge drawing room. The estate manager and Patrick took their revolvers with them. The drawing room, which reached up through two floors in height, had an enormous, baronial fireplace. Compared to the day time warmth, it could feel cool at night at this altitude, and a fire of aromatic cedar wood was burning in the grate, scenting the room. The walls, for half the room's height, were panelled in a rich golden polished iroko wood, which gleamed in the light from the electric lamps. (Electricity on the estate was provided by a powerful diesel generator. After eleven o' clock at night, the generator cut out, but was reactivated again each time a light switch was flicked). Oil paintings – many of them family heirlooms from Scotland – and water colours were hanging on the walls, and above the fireplace was mounted a gigantic buffalo head with a great sweep of horns. Matching elephant tusks, mounted in silver, stood on either side of the fireplace. There was a leopard skin rug at the hearth, and the skins of zebras and a variety of antelopes were scattered on the floor. The furniture was an eclectic mix of local country-made pieces and fine eighteenth and early nineteenth century antiques from Scotland. In the centre of the room, on a broad Wilton carpet, stood an eighteenth century circular mahogany table, gleaming with well cared for age, on which, in a copper basin, was arranged a large display of roses from the garden. Despite its size, this was a very welcoming room.

'You should see this room when there's a dance,' remarked Marjory, seeming to discern Michael's approval of it, 'crowded with people enjoying themselves. Then the carpet is rolled up and the animal skins are removed, and the furniture is cleared away to the sides, and a Goanese band plays at one end of the room.'

'It sounds wonderful,' Michael responded.

'Of course, there have been no big dances for two or three years now. People don't like to travel at night anymore because of the *Wa Chui*.'

Chapter Four

The tourist industry had of course collapsed in the colony, excepting only along the coast, where visitors from abroad continued to arrive, assured that the *Wa Chui* were not present in the coastal region. In happier times, Patrick would have organised a round of excursions for Michael, and a full scale safari under canvas to one of the game regions, but these days that was impossible – or if not impossible, extremely foolish to attempt. So Michael was shown around the estate, all five thousand acres of it, by his friend, and after a while he began to take a horse from the stables in the morning (having first asked a *syce* to saddle up for him) and go for a long ride just after breakfast. Sometimes Marjory happened to be paying a visit, and the two would then ride out together.

Marjory was an excellent rider, better, in fact, than Michael, who was himself more than merely competent. She rode as if she had been born in the saddle – as indeed, metaphorically, she had, for she had grown up with horses and riding on her parents' farm. She made (Michael thought) a very attractive, but somewhat assertive, figure on horseback, with a man's cotton shirt open at the throat, riding breeches, a soft, wide brimmed hat, and either chukka boots, or very well polished riding boots. These latter she did not bring with her on her visits, but rather, she borrowed a pair of boots that had belonged to Lady Pencaitland, who no longer rode. Her outfit was completed by a holstered revolver on her hip. Michael wore an old pair of cavalry twill trousers, a soft brushed cotton shirt, a bandana around his neck, chukka boots, and a tweed flat cap – which (lacking only a woollen waistcoat and his old tweed jacket) was what he had often worn when hacking around the Oxfordshire and Gloucestershire countryside. He too had been familiar with horses since his childhood, for his parents had always kept two or three horses at the family home, but horses had featured far less in his life than they clearly had in Marjory's.

Patrick had insisted that Michael take a revolver with him when he went riding, so he wore a revolver that Patrick had loaned him on his hip. He had not carried a sidearm since the end of the War.

It was during their rides together that Michael fell in love with Marjory. Soon, it seemed to him that he was living from one ride with Marjory to the next, anticipating their next ride together across the African landscape with more eagerness and greater desire than he had anticipated anything for a long time. They rode together across hard red earth and through high golden grasslands, in which herds of impala and zebra, seemingly untroubled by the presence of the horses, grazed peacefully. This upland terrain was decorated with large aloes, decked with tall spikes of red blossoms. Near the house they had passed meadows in which horses and dairy cattle were grazing, then they had ridden through herds of native beef cattle, grazing on ground that had never seen the plough, in which indigenous grasses grew, and they had passed wide, open fields in which, within a short while, maize would be growing (the soil as yet uncultivated, for the rains and the planting season were not yet due). Michael would sometimes allow Marjory to ride a length or two ahead of him, so that he could gaze at her without her becoming aware of his interest. He drank in her graceful, supple form, moving in perfect union with the horse; he experienced both joy and torment as he admired her; he yearned to clasp her and kiss her. But Marjory was (it appeared) unaware of his feelings for her, and he feared an end to these shared rides if he made those feelings clear.

'You see that *donga* ahead?' she asked. 'I'll race you to it, Michael!' And she dug her heels in and her horse broke into an immediate gallop, and Michael spurred his mount, and the two of them thundered across the hard red earth, and when, two lengths ahead of him, she reached the deep eroded cut in the earth and pulled up hard, she was laughing, flushed, more beautiful than anything he had ever seen, but all he could do was grin in response and say 'You're a centaur!'

She grinned back. 'Were there female centaurs?' she asked, laughing again.

'There must have been,' Michael responded, 'unless there were a given number created by the gods, and they were immortal.'

'Well, I'm sure as a writer you know more about it than I do, Michael. I would quite like to have been a centaur.' She curvetted her horse. 'But what would happen when I met a mortal man one day and fell in love with him? That must happen one day, although it hasn't happened yet.' She laughed.

Oh, she was cruel, Michael thought.

February arrived (and the British Prime Minister, Harold Macmillan's "Wind of Change" speech in Cape Town on the 3rd February, caused many in the colony some disquiet), and towards the end of the month, Michael turned forty. Through the month of February Michael became ever more deeply infatuated with Marjory (who visited *Mahali pa Kupumzika* frequently, staying a night or two at a time), and as a consequence, ever more torn between joy and pain. His fortieth birthday was, like his welcoming dinner, celebrated with a black tie evening, and the gift of a very beautiful nickel plated Colt revolver with an ivory grip from Patrick. Michael owned a couple of shotguns and a .22 rifle which he kept at his mother's home – his childhood home – in Oxfordshire, but he had never (outside of his years in the army) possessed a sidearm before. However, he was beginning to feel undressed if he left the house without a revolver at his hip, and he was deeply touched by the gift, which must have been very expensive. He could not, however, see himself being able to return to England with it. Perhaps Lord Pencaitland could advise him? (As it happened, Michael was to leave the revolver in Patrick's keeping when, eventually, he returned to England, to take possession of it again when next he visited the colony).

At tea time, which today was being served in the drawing room, Michael saw a stranger wearing a clerical collar. He was a tall man in his early middle age, his hair very dark, his face very tanned. His eyes were a deep blue, and they shone with good humour.

'Michael, meet the Reverend Alastair Fleming, of the Church of Scotland Mission,' said Patrick. 'Alastair, this is Michael Hood, a friend visiting from England.'

'I'm very pleased to meet you,' the man responded, shaking Michael's hand. 'Is this your first visit to Equatoria, Mr. Hood?'

'It is,' Michael responded. 'I hope however it wont be my last.'

'You may have gathered, the Colony is going through a wee upset right now, but I'm sure that with the good Lord's help, that will be sorted out in time. It's a braw country, with a grand people.'

Michael smiled. The minister's accent reminded him of that of his paternal grandmother, a Scotswoman from Fife. It was a pleasant accent, not at all the music hall "Scotch" that the English so enjoyed making fun of.

'Reverend Fleming runs a CSM mission about ten miles to the south, at Jituamba,' Patrick told him.

'Aye – and Lord Pencaitland is a generous benefactor of ours.'

The Reverend Alastair Fleming and the two Hepburn men

discussed farming, and cattle, and preparations for the planting season. At *Mahali pa Kupumzika,* the wide, open fields that Michael had so far only seen left bare, untouched red earth, had just begun being ploughed and harrowed by a pair of Massey-Ferguson tractors. 'The rains are close upon us,' Lord Pencaitland asserted.

Michael had nothing to add to this conversation; his ignorance in these matters was profound, although had this discussion of farming prospects taken place in the Cotswolds, he would not have been entirely at a loss. However, Michael was interested in the work of a missionary in Equatoria, and he asked the Reverend Fleming a number of questions relating to his missionary activities. He brought the conversation around to the Emergency.

'Do you find, Reverend, that the Emergency is affecting your work?' he asked the missionary.

'Some of the missions have lost members of their flocks,' the Reverend Fleming answered Michael. 'But at Jituamba our people have been faithful, and there has not been any trouble so far.'

Within days of the Reverend Alastair Fleming's visit, Lord Pencaitland's conviction that the rains were imminent seemed borne out by the weather: ever heavier cloud formations, the colour of bruised plum, began to build up across the Cairngorms Range, and there was a gathering, heavy humidity to the air, with sheet lightning playing on the eastern horizon at night. Then one afternoon the anticipatory hush of the dry land was broken by great rolling peals of thunder, and then the heavens opened up. The rain beat on the hard ground like the drumming of a thousand timpani, and the long rains had set in. With the coming of wet weather, that year's maize crop was planted. Whereas by late January, the quick flowing streams that usually cut across the Hepburn land from the high, forested hills to the east had either dried up, or been reduced to mere trickles, they now became surging torrents laden with red soil. By the end of February the long golden grass, where the cattle had not yet grazed it to the ground, had become brittle and dry, but now fresh new blades began to spring up from the red earth. Only the fields of lucerne, and the nearer paddocks where the horses were corralled, were still green before the coming of the rains – watered as they were from wind pumps reaching to aquifers far beneath the ground. The horses and cattle were watered from troughs kept brimming by these wind pumps, and during the dry season they had had to be fed almost entirely on animal feed, derived from a mix of maize and lucerne (both produced on the estate), to which were added oats and bran. The oats and bran had to be bought at Jiljil and transported to the estate by lorry. With the new year the cost of animal feed (along with bulk fuel deliveries, and every other requirement that had to be brought in) had soared, because haulage costs (due to very much higher insurance premiums, and the requirement that every driver be accompanied by a mate who was, literally, riding shotgun) had shot up.

However, at present, truck and lorry deliveries to farms like *Mahali pa Kupumzika* – deep in the countryside – were still being made. Commercial transport and long distance haulage were vital to the colony's production of agricultural produce for export and the acquisition of much needed foreign exchange. Equatoria's economy was an agricultural and a mining one (copper and gold were the two most important minerals mined); the country had only minimal tertiary industry; little was manufactured within the colony.

From March through to late May it rained almost every day, and when it was not raining, the sun rarely broke through the cloud cover. It was cool, even cold, at night: the fires were built up in the drawing room and the dining room in the evenings, and there was a fire burning in the library from mid afternoon onward, for Lady Catherine and Lady Pencaitland favoured the library in the afternoons in the wet weather. When Michael went to bed, he was glad to crawl beneath the blankets. He saw less of Marjory during this wet season, at first because she was busy helping with the planting on her family's farm, and later on, because the weather was so off-putting. And anyway, riding was not much fun in this weather. Michael read books he found in the library, a very attractive room panelled in dark wood, with two of the walls lined with books.

Michael found the entire series of C.S. Forester's *"Hornblower"* novels on the shelves, and he began rereading them, not having read them since his adolescence. He also reread some of G.A. Henty's historical novels, in particular those set in Africa. Although aimed at somewhat younger readers than himself, he enjoyed the refresher course in plot construction these novels offered him, and in the techniques of sustaining a high level of action and excitement.

Sometimes Michael would find either Lady Catherine or Lady Pencaitland (if not both of them) sitting reading in front of the fire in the library. Lady Pencaitland always smiled at him and asked him whether he was comfortable. Lady Catherine in particular seemed glad of his presence, sometimes addressing him as "Mr. Umm . . . Ahh . . ." and sometimes as "Malcolm," and either embarking on stories from her girlhood about people he had never heard of, or asking him how his girls were, under the impression that he was Patrick's deceased younger brother, the father of the two teenage girls Michael had yet to meet. 'How are the girls?' she would ask him, and Michael would respond, 'They're well, I believe.' And as far as he knew, they were well. Patrick's nieces were away at boarding school in Naburu, and although school broke up over March and April for two weeks, the girls had not come home this time, but had gone down to the coast to stay with friends for the Easter holidays.

Michael gathered from Patrick that the two girls – aged thirteen and fourteen – were something of a handful. 'They're high spirited,' Patrick explained, 'and they're not very amenable to discipline. But there's no real wickedness in them.'

Chapter Four

Michael, since his school days, had always been rather awkward with adolescent girls, especially "high spirited" adolescent girls, and he was in no great hurry to meet the Hepburn girls.

As for Lord Pencaitland, he did not enjoy the rains. He felt his age; his rheumatism played up badly, and he spent much of his time hidden away upstairs with the Alsatian dog, even having his meals sent up. Right through the rainy season, Michael barely saw him. But Patrick visited his father every evening, spending an hour with him in his parents' sitting room upstairs, discussing (Michael assumed) estate matters. During the day Patrick, accompanied by the two Rhodesian ridgebacks, would often be gone for hours at a time, taking the Land Rover, which was (apart from the tractors) the only vehicle capable of navigating the tracks on the estate at this time of year, for the terrain was often deep in mud. Michael rarely saw the estate manager, André Myburgh, who also drove a Land Rover. His absence caused Michael no great regret.

In late May the rains cleared up almost overnight. The sun shone again, and the air was fresh. Sitting on the veranda Michael enjoyed watching the lilac breasted rollers – those beautiful birds in which turquoise blue and lilac predominated – as they performed their aerobatics above the garden. There would often be a flock of guineafowl on the lawn, going chi-chi-chi. Sometimes a troop of black faced vervet monkeys would visit, making their way into the garden from a semi-wooded area to the north-west of the house. Very occasionally, Michael would see colobus monkeys, their black and white colour scheme most striking. Michael always had a book with him, but it lay closed on his lap as often as not. With the passing of the wet weather, Lord Pencaitland had come downstairs again, and he and the Alsatian dog (which had grown fat for lack of exercise) would sometimes join Michael on the veranda. Occasionally the two men would take an easy stroll along one of the tracks past the fields near the house, and the Alsatian dog would come with them. So too would the two ridgebacks, if they were not out with Patrick. Lord Pencaitland would tell tales about the colony's early days, when the country was barely settled, and the land teemed with game. Lord Pencaitland had gentle, rheumy, pale grey eyes. But Michael knew that he had been a great hunter as a younger man. The pair of enormous elephant tusks mounted in silver on either side of the fireplace in the drawing room were from an elephant he had shot.

Patrick shot for the pot, rather than for sport. However, his mother would not allow him to bag guineafowl anywhere near the house. Like Michael, she enjoyed watching these gregarious birds on the lawns. Within a week of Michael's arrival, back in January, he had accompanied Patrick in the Land Rover as they set off to shoot an impala antelope for dinner. In the high grasslands in the east (in which scattered trees, the outliers of the Nyahurari Forest, stood) they drove the Land Rover (in the back of which were the two Rhodesian ridgebacks, along with Patrick's gun bearer, and a farm worker) within thirty yards of a herd, and without leaving the vehicle, using a .30-06 sporting rifle, Patrick had put a bullet cleanly through the shoulders of an impala buck. The animal had dropped where it stood. The two black men had commenced gralloching the animal immediately – saving the liver and kidneys, which they wrapped in pieces of cloth, for themselves – the two dogs being tossed an occasional piece of offal, and then they loaded the carcass into the back of the Land Rover. The two men were rewarded with a shoulder each. This had been mere butchery, Michael thought, not sport – but then, Patrick had made no pretence that it was anything but a necessary task, to be carried out quickly and efficiently.

One morning after the rains, Patrick said to Michael, 'The *Watu* have told me that the buffs are eating the new barley. We'll have to shoot one, to discourage the others. Would you like to come?'

Michael was to see butchery on another scale altogether. The barley was growing below the first of the forested ridges towards the east, where the estate's land rose to its highest elevation. In the open body of the Land Rover, along with the two Rhodesian ridgebacks, were Patrick's gun bearer and a farm worker. Patrick and Michael of course were sitting in the cab. It took them forty minutes of driving slowly, over very rough tracks, to reach their destination. The terrain – hilly, grassy country with scattered stands of acacias and groups of two or three cedars – was particularly lovely now that the rains had watered the soil. Everywhere there was bright new growth, a range of greens from pastel through to the dark foliage of the cedars. They crossed a number of streams, flowing clean again, climbing higher all the time. The pure clean air was invigorating. They were about eight thousand feet above sea level now. They saw the large buffalo herd spread out on the estate's eastern boundary, beyond which the ground rose in steep forested ridges to the distant Cairngorms Range. The buffalo had not moved far from the barley fields.

'I'll be surprised if there's any barley left,' Patrick remarked. 'We'll drive a little closer, then we'll walk. I'm afraid we'll spook them if we drive much closer.'

A little over one hundred yards from the buffalo, Patrick stopped the car and turned off the engine. 'Stay!' he commanded the dogs. 'Karanja!' Patrick turned to his gun bearer. *'Njoo na mimi!'*

With Karanja (who was carrying a second rifle) walking just behind them, Patrick and Michael set off parallel to the herd, with the grass, which was already long, brushing at their trouser legs. Amaryllis, with brilliant red flowers, grew along the edges of the path. They walked until a large stand of black ironwood stood between them and the herd, and using it as cover, they drew nearer the buffalos. At the edge of the thicket Patrick halted, his two companions behind him. Patrick raised his heavy Westley Richards .425 rifle and sighted, then fired. The animals all raised their heads, then, as a big bull buckled, fell, and lay on its side, the herd broke into a lumbering gallop to the east, heading for the cover of the forested ridge.

'Good,' Patrick declared. 'That'll teach 'em!'

The two black men set to work butchering the enormous carcass. Michael could see the ticks, swollen and vile, clustered beneath the creature's throat and around its ears. The animal's eyes were completely glazed over. The spread of double-curved horns was impressive. The animal's head and horns were almost as big as those of the buffalo head mounted above the fireplace in the drawing room back at the house.

Speaking *Kiswahili*, Patrick said to the two native men, 'I will send a tractor with a trailer. You stay here.'

'*Ndiyo Bwana,*' they answered. They would stay with the carcass, to guard it from vultures, until the tractor arrived. Patrick tossed them a half empty packet of cigarettes and a box of matches to keep them company, and he and Michael walked back to the Land Rover, in which the two dogs, very obedient, were still sitting quietly.

Chapter Five

Michael began thinking of returning to England. It was now mid June. He had been away for five months. How glorious a summer in Oxfordshire would be, where his mother kept up the old family home; a summer away from the crowds, traffic, noise and visitors of London; a summer beneath a fresh, blue sky, rather than trapped beneath London's brassy, humid summer sky. In London Michael had the top two floors (and the attic above them) of an eighteenth century merchant's house in Frith Street in Soho. He enjoyed springtime in London (he had of course missed the spring this year), and there was a strange appeal to wintertime also (perhaps explained by the absence of crowds of visitors), but he did not enjoy the summer in London.

However, Michael had yet to broach the subject of his departure with Patrick, when the Hepburn household learned of a *Wa Chui* night attack on the Reverend Alastair Fleming's mission at Jituamba, ten miles away. The Hepburns learned of it the next afternoon, when the Police paid the house a visit. Lord and Lady Pencaitland, Patrick and Michael were sitting on the veranda with the three dogs. Karim was standing nearby.

'And the Reverend Fleming? How is he?' asked Lord Pencaitland.

'I'm afraid he was one of the eleven people murdered, Sir.'

'Oh, the poor man,' Lady Pencaitland said.

Lord Pencaitland blanched, and said, 'I need a drink. *Karim, niletee whiskey.*'

'What exactly happened?' asked Patrick, as Karim went inside the house.

'The *Wa Chui* descended on the mission in force, round about midnight. Most of them were carrying *pangas*. Some were armed with automatic weapons – we have the Chinese to thank for that. They gathered together the people who had not managed to flee, and lined them up, including the Reverend Fleming, and gunned them down,' answered the Police captain. 'Survivors say that the Reverend Fleming tried to talk to them,' he continued. 'He was slashed across the face with a *panga*, and fell to his knees, at which point some of the people with him also fell to their knees, and begged their attackers for mercy. There was no mercy shown to them.'

Karim returned with a large whiskey and a soda siphon on a silver tray, and placed the objects on the small table alongside Lord Pencaitland. Patrick and Michael, who had got to their feet when the Police arrived, now sat down again. Lord Pencaitland ignored the soda siphon and reached for the whiskey.

Lady Pencaitland's face showed no unusual emotion. Her vague half smile was in place, as always. But when she reached for her tea cup, her fingers trembled, and for a moment there was a small audible vibration of cup against saucer.

'Your physical location,' the Police captain continued, 'with your land running to the edge of the Nyahurari Forest, makes you vulnerable, Sir. I would consider yourselves under threat, and take all precautions,' the Policeman told Patrick.

'I think we are already being careful, Captain,' Patrick responded. 'The exterior doors are locked soon after dinner, if not earlier, and are only unlocked again after sunrise the next morning, and no servants – no natives – are permitted in the house during the interval – oh, excepting Karim of course, but he's a Somali. The dogs sleep on the veranda. We're armed – there are always guns within reach. Even my mother knows how to use a revolver.'

'Those measures sound sensible, Sir. Tell me, do you have any idea how many of your estate workers have taken the oath, and who they are?'

Patrick looked thoughtful. 'No, not really.'

'If you were able to find out, and let us know, that would be useful. Perhaps you could let it be known that you would reward informers.'

'No!' Lord Pencaitland interjected. 'I'm paying no informers!'

'Father, these are no longer normal times. I think it would be a good idea to consider such a step.'

'I wont stand for it,' Lord Pencaitland declared. 'I will not live that way.'

Patrick let the matter drop.

That evening after dinner (which had been served by Karim and his young Sikuyu assistant, Mwara), as Michael and Patrick sat smoking on the veranda, the Rhodesian ridgebacks at their feet, Michael said, 'I had been thinking about going home. But I don't want it to look as if I'm running at the first sign of trouble. Perhaps I should stay a while longer. If you will have me.'

'It's up to you, old boy. It's good of you not to want to cut and run. But I doubt that times will get better for a long while yet. No one will think the less of you if you were to leave now – though you're welcome to stay as long as you like, you know that.'

Patrick and Michael stared out at the darkness. Michael felt a sudden shiver of apprehension, which he dismissed immediately, as the product of an over imaginative mind. Above the trees at the bottom of the gardens a thin sliver of moon was just rising. The relentless high voltage whine of millions of night insects had become something that the mind completely blanked out. The night calls – bird and beast – had by now become a customary backdrop for Michael; sounds which had sometimes disturbed him at night during his first few weeks here, rarely did so any longer. But the shriek of the hyrax that lived in the cedar tree, when heard in the early hours, could still make his blood curdle.

After a while, his cigar in one hand, Patrick spoke again. 'You know that Marjory and I are getting married next month?'

Michael experienced a sense of sudden shock. He had not even realised that they were engaged. 'I should have seen it,' he thought. 'So much makes sense now.'

'Congratulations, old Pat. She's a wonderful girl.'

But he asked himself: Does she even love him?

'We have had a sort of unofficial understanding for years,' Patrick told Michael. 'The last couple of years we kept thinking, we will wait until the Emergency is over. But I fear that would mean us waiting a long time. So we're going ahead.'

'I agree. Seize the day. Life must carry on.' Michael realised that he was babbling, so he shut up. He sipped at his whiskey. Then he had a thought. 'Of course there's no question of my leaving yet,' he said. 'I'm staying for the wedding.'

'I'm glad, Michael. I want to ask you to be my best man.'

'I'm honoured! Of course I will.'

Patrick and Marjory were married on a Saturday at Saint John's, the pretty stone-built Church of England church in Jiljil. Patrick's nieces, his deceased brother's two daughters, were home from school for the holidays, and served as bridesmaids. Michael met them for the first time. They were both pretty girls, aged thirteen and fourteen. They were entirely free from the brooding, sulky air adopted by many teenage girls of that age, and they both engaged in somewhat puppyish flirting with Michael. He was polite to them, smiled, but (his own teenage shyness with adolescent girls never having been entirely overcome) he made

Chapter Five

no attempt to be a great friend to either of them. This only intensified the girls' interest in him, especially the interest of the older girl, Eleanor.

The interior of the church was laden with cut flowers from the two Hepburn establishments. Despite the Emergency, and the potential dangers of travel, there were upwards of fifty people in the church. The Hepburns were the nearest thing to a founding family that Equatoria had, and the Hepburn name carried a great deal of weight in the colony. Michael (wearing a pale grey double breasted summer weight suit, for he had not packed his morning clothes) carried out his duties as best man adequately. In his best man's speech at the reception on the lawns of *Mahali pa Kupumzika* afterwards, he told a few obligatory comical stories – amusing tales of his and the groom's shared schooldays. As always at this time of year (it was mid July) the sun was shining. The gardens at *Mahali pa Kupumzika* looked splendid, a mass of colour and blooms. All that marred the idyllic picture was the number of guests who were wearing sidearms.

Seeing Marjory standing with Patrick in front of the altar, Michael had felt a pang; not so much of loss (he had lost nothing he had in fact possessed), but of what might have been. There had been times, especially when he and Marjory had gone riding together, when he had dared to imagine taking her home to England as his bride one day. Oh, how presumptuous I was, he thought to himself.

Michael neither wished nor expected to be driven down to Port Hardinge. He tried hard not to resent his friend his happiness, nor to feel an irrational sense of betrayal by Marjory, but he did not wholly succeed. He had no wish to make a long journey by road with the newly-weds for company. So Patrick used the radio telephone to instruct the Hepburn family's man of affairs in Namuri to make a booking for Michael on the next British India steamer home, and he himself made a reservation for him in a first class sleeping compartment on the train from Port Caroline, which halted at Jiljil on its way to the coast.

Michael said his goodbyes to Lord and Lady Pencaitland, and to Lady Catherine (who, right to the end, remained uncertain as to who he was). As Patrick and Marjory drove him to Jiljil (all three sharing the wide bench seat in front, with Karim sitting in the back of the car), he thought the countryside had never looked prettier. The maize was ripening in the fields. The cattle were fat and content. The sky, an intense blue, was dotted with brilliant white cumulus clouds. At Jiljil Station, a noisy, colourful throng of local people – natives and Indians – was boarding the train at the far end of the platform, where the second and third class coaches had pulled in. Many of the natives were carrying trussed chickens, and some had a goat kid or two with them. Karim and the porter loaded Michael's luggage into the first class compartment. Michael tipped Karim generously, a sum sufficient to divide up among the other servants, if Karim so wished. Michael took Marjory's hand and kissed her on the cheek.

'Dont forget us, Michael,' said Marjory. 'You must be sure to visit us again.'

But Michael, who had not yet made up his mind whether he could bear to visit again, now that Marjory was married to another man, just smiled.

Up ahead, the big articulated Garratt engine, with its sixteen driving wheels, steamed and hissed. Michael climbed aboard the carriage, made his way down the narrow corridor to his compartment, lowered the window and leant out. At the rear of the train, the guard blew his whistle twice, and waved a green flag up and down. There was a last scramble, with much shouting, from the native contingent, and from the few Indians still boarding the train. The latter were travelling second class. First class of course was reserved for Europeans.

'Come back next year,' Patrick told him, as they shook hands again through the open window.

Chapter Five

'Visit us again!' shouted Marjory, as the train, with enormous blasts of exhaust steam from the engine's piston boxes, its whistle blowing loudly, began to pull away.

'Have a good journey Michael! *Kwaheri – kwaheri!*' they both shouted, and the train slowly gathered speed, and Jiljil was left behind. They would reach Namuri in the late afternoon, and travel through the night, arriving at Port Hardinge around one o' clock the next day. With the Emergency, the train journey took longer than it had in the past. The BI steamer for England departed Port Hardinge two days later. Michael was booked into the Imperial for two nights.

'I'll have time to look around the port,' he thought, and settled back in his comfortable seat. But before long he began pondering his recent visit. Would he ever return to *Mahali pa Kupumzika* again? Right now he doubted it. In having (seemingly effortlessly) gained Marjory's hand in marriage, Patrick had (Michael could not help feeling) compromised the friendship between the two men. And the romance that Michael had imagined he was having with Marjory had been shown up as nothing but an illusion. Michael could not avoid feeling not only bitter, but foolish.

Chapter Six

July was almost over by the time the ship docked at Tilbury. It was drizzling, and cool. Welcome home, Michael, to an English summer! Michael spent two days and nights at his home in Frith Street, near Soho Square, catching up with his personal mail. The bills that had fallen due during Michael's absence had been settled by his agent, who, with a front door key Michael had left her, had called at his home once a week and sorted through his mail. Michael had also left her a dozen signed, blank cheques. He met a few casual acquaintances for drinks the second night, at The Crown and Two Chairmen in Dean Street, then he packed a suitcase and walked to Tottenham Court Road Tube Station. Here he took the Central Line west to Notting Hill Gate, changing there for the north bound Circle Line. Two stops later he alighted at Paddington Station, which was, for Michael, a gateway to bucolic serenity and contentment. Here he caught the 13.50 for Kingham, the Cotswolds station nearest his mother's home.

Michael felt his spirits rise as the English countryside enveloped him. His family home was in a beautiful part of England, a few miles from the ancient market town of Chipping Norton. The old house, built, like most houses in the region, of weathered grey Cotswold stone, stood in a landscape made up of sometimes rather steep sided, but generally low, often wooded hills, and hidden combes, in which clear shallow streams flowed rapidly. The picturesque villages were linked by narrow lanes, often sunken between high hedgerows or dry stone walls. The mellow stone of the houses, the one or two shops, and – inevitably – the church in each village represented a simple, English vernacular architectural style that Michael found very attractive. This was where he had spent most of his school holidays; this was where he still came to recuperate, to recover from the exhaustion that London eventually induces; here he came to get over a broken heart (of which he had had a number during his lifetime); here he returned to overcome a writer's block if he was having no success with a novel he was working on. Here he came to visit his mother. This was where he came now, to purge his system of Africa, and Marjory, and to reclaim his roots.

It was a walk of more than half a mile from the station to Michael's family home. His mother would happily have met him at the station with the car, but Michael had been looking forward to the walk. The roadside verges were thick with nettles, dock leaf, Queen Anne's lace, and tall foxgloves, decked for half their length with thickly clustered purple-pink blossom. In the hedgerows, dogroses bloomed – pink, purple and lilac. The sun had come out and Michael saw butterflies by the score. Brimstones (sulphur yellow, thus their name), meadow browns, and large and small whites predominated, but he noticed with pleasure a couple of red admirals, and several splendid peacock butterflies. There was little road traffic.

Michael spent the entire month of August in the Cotswolds. He spent much of the day reading on the veranda; he certainly did no work. Twice he went out to dinner at local houses; people he had known when growing up, and as a young man. Michael had packed no dinner jacket, but he was able to wear that of his father, which was still hanging in the wardrobe, along with so many of his father's clothes his mother had not found it in herself to get rid of. His mother no longer kept horses, so he went for walks instead, accompanied by his mother's red setter, who was seven years old and still up to long traipses across the fields and through the woods. Michael stuck to the rights of way he knew so well, those often very ancient public footpaths which cut across private land, and gave you a feel for the countryside which could not be gained by driving through it in a car, or by limiting your walks to the narrow lanes. He helped his mother with some gardening, but his help was not really needed, for his mother had a man who came in once a week to mow the lawns and do any heavy work in the garden.

Michael particularly enjoyed sitting on the veranda with his mother and her dog after dinner, a lager beer within reach, a cigar between his fingers, the long summer day not yet done. There was little rain that August. In the evenings especially, recalling another veranda thousands of miles away, under a different sky, Michael's thoughts kept returning to Equatoria, to *Mahali pa Kupumzika*, and inevitably, to Marjory. How far away it all seemed, those recollections; how little relation they bore to his present circumstances. His stay at the Hepburn estate, and the people he had known there, had assumed something of a dreamlike quality for Michael. He was no longer hurting over Marjory; he had known her but briefly, and clearly, he had not known her very well. He thought he would probably never see her again. In this assumption, he was mistaken.

By mid September, Michael was working on a new novel in his Soho home. The weather had broken, whittling down the number of visitors to London. Cold rains had set in, a foretaste of the coming autumn, and London was slowly being returned to its true residents, the people like Michael who made their homes there. Towards the end of September, he received a letter from Patrick: old

Chapter Six

Lord Pencaitland had died suddenly, in his sleep. He was well into his mid eighties. This meant that Patrick and Marjory were now the Earl and Countess of Pencaitland, and Fiona Pencaitland, Patrick's mother, was now the Dowager Lady Pencaitland. The three of them (along with Lady Catherine, and Patrick's nieces, when they were at home) continued, however (in light of the unrest), to live *en famille* in the big house. The house was certainly large enough that the Dowager Lady Pencaitland did not have to feel that she was imposing on her son and daughter in law.

By the time Michael received the letter from Patrick, the funeral service had already taken place. There were very few of the original Equatorian pioneers still living now. Indeed, for many in the colony, old Lord Pencaitland's death marked the end of an era. Michael wrote back, a thoughtful, sensitive letter, and he sent his love to Marjory also. He took a break over Christmas from the novel he was working on, returning to his family home for a few days. He took a friend with him, a man slightly younger than himself who had no near family with whom to spend Christmas, and whose quiet, thoughtful manner Michael found restful.

'Mother, this is Maurice Grainger, the friend I wrote about. Maurice – my Mother, Jessica Hood,' he said, introducing the two on finding his mother in the drawing room. A fire was burning in the grate. There had been a snowfall the night before, but London had seen only a few stray snowflakes. Travelling through the snowy countryside by train was like traversing a fairytale land, a land drained of all colour but the white and shadowed blue of the snow, the stark silhouettes of the leafless trees, and the dark, almost black pulsing of the rivers and streams they crossed, for they alone were not iced up. As Michael and Maurice had left the station at Kingham on foot, Michael had felt the cold acutely on his nose and cheeks, the only unprotected parts of his body. He experienced a sudden, incongruous flash of memory: a momentary recollection of the warmth and colour of *Mahali pa Kupumzika*.

But Equatoria was a troubled Paradise, and he decided to write to Patrick again soon.

Offered two days' wages, and the promise of Boxing Day off, the cook-housekeeper (a widow whose two grown children were living in Australia) was happy enough to work on Christmas Day, and so the Hoods and Maurice Grainger sat down to a proper Christmas lunch.

When Michael had been a boy, there had been a cook-housekeeper, a kitchen maid, a laundry maid and a parlour maid, and outside the house there had been a full-time gardener and a stables lad. Now a village girl came in twice a week to do the house and the laundry, a gardener once a week, and Mrs. Hughes had no one to help her in the kitchen.

The two men were back in London before the New Year. Michael had been invited to a New Year's supper and ball at a house in Holland Park. That evening he walked up Frith Street towards Soho Square, wearing a charcoal grey overcoat over his dinner jacket and white silk scarf. It was clear and very cold. At Soho Square he was able to flag down a taxi. Antonia Thrupps, the girl Michael had taken out a few times in the past, was at the ball. For old times' sake the two kissed for a while in what appeared to be the library, but their hearts were not in it, and Michael knew that that particular flame could not be rekindled. Michael was as alone on returning home in the early hours of 1961 as he had been when departing his Soho residence in the last hours of 1960.

Later that month Michael wrote to his friend Patrick. He received a letter in reply a month later:

"... the authorities have now surrounded the native compound with barbed wire, and a gate that is locked at night, and it is my responsibility, a task I delegate to André Myburgh, to see that the workers on the estate are shepherded within the compound at the end of the day. Of course I do not apply this to Karim, whose loyalty I trust absolutely."

Michael understood: the Somalis looked down on the Sikuyu, considering them savages, and pagans to boot. Karim was, like most of his compatriots, a Muslim. The letter continued:

"A couple of European Equatoria Regiment Reservists and a platoon of loyal Sikuyu guard the compound through the night. I billet the two European officers, a second lieutenant and a sergeant. They are decent young fellows – I know their families – and I've put them up in the house. You probably know that there are some British forces now in the Colony. Members of a special unit of Equatoria Regiment Reservists (they call themselves the *'Simbas'*) mount forays into the Nyahurari Forest, and the forests around Mount Kirinjogu, and up and down the length of the Cairngorms Range, trying to flush out the *Wa Chui* who hide there. But the outrages grow more frequent and widespread; with so much of the workforce in the Highlands having taken the oath, you cannot be sure who is *Wa Chui* and who is not."

A flawed Paradise, Michael thought, reading these lines. He continued reading:

"The population on the Sikuyu reserves has been concentrated within about twenty-five protected villages, as they're termed. This means that they have to be fed at government expense, since for the most part they are unable to work on their *shambas* any longer. And the villages have to be guarded by the military. The government calls this policy 'villagisation.' It has a double purpose: to close down *Wa Chui* recruitment, and to protect the Sikuyu from intimidation by the *Wa Chui*. The European farms are suffering from the absence of their young men, the sons of the farmers, who would have been working their family farms with their parents. Instead they're with the Reservists. Only those young men between the ages of eighteen and twenty-seven have been called up so far, but most of the young men into their thirties have volunteered for the Reservists."

Michael, who was reading this worrying letter in his sitting room at the tail end of February, the day after his forty-first birthday, and who was thoroughly tired of the English winter, felt a sudden yearning to see Equatoria again, to feel the hot sun on his face, to smell the red dust, to marvel at the brilliant colours. He continued reading:

"Here at *Mahali pa Kupumzika* I have engaged a local *fundi* to make strong interior shutters of steel for the windows downstairs. It is, as you can imagine, quite a big task. We will close the shutters every night. On the broader front, the Colony's economy, particularly the Highland farming community's economy, is suffering. There is a shortage of native labour due to the 'villagisation' on the Sikuyu reserves, and a bleeding away of existing labour (especially on farms like ours which adjoin the Nyahurari Forest and the foothills of the Cairngorms Range), as workers on the farms disappear to join *Wa Chui* guerrilla groups; after that, there's the near collapse of local commercial transport. The haulage companies are carrying the costs of very much higher insurance premiums, and the wages for two men in the cab where once there would only have been one, and they're reluctant to make deliveries to isolated farms such as our own. The delivery of bulk supplies such as fertilizer, fuel, pesticides, animal feeds, in fact, everything we rely on trucks and lorries to deliver to the estate, has risen hugely in cost. This feeds into the prices we must ask for what we produce, and makes it difficult for our produce to compete on the international market. People are struggling. Even here on the estate, we are beginning to find it tough.

You probably noticed how slow your journey to the coast by train was; that was because in front of the engine, there was an open car attached for much of the journey, with an Army machine gun detachment aboard. There's one at the rear of the trains also, now."

Michael paused in his reading the letter, thinking that perhaps he ought to ask Patrick whether he could be useful to him if he were to visit for a while. Then he picked up the letter again.

Chapter Six

"Food production for local consumption is down, so local food costs have risen," Patrick continued. "This is because the native *shambas* are no longer functioning, and because with their transport and labour problems, and so many of their young men away with the Equatoria Reservists, the European farms in the Highlands particularly are not producing the quantity of food they once did."

In the letter's final paragraph, Patrick wrote, "Do not think that we're complaining; we'll come through this eventually. And we are well: Marjory (who sends her love), my Mother, Lady Catherine, the girls, and I. I imagine the first daffodils will be out in London's Royal Parks by the time this letter reaches you. With all our troubles and problems, I would rather be here, in Equatoria, than having had to endure an English winter!"

Michael smiled. He went through to his study, which overlooked the garden at the back of the building, sat down at his desk beneath the tall window, unscrewed the cap of his fountain pen, and began to write a letter to Patrick. In it, he asked whether he might visit again. Michael had the letter weighed and stamped at the Poland Street Post Office. It would take about three weeks to reach Equatoria by sea, or a week by airmail. He chose airmail, even though it was so much more expensive.

A week into April, Michael received another letter from Patrick.

"Yes, we would very much like to see you again," (Patrick wrote), "if you still wish to visit. We are in the middle of the long rains right now, so perhaps late May might be the best time to arrive. What do you think?"

Just over a week later, Michael posted a brief one page reply by airmail: "Late May it is. I have booked a berth on the SS Uganda, arriving at Port Hardinge on the 24th May. I shall overnight in Port Hardinge, then take the train to Jiljil, arriving on the 26th May. Can you meet me?"

Patrick replied by telegram, which Michael received with only just over a week to go before he was to board the British India liner at Tilbury Docks.

"WILL MEET YOU JILJIL STATION 26 MAY STOP BEST WISHES STOP PATRICK"

Michael's novel, begun in September the previous year, remained unfinished.

Chapter Seven

They pulled out of Port Hardinge Station in the early afternoon. Once they had left the densely cultivated coastal strip behind, the journey might have become rather dull, for the railway line ran with few deviations, and after a while the endless plain and the unvarying cover of bush became tedious. There was no fence alongside the track, only the telephone poles marching in infinite progression. Changes of direction, when they occurred, were miniscule, before the track settled into another seemingly limitless stretch of straight run, mile after mile after mile. However, from his window Michael twice saw elephants, a sight which thrilled him, these huge animals, the very image of an unspoiled, untamed Africa, and once, he saw a large herd of buffalo. There were numerous herds of zebra and antelope, and occasional groups of giraffes, the latter moving in graceful slow motion, like a bush ballet performed at half speed. The train only rarely moved any faster than twenty-five miles an hour on the narrow three feet three inch gauge that was employed within the colony; Michael had ample time to view anything of interest that presented itself through the window, but it would soon be dusk – that brief, momentary dusk of equatorial Africa – and he was looking forward to dinner, for he had had no lunch at Port Hardinge. Soon, he heard the three toned dinner gong (which was held suspended from one hand and beaten with a padded stick held in the other) being sounded up and down the corridor, and he repaired to the dining car, where the waiters wore gleaming white *kanzus* and black sashes, with a black fez on their heads. (This indoor male Native servants' uniform was ubiquitous in the colony).

The cutlery was of heavy electro-plated silver, the heavy duty chinaware had the Equatorian Railways logo in blue on each piece, the table cloths and napkins were of amply starched, gleaming white linen. Michael ordered a pea soup, for its happy associations with childhood, and for the fish course he ordered the grilled dorado steaks on offer, which were served with a sweetcorn salad. The waiter assured him that the fish had been caught that morning. The flesh was firm, dense, and reminded Michael of swordfish. Had he been travelling on the down train, the Nile perch fillet might have been worth sampling, but it had been caught a long way inland, and Michael thought it wise to give it a miss. For his main course he ordered a springbok steak served with sautéed potato slices and onion rings, along with peas and carrots. Declining the wine list, he asked the waiter to bring him a Tusker beer. Although a steamed treacle pudding was on offer, Michael thought it might be a bit much after his generous meal, so he ordered tinned peach slices (probably, he thought, from South Africa) served with ice cream. He followed the meal with the excellent coffee that was so commonplace in the colony. He lighted up a cigar with his coffee, ordering a second cup as he did so. When he returned to his coupé, feeling comfortably replete – the dorado steaks had been substantial, almost a meal in themselves – he found that the banquette seat had been made up as a bed, complete with starched white linen sheets, and a blanket, with two pillows in crisply ironed, white cotton pillowslips, unmarked by any blemish. He was still smoking his cigar when the whiskey he had ordered before leaving the dining car was brought by a steward.

During the night the regular clackety-clack of the wheels crossing the joins in the rails, and the steady, rapid beat of the pistons from up ahead, were comforting sounds each time Michael awoke. The second time he awoke, he heard the long, mournful wail of the engine's whistle, a brave challenge to the immensity of the dark, limitless hinterland of Africa. Perhaps the engine driver sounded the whistle simply to declare his (and the fireman's) presence in this vast countryside, which was almost devoid of human habitation. Michael felt strangely moved, but he was soon asleep again.

As Michael ate his breakfast in the dining car the next morning (toast with marmalade; smoked kippers; two fried eggs with sausages, bacon, toast and fried tomatoes; and a glass of fresh orange juice, followed by a cigarette with the wonderful Equatoria coffee – two cups), he knew they were approaching Namuri, for the small *shambas*, hacked out of the bush, were seen more and more frequently, but prickly pear and kei apple thorn were taking over the tiny plots, for the Sikuyu who had worked this land were now being held within "protected" villages, or more accurately, within compounds surrounded by barbed wire. They were denied even the limited freedom of movement that farm labourers in the Highlands necessarily enjoyed. Effectively (like the Sikuyu on all the native reserves), they were being held in concentration camps, a policy which met with very vocal opposition from a small body in the colony. In this way the authorities hoped to deny the *Wa Chui* further recruits. These abandoned native farms were for Michael his first visible indication of the economic impact of the Emergency on the colony.

Namuri Railway Station was, however, quite busy, with a number of Europeans and Indians on the platform, waiting to travel upcountry. Native Police *askaris* armed with *lathis* (long, heavy sticks of bamboo, shod and bound with iron), and officered by a pair of Europeans wearing Sam Browns and sidearms, were very much in evidence on the platform. An Indian coffee seller circulated with his brass urn slung from one shoulder, the spout against his hip, and several small brass cups clinking against each other. His customers consisted only of Muslim Indians, for the Hindus were afraid that their caste would be compromised by sharing the brass cups with others. There were native food vendors (who, possessing Police passes to dwell within Namuri, were not obliged to be held in protected villages) selling roasted corn cobs, bags of peanuts, bottled mineral water and Coca Cola, *samoosas*, and dubious preparations whose composition Michael could only guess at. Michael shuddered to think what discomfort his Westerner's stomach might endure if he were to dare to sample such as these. The train spent more than half an hour at Namuri Station, while the engine was re-watered and re-coaled, and the train's catering and household departments replenished their depleted stocks.

It was about midday when the train drew into Jiljil Station. Michael saw Patrick waiting on the platform, with Karim standing just behind him. Patrick was wearing wide, starched khaki shorts reaching to his knees, with long socks, and his old slouch hat with a leopard skin hat band. There was a holstered revolver against his hip.

'Patrick!' Michael called from his window. '*Jambo!* Over here!'

Michael and Patrick shook hands through the open window. '*Jambo* Michael. *Karibu!*' Patrick declared.

Karim entered his compartment to fetch his luggage, and greeted him, '*Jambo Bwana* Michael.'

'*Jambo* Karim. *Habari?*'

'*Nzuri sana, Bwana,*' replied Karim. '*Habari?*'

'I am well, thank you Karim.'

'You are looking *nzuri sana*, Michael,' Patrick said. Michael wished he could say the same of his friend, but Patrick was beginning to have the look of a heavy drinker about him, with a high complexion and broken blood vessels on and around his nose. Michael guessed that his friend was having recourse to the bottle more than ever before.

Patrick had brought the Land Rover. 'We would not have managed the roads with the Chevvy,' he explained. To add emphasis to his remark, it began to rain. 'But the long rains are petering out; they'll be gone within another few days, I think.'

Karim joined the two men in the front of the Land Rover, seated in the centre seat, for the back of the Land Rover was already fully laden with boxes of groceries and supplies from Hari Patel's *dhuka*, as well as a large drum of diesel fuel – to all of which, Michael's luggage had now been added. As Jiljil's Main Street gave way to murram, Patrick said, 'I've been using her in four wheel drive. We will need it from now on.'

They rarely got above twenty miles an hour, and once they had turned off the north bound road onto the narrow single track road headed east, their speed at times was barely above walking pace, as the vehicle progressed in serpentine fashion from one side of the track, deep in mud, to the other, Patrick wrestling with the heavy steering. The long private road leading to the house was on the whole in better condition: Patrick had had it graded, and resurfaced at critical junctures, before the rainy season, but there were places where their speed still dropped right down. At one point they passed a herd of zebra, all standing facing the same way, their rumps to the weather, their heads down as they cropped the bright new grass.

'Damn *pundas*,' Patrick exclaimed. 'They'll be after the new corn next. I think we'll have to shoot one or two.'

'Can you eat zebra meat?' Michael asked.

'You can, if you don't mind eating second cousin to a horse,' Patrick replied. 'It's actually very good for you, it's so lean. But it's tough – the *Watu* will roast it, of course, but in my opinion it's best served stewed for a long time. But the meat wont go to waste if I shoot a couple of the stripey donkeys. The *Watu* will get it.'

The rain eased off, and the sun broke through, making the wet cedar shingled roof of the distant house glisten. 'It will do my mother good to have a house guest – take her out of herself.' Patrick commented. 'Aunt Catherine is still with us, but battier than ever.'

Michael thought that the gardens, which had been so splendid during his first visit, were looking neglected. Perhaps it was just the rain. But the lawn had not been mown for a while, and there were weeds growing between the gladioli and roses in the flower beds. The shrubbery looked unkempt, in need of pruning. But the gardens were still beautiful, the flame trees still covered in bright scarlet blossom, and the magnificent cedar tree in one corner was as impressive as he had remembered.

The three dogs bounded forward as the Land Rover pulled up at the foot of the steps to the veranda. Patrick fondled the flat heads of the ridgebacks, who then came to sniff Michael's legs. The Alsatian rejoined Lady Fiona Pencaitland on the veranda. She extended her hand and smiled at Michael. 'How nice to see you again, Michael. We have been so looking forward to your visit.'

'I am very glad to be back, Lady Pencaitland,' Michael responded, shaking her hand. 'My condolences for your loss. Lord Pencaitland was a fine gentleman.' He looked around. Where was Marjory?

'*Mpishi Moja* has prepared a late lunch for us. I believe there was some sort of a crisis in the kitchen which Marjory had to attend to. I expect she will be with us shortly,' Lady Pencaitland remarked.

There was a cloak room with a basin below a gilt framed mirror, and a lavatory cubicle, opening off the hallway, which Michael had to visit. When five minutes later he entered the dining room, he found Marjory there with Patrick and Lady Fiona.

Chapter Seven

'Dear Michael, how lovely to see you again, and you look so well.' Marjory smiled broadly, and took Michael's hand in both of her own. He kissed her on the cheek, then loosed his hand and stepped back. He experienced a confusion of feelings: on the one hand, there was the residual hurt at the way Marjory had (as he sometimes felt) misled him; on the other, a simple delight in seeing her again. Marjory was wearing dark blue slacks, a cream silk blouse with a gold locket around her neck, and an unbuttoned caramel coloured woollen cardigan. Her lovely golden hair was much as he remembered from his previous stay: gathered in a chignon off her fine neck. But she was paler than he remembered; perhaps the result of almost three rainy months during which the sun had rarely shone. Michael fancied that it was more than simply a chance arrangement of proportions, planes and angles that attracted him so much to her face; he thought that he could read Marjory's character – one of spirit and pluck – reflected in her beautiful features. He found her grace and beauty utterly compelling.

Michael had to make a conscious effort not to stare at Marjory during the late – but more than adequate – lunch. (A clear chicken consommé, followed by a beef curry served with rice and plump, greasy chapattis – the beef raised on the estate – accompanied by small dishes of grated coconut, chopped raw tomatoes, and fruit chutney, with tiny mango cubes, deliciously sweet and juicy, and homemade ice cream, for dessert). In an attempt to direct his thoughts elsewhere, he asked Patrick, 'Have conditions deteriorated much in the Colony? I could not help noticing, on the way up, the *shambas* outside Namuri were abandoned, returning to nature.'

Patrick looked up from his plate. He had been partaking generously of the red wine that Karim, standing just behind him, kept pouring for him. 'A lot of farmers are struggling financially now,' he replied. 'Supplies cost a lot more if you want them delivered to your doorstep. Deliveries have anyway grown infrequent. It costs us more to grow our produce now, and we are no longer as internationally competitive.'

Patrick paused, and gulped at his glass of wine. 'Despite the villagisation programme, the *Wa Chui* are still gaining recruits,' he continued. 'And their weaponry is growing more sophisticated, thanks to the Chinese. Not long ago, a *Wa Chui* band ambushed an Equatoria Reservist unit about to pursue them into the Nyahurari Forest, not far to the south – and they used mortars! Three Reservists were killed. Just before the rains began, a railway bridge on the mainline between Namuri and Port Caroline was blown up. Fortunately, the train had already crossed before the charges went off. Perhaps the most horrifying recent incident was when the *Wa Chui* overran a protected village in the Sikuyu reserve, and murdered fifteen Sikuyu villagers – presumably because they would not swear the *kiapo*. The six men of the British Army unit guarding the compound were also killed.'

Patrick looked around the table angrily, his colour very high. (It seemed that his mother, along with Marjory, had delayed their own lunch so they could join the two men at table). 'It's the British government I blame, with their talk of *Uhuru* for the Colony. Those left wingers at Westminster have never had a clue what the realities of colonial life are about. Their promise of independence in the foreseeable future has fired up the *Wa Chui*, and encouraged them in their outrages. The *Wa Chui* are trying to make Equatoria ungovernable, and destroy the Colony's economy, in the expectation that Britain would then pull out.'

'Which the British government would never do,' responded Michael. 'I'm quite sure that Britain will only grant Equatoria independence once the Emergency is over, and they can hand over a viable country. What do you think, Pat?'

'I think you are absolutely correct – but that is not what the *Wa Chui* believe. The *Wa Chui* have been hugely encouraged by the granting of self rule to Tanganyika earlier this month. Tanganyikan independence seems imminent now.'

Lady Fiona Pencaitland, who had been gazing into the far distance with a half smile on her face, spoke up suddenly. 'But we will be alright, no matter what happens, wont we, Patrick?' she asked.

Patrick smiled at his mother. 'I'm sure we will, Mother,' he replied. Michael realised that his friend was not sure at all, or he would not have been so worked up. His anger (which, if it had a target at all, was directed against the British government at Westminster) was the product of anxiety for the future.

Chapter Eight

After the late lunch (it was almost time for tea), Michael found his luggage in his bedroom upstairs and removed the gifts he had brought for Marjory, Patrick, Lady Fiona Pencaitland and Lady Catherine. He went back downstairs with them. The rain had not returned. Marjory and Lady Fiona Pencaitland were sitting on the veranda with Patrick, drinking coffee. Lady Catherine had not yet awoken from her afternoon rest. The two Rhodesian ridgebacks and Lady Fiona Pencaitland's Alsatian were lying down nearby. There were two young men in army uniform present.

'Will you join us for some coffee, Michael?' Marjory asked.

'I will, thanks.'

Mwara, the young Sikuyu houseboy, was standing nearby. *'Leta kikombe na sahani kwa Bwana* Michael,' Marjory ordered him.

'Ndiyo Memsaab,' the young man replied, and disappeared into the house, returning a short while later with another coffee cup and saucer on a tray. While he was gone, Patrick introduced Michael to the Equatoria Regiment Reservist lieutenant and his sergeant. The young lieutenant had short cropped blonde hair and a friendly face with a fading tan.

Chapter Eight

'Michael, this is Lieutenant Anthony MacDonald of the Equatoria Regiment Reserve.' Patrick turned to the young man. 'Lieutenant – meet Michael Hood, a friend from England.' The two men shook hands. 'And Sergeant Jack Cunningham.' Michael shook hands with him also. This young man looked as if he barely shaved yet. He too had a fading tan, with short dark hair. They were both drinking coffee with the Hepburns. They had only recently awoken and ate what was their breakfast, in the small parlour adjoining the drawing room, for they slept all morning, and into the afternoon, as they were on duty with their unit guarding the Native compound during the night.

The sun was shining brightly now. The air, washed clean, seemed to sparkle. A pair of black collared barbets was singing their antiphonal duet to each other, "too-puddly too-puddly too-puddly," back and forth between two of the flame trees in the garden. Nearer to hand, three or four tiny sunbirds with vivid scarlet chests were probing with their long curved bills in some white buddleia flowers. Michael reached into the bag he had with him, and removed a small package in Harrods gift wrap.

'I hope you will like these, Lady Pencaitland,' he addressed Patrick's mother, giving her the small package. She smiled and unwrapped it.

'Oh – these are lovely, Michael.' Inside the gift wrap were four hand-made scented toilet soaps. 'You cannot get this sort of thing in the Colony. Thank you.'

Michael handed Marjory a bottle of Bénédictine liqueur with a russet coloured ribbon tied around the neck. 'Yum-yum,' she said, and stood and kissed him on the cheek. 'Thank you, Michael. I am tempted to drink some straight away, but I shall wait until after dinner, I think.'

Then Michael extracted a Macallan twelve year old Scotch whiskey in a presentation canister, which he gave to Patrick. 'And for you, old Pat, hoping that you will enjoy it.'

Patrick smiled, a rare smile of unfeigned affection for his friend. 'I certainly shall! A rare treat indeed. You can help me drink some once the sun is over the yardarm. There's just something I have to see to first.' In Equatoria, the sun was generally considered to have attained that mythical position in the sky by five o' clock in the afternoon. It was already four o' clock. After Patrick had driven off in the Land Rover (he had some chore to attend to on the estate), the two ridgebacks with him, Michael and Marjory remained alone on the veranda. After declaring that tea time would be late this afternoon, the Dowager Lady Pencaitland and her Alsatian dog had gone indoors.

'How is your family, Marjory?' Michael asked her.

'My mother, father and brother are well, but like every farmer in the Highlands, they're finding things a struggle right now. I think a lot of farmers are on the very edge of financial viability now.'

How beautiful she is, Michael thought. Her narrow head sat so proudly and elegantly on her slim neck. 'And here, at *Mahali pa Kupumzika?*' he asked. 'I get the impression that Patrick is rattled.'

'Production costs have mounted, and transport is erratic. And we're short of labour. But we're still slightly ahead, though if things get much worse, that could change.'

'I'm sorry,' Michael said. 'It seems such a waste of so much beauty and potential.'

'Equatoria will always be beautiful. I hope we don't have to leave.'

So they had discussed leaving the colony, or at least, it had been in Marjory's mind, Michael thought.

'Is there anything I can do to help?'

'Your being here will help take Pat's mind off his worries, I hope. Unfortunately LegCo – you know, the Colony's all-European Legislative Council – sits in Namuri for the next three months, every Thursday and Friday, and Patrick has to attend.

He's the Member for Nyarua District. I expect they'll be debating our response to the growing menace from the *Wa Chui* – that, and the threat of *Uhuru*. Patrick tells me that the Council of Executive Members' delegates in London are not making much progress with the British government. It's the future status of the Europeans in the government of an independent Equatoria, that is the sticking point.'

In 1946, as a reward for the colony's unstinting help with men and materiel during the War, Equatoria had been granted semi-autonomous government by Britain. A Council of Executive Members, made up of LegCo Members appointed by the First Councillor (equivalent to the Prime Minister of a Dominion territory such as South Africa, Australia or Canada), constituted a cabinet (although it was not called that). The colony retained a Governor appointed by Britain.

Patrick was back by half past five. He joined Michael, who was drinking tea on the veranda, gazing at the plate of fresh scones *Mpishi Moja* had made. Michael was still dressed in the white linen suit in which he had travelled up from Port Hardinge. Marjory had gone upstairs to change. The two ridgebacks went and had a long drink of water from their water bowls, then lay down on the floor, their tongues out.

'Hullo old chap,' Patrick greeted Michael. 'How about we sample that Macallan?'

'I'll gladly join you,' Michael replied.

'Mwara – *Kuja hapa!*' Patrick shouted. Mwara appeared from within the house. *'Kioo cha whiskey mbili,'* Patrick ordered him. While the houseboy was fetching two whiskey glasses from the drinks cabinet in the drawing room, Patrick fetched the cylindrical carton of Macallan from the hallway, where he had left it before going out. He poured Michael and himself a generous double tot into each of the two heavy lead crystal glasses Mwara provided.

'Cheers!' Patrick declared.

'Cheers.'

Marjory joined the men a few minutes later, as did Lady Fiona Pencaitland, the Alsatian dog at her heels. Marjory had changed into a very pretty cocktail dress of pale green silk, supported by narrow shoulder straps over her bare shoulders. She was wearing an emerald and pearl necklace (a Hepburn heirloom). Michael wondered when he would see Lady Catherine. He had a gift for her, a round Wedgwood lidded box in which she could keep hair clips and suchlike. Perhaps she kept to her room most of the time? In fact, Lady Catherine had a comfortable bed-sitting room and a bathroom of her own upstairs.

When Michael had finished his whiskey, he went upstairs to change into his evening jacket, for dinner was to be black tie. By the time he came back downstairs, Marjory and her mother in law had joined Patrick in a drink. Only Patrick had touched the scones. The group continued to sit and chat on the veranda for a while, night sounds now coming from the garden, for here, on the equator, the sun had set promptly at six o' clock. After a while, the group went indoors to the drawing room. Marjory wished Michael to tell her about the plays he had seen and concerts he had attended in London. The Dowager Lady Pencaitland sat silently, her features in repose, a glass of sherry to hand, the Alsatian at her feet. Patrick was still drinking whiskey. Michael joined him in another. When Lady Catherine appeared, both men stood, and Michael went forward to greet her. Smiling at the old lady, he said, 'Good evening Lady Catherine. I hope you are well.'

'Good evening, Malcolm,' Lady Catherine responded. 'Have you been away?' She was wearing a black silk dress of extremely antique styling, reminiscent of the 1920s, with a long string of pearls hanging across her bosom. The dress was however rather longer at the hem than the young flappers of the 1920s would have worn it.

Chapter Eight

At one point, Patrick left the room. When, after some minutes, he returned, he had buckled on a gun belt with a holstered revolver attached. He was carrying another holstered revolver and a gun belt in his hand. 'We should be wearing these,' he remarked. 'I have your revolver with me, Michael.' He handed Michael the gun belt and holstered revolver he was carrying. Michael had almost forgotten the beautiful ivory handled Colt revolver, his fortieth birthday present from the Hepburns. He took the gun belt from Patrick and withdrew the revolver from the holster, and admiring it, he said, 'What a lovely weapon. I see that it's loaded.'

'Of course,' Patrick said. 'We should have them with us in the evenings. And you must carry it whenever you go any distance from the house during the day. If you go riding, be sure to take it with you.'

Michael, who felt no foolish inclination to downplay the threat posed by the *Wa Chui*, responded, 'I shall do that. But I doubt I shall be going riding as often this time.'

There had been a slow bleed of labour from the estate. At least once a week now, another black farm worker was absent – sometimes two at a time. These workers were not after all forced labour, although the native compound was surrounded by a barbed wire fence, and guarded at night by its small unit of Equatoria Regiment native troops, officered by the two European Reservists. This was not done in order to imprison the estate workers (although soon after sunset, the gate to the native compound was closed until dawn, and there was no freedom of movement during that period), but to protect them from *Wa Chui* reprisals. It was possible to slip away during the day, and head for the *Wa Chui* camps in the Nyahurari Forest in the foothills of the Cairngorms Range.

One morning, Karim told Patrick that Mwara, the young Sikuyu houseboy, was absent. Patrick sent a message requesting the presence of the village Headman. He spoke to him on the veranda in *Kiswahili*. 'Where is Mwara?' he asked the late middle aged, grey haired man, after the usual greetings and enquiries after one another's health.

'I know not, *Bwana Mkubwa*.'

'He has gone to join the *Wa Chui*, has he not?' Patrick stated.

'It is possible, *Bwana*.'

'Tell me if you hear news of him.'

'*Ndiyo, Bwana Mkubwa.*'

Patrick gave the man two cigarettes, which he took in cupped hands, bobbing his head.

'That is all then. *Kwenda vizuri*, Kimathi.'

'*Weka vizuri Bwana Mkubwa. Kwaheri, Bwana.*'

Michael noticed that Mwara's defection marked an increase in Patrick's drinking. No doubt this was coincidental: none of the Hepburns had had anything like the relationship with Mwara that they had with Karim. Patrick no longer waited until the sun was "over the yardarm" before switching from lager beers to whiskey.

A few days after Mwara's disappearance, Michael and Marjory went for their first ride together since his return to Equatoria. The streams from the high forested ridges on the estate's eastern boundary were still flowing fast and clear. They reined their horses in below a rocky outcrop. A tiny watercourse tumbled in a series of miniature waterfalls down the rock face, upon which moss, ferns and lianas grew. A grove of cedars (which were more accurately known as African junipers) had escaped the axe, and grew below the rock face. It was like a setting from Arcadia, Michael thought. The location was not new to Michael: the two of them had visited it before when out riding, during his previous stay.

'This is a favourite place of mine,' Marjory remarked, as she had once or twice before in the past. She dismounted from her horse, which she led to the stream, where the animal drank for a while, before she walked it away and let it graze on the green grass nearby, throwing the end of the reins around the branch of

Chapter Eight

a Spanish tamarind. Michael dismounted also, and after his horse had drunk, he too threw the reins around the large shrub. The two horses could graze on the thick green grass while Marjory sat down, her legs elegantly arranged, in the shade of the nearest cedar, for the sun, almost directly overhead, was very warm. Michael joined her, shifting his holstered revolver around more comfortably as he sat down alongside her. A pair of cinnamon chested bee-eaters, strikingly pretty with their bright yellow chins and cinnamon coloured breasts, perched on the lowest branch of a nearby cedar.

Michael wished to ask Marjory a question. He thought the best thing was to come straight out with it. 'Marjory, if I may ask – Patrick is my oldest friend – is the Emergency causing you real financial concern at *Mahali pa Kupumzika*?'

'*Mahali pa Kupumzika* is surviving at the moment – just,' Marjory responded. 'It's the smaller farmers, like my parents, who are really struggling financially, like most farmers in Equatoria. Our farm is much smaller than *Mahali pa Kupumzika*; we cannot apply the economies of scale that the big estates can.'

Michael noted Marjory's use of the words "our farm," and "we," as applied to her parents' farm. Were they significant? How closely did she identify with *Mahali pa Kupumzika*? He also wondered (as, he was sure, did many other people) why Marjory showed no signs of falling pregnant after a year's marriage. How happy was she? That was something he could not ask her.

Instead, he asked, 'Are you anxious for the future, Marjory?'

'Yes,' she replied, 'I am. How can there be a future for European land owners in an independent, black ruled Equatoria, especially after the bitterness the *Wa Chui* have sown?' Marjory smiled ruefully at Michael. 'I don't want to leave. I was born here! This is my home! But right now, this is a country of sorrows. I think most of us will end up leaving – unless the Council of Executive Members' discussions with the British government in

London reach a happy conclusion. Which seems unlikely, from what Patrick tells me.'

Michael himself was in two minds about Britain's imperial mission. On the one hand, he believed that British rule in the colonies had been based upon a moral superiority; that it had been benign, and that it had brought stability, peace and prosperity (generally speaking) to regions that had known none of these things before the British had arrived (and would in all probability know none of them after Britain had pulled out). Yet, to belie his beliefs, there was the bloody and oppressive history of British rule in Ireland, and the questions that had arisen in his mind about British rule in India, once he had begun researching for his historical novels set in the days of the Raj. And now, in Equatoria itself, there was the often extreme violence and economic instability of the Emergency.

Sometimes, Michael found himself wondering whether Europeans had any business ruling anywhere in Africa. We are, he thought, an utterly alien people who shared nothing with (and often showed little desire to understand) the cultures of Africa, but by virtue of our advanced technology and weaponry, we have imposed our rule over much of Africa. (And where British rule had not reached, that of the French and the Portuguese had). Michael understood that the Empire was essentially an economic construct: it was of economic benefit to British holders of capital seeking new outlets for investment, and to British manufacturers and bankers; it was an exploitative organisation which sought to disguise its primary objective by donning a cloak of high moral purpose. Yet within Michael's own family history there had been administrators and soldiers in British India; these, his ancestors, had not been there to get rich, but to serve some higher ideal. One of his own grandparents had been born in India.

Michael was aware that that the contemporary *zeitgeist* was now anti-colonial, anti-imperial. Which was why he was certain

Chapter Eight

that the Hepburns' days in Equatoria were numbered, whether the government defeated the *Wa Chui* or not. And he was no longer sure that the *Wa Chui* could in fact be defeated.

How could Marjory be expected to be "happy?"

Chapter Nine

In mid June Patrick and Michael, accompanied by Karim, drove the Land Rover to Jiljil to fetch a drum of diesel fuel and a drum of petrol. (The Standard Vacuum tankers would no longer deliver as far as *Mahali pa Kupumzika*, because of the threat of a *Wa Chui* ambush). There were also feedstock supplies to collect for the horses, specifically oats, bran and molasses. The estate of course grew its own maize. In whatever space was left over in the back of the Land Rover, they would cram groceries and household necessities from Hari Patel's *dhuka*. Hari Patel no longer made deliveries as far as *Mahali pa Kupumzika* either. There was no rain at this time of year; they could make good progress on the narrow dirt roads.

One day in the far from distant future, with the relentless increase in Human population numbers in Africa, the entire Equatorian Highlands would become a vast, high density semi-rural slum, but that day was still twenty or thirty years hence: for now, the countryside was given over to spreading European farms between which were stands of indigenous forest, and stretches of shrub and grassland, in which game was still far from absent. Driving through such country reminded Michael of some of the films set in Africa he had watched in recent years: there was of course *"African Queen,"* Starring Humphrey Bogart and Audrey Hepburn (there was a surname that was close to home!) But as he had yet to see one of Africa's mighty rivers, much of its setting was alien to his experience. Perhaps the film that Michael felt most closely mirrored his current circumstances was *"Safari,"* in which Victor Mature and Janet Leigh had starred. It was set during a very recent native uprising in a neighbouring colony, similar to that which Equatoria was now suffering, and the scenery was authentic, and the background was so very similar to his experience of Equatoria. He had also enjoyed watching *"King Solomon's Mines,"* starring Stewart Granger and Deborah Kerr, and he was sure he recognised some of the settings from that production.

Hari Patel, who had arrived from Gujarat in the 1930s, gave the two men strong, gritty coffee from tiny enamelled brass cups, washed down with a glass of water. The water glasses were very *maridadi* (which in *Kiswahili* meant something like "stylish," but in colonial slang meant over decorated), and were of yellow glass decorated with gold embossed designs. Hari Patel's native assistant, with Karim overseeing him (for hard labour was on the whole beneath Karim; that was what the Sikuyu were for), loaded the back of the Land Rover, while the two Europeans drank their coffee. Patrick and Michael had first called at the oil company's sub-depot to collect the two drums of fuel, after which they had made a stop at the animal feed store. When they drove down Jiljil's Main Street, Karim sat in front between Michael and Patrick, his legs, hidden by his *kanzu*, to the left of the gearbox hump, for there was no room for him in the back of the vehicle now.

They had travelled about twenty miles on their return journey, not yet having reached the narrow turnoff to the east, and were passing through a wide area of heavily wooded, uncultivated land, when Karim (whose vision was singularly acute) said, '*Bwana!* There are *Watu* blocking the road, and they are armed!'

Both Europeans peered ahead, and Patrick (who had not seen action during the War, having commanded a desk in Cairo) began to reduce his speed. Michael (who had seen a great deal of action during the War) said, 'Keep your speed up, Patrick!'

Karim had turned and was peering through the window at the rear of the cab. 'They are behind us also,' he announced.

Michael twisted round and looked through the rear window. Karim was correct: a group of armed men now blocked the road behind them.

Patrick wore his holstered revolver on his left hip, butt facing forward. 'Pat,' Michael said, 'Can you draw your revolver?' Michael already had his Colt in his hand. 'When we're a little closer, I want you to start firing at them – you can drive with one hand.'

Patrick reached across his right hand and drew his revolver from its holster. Michael leant out his window on the left hand side. He could see the men clearly now. There were five of them, and three were aiming guns at the advancing Land Rover – whether bolt action rifles or automatic assault rifles, he could not be sure. Then gunfire erupted, short rapid bursts typically associated with automatic assault weapons. The windscreen shattered and Michael felt glass cut his face. He leant over Karim (who had hunkered right down) and used the butt of his revolver to clear the remnants of glass in front of Patrick, then did the same for his side of the windscreen. He could hear bullets pinging and whining off the front of the Land Rover. He hoped the radiator was not holed.

'Open fire, Patrick,' he commanded, not particularly urgently, 'and go as fast as you can.' And he himself opened fire with his revolver, shooting directly ahead of him, with no windscreen glass now to impede him. Patrick did likewise. Michael rapidly emptied the six chambers in his revolver. He reloaded as fast as he could, having grabbed the box of cartridges from the shelf below the dashboard and placing the box on the seat between Karim and himself, spilling cartridges on the car's floor as he did so.

Chapter Nine

Patrick had also emptied his revolver, and he tossed it to Karim, who had raised his head again. 'Reload please Karim!'

Karim reloaded Patrick's revolver as rapidly as he could, and Michael had already opened fire again – then they were flashing past the men either side, and the three men in the cab ducked down instinctively, Patrick letting out a yell as he dropped his revolver on the floor. His right hand was wounded, and it began to bleed copiously. Michael was, miraculously, unscathed, apart from the glass cuts to his face, and what he quickly established was just a bullet burn to his chest, although he could see bullet holes in his door. Nor was Patrick harmed, apart from the injury to his hand. Karim appeared to be unharmed also. Later Michael was to notice that the rear window was shattered and that there were exit holes in the rear of the cab. It was a wonder that none of the three men was badly harmed.

'Are you OK, Karim?' Michael asked the Somali, whose face was also cut by glass.

'*Ndiyo Bwana.*'

'Pull up a few miles ahead, Pat,' Michael told his friend. 'We'll look at the car, and your hand. Then I'll drive.'

'Right-O Mike.'

He hasn't called me Mike since we were at school together, Michael thought. His chest was bleeding freely; his shirt was red with blood. He struggled out of it, rolled it up, then, using the sleeves, tied it over one shoulder and across his chest, covering the wound. He had applied emergency dressings to wounds before.

A few miles ahead, round several bends in the road, Patrick pulled up. The *Wa Chui* had probably been using Chinese-made Type 56 assault rifles, a variant of the Soviet AK-47. These weapons had small, 7.62mm calibre rounds. A bullet had scoured a burning channel along the fleshy part of Patrick's right hand on the outer edge, abrading the small bone there.

Michael used his handkerchief to wrap and knot around

Patrick's hand. Patrick's normally ruddy complexion had turned very pale beneath the glass cuts he too had sustained. 'I could do with a cigarette,' he remarked. Michael lighted him one of his own and passed it to him. Then he turned to Karim.

'Karim, is there any whiskey in the back?'

'*Ndiyo Bwana*. There is a box with twelve bottles.'

'Bring one here, please.' Michael got out of the cab, and Karim went round behind and found the crate of Bell's, removing a bottle, and bringing it to Michael, who unscrewed the cap and gulped at it, then handed the bottle to Patrick.

'Have a slug of this, Pat,' he told his friend. Patrick drank from the bottle, a very hefty, prolonged draught. Michael took this opportunity to offer Karim a cigarette, who took it with thanks, then he lighted himself a cigarette. He would have offered Karim a drink, but he did not wish to offend Karim's Muslim sensibilities. Michael saw a spot of bright colour blossom in each of Patrick's cheeks. Patrick gulped again from the bottle.

Incongruously, Michael was suddenly aware of the harsh call of a bushshrike. He had been teaching himself about the birds of the Equatorian Highlands (both with the aid of a book on Equatorian birds he had found in the library at *Mahali pa Kupumzika*, and with Marjory's help in identifying their calls when they were out riding together). Although he could not see the bird, he could visualise it: a very pretty, colourful creature. He went round to the front of the Land Rover. The wings were holed by bullets in half a dozen places, and the top of the bonnet was scoured by the tracks of bullets, several of which must have hit the spare tyre on top of the bonnet. (They had been shooting high, thought Michael, like most beginners with automatic weapons). Raising the bonnet, he found that the radiator was almost undamaged, except for two neat bullet holes, through which water was issuing in thin streams. Michael looked around and saw a very thin, tough, straight stick at the side of the road. He broke two pieces about seven inches

Chapter Nine

long from it, and with a large stone he hammered these into the holes in the radiator, until they had gone right through and were showing the other side. They would hold at least until they got home.

'Karim, is there any water in the car?' he asked the Somali.

'*Ndiyo Bwana*. It is underneath the seat where you were sitting.'

Michael raised the seat cushion, and found a four gallon jerry can of water beneath it. With a handkerchief leant him by Patrick, he removed the hot radiator cap, then topped up the radiator, replacing the radiator cap before dropping the bonnet down again with a clang.

Patrick slid across the seat to the left, Karim climbed back in next to him, and Michael got in behind the wheel, and put the Land Rover in first gear, then pulled away. His chest was burning where the round had scoured the pectoral muscle.

'We were lucky they were such rotten shots,' Patrick said. Michael admired his efforts at making light of the incident. He knew that it had shocked Patrick. 'I wonder whether we got any of them?' Patrick continued.

'I couldn't tell. We will clean up your hand properly when we get home. You're right; we were very lucky. That could have been much worse.'

'The bastards!' Patrick exclaimed. 'They'll be making for the forest now, I would think. Through Keith Hepburn's land.' Keith Hepburn was Marjory's father. 'We must try to raise Keith or Eileen on the radio telephone and warn them.'

'And the Police,' Michael added. 'It's a pity we don't have a radio in the Land Rover.'

Michael was aware that during the engagement he had felt more intensely conscious of being alive than at any time since the War had ended. He felt almost intoxicated with elation.

Keith Hepburn and Eileen, Marjory's parents, were not

molested by the insurgents, but neither the Army unit that guarded the estate's native compound at night (whose two officers Michael had alerted immediately upon reaching *Mahali pa Kupumzika*), which set off to the south-east in two Land Rovers in an attempt to cut across in front of the insurgents, nor the Police, could catch them. By the time the Police at Jiljil had reached the district, the *Wa Chui* had almost certainly reached the sanctuary of the forest, for there were no direct roads between Jiljil and the eastern boundaries of either of the Hepburn holdings. At *Mahali pa Kupumzika*, Marjory had cleaned and dressed the two men's wounds properly, and dabbed TCP to the glass cuts on the three men's faces, applying sticking plasters to the worst of the cuts.

At dinner that evening, at which the young Equatoria Regiment Reservist Lieutenant, doing more listening than talking, was present, Patrick (whose wine glass was being frequently recharged by Karim) said, 'In future, when we visit Jijil, we will take the two Land Rovers. André will drive his Land Rover. We're going to need more carrying capacity anyway, with deliveries to the estate so disrupted.'

Patrick reached for his glass of wine. 'During the dry season we can also take the Chev – if we have someone to drive it. Perhaps that's something you could do, as long as you're here, Michael? Its loading capacity will be useful. We'll be safer with two or three cars travelling together.'

'OK. I can drive the Chevrolet, if you wish,' Michael responded.

Marjory spoke up. 'Perhaps we should be looking to travel in convoy with my father each time we visit Jiljil,' she suggested. 'It seems that we're pretty much on a war footing now, and I expect my father would welcome the company.'

'That's an excellent idea, Marjory,' Michael interjected.

'I agree,' Patrick said. 'I shall talk to Keith about it.'

'If I was the *Wa Chui*,' Michael said, 'I would be trying to obtain land mines from the Chinese next . . .'

Chapter Nine

'Yes, that's probably the next step,' Patrick agreed. 'The *Wa Chui* are clearly becoming better organised, with access to more and better weapons.' He smiled lopsidedly. 'Though that ambush wasn't very professional.'

Lady Fiona Pencaitland sat with a half smile on her patrician features. The focus of her gaze seemed far distant. Her Alsatian dog lay at her feet beneath the dining table. Lady Catherine remarked suddenly, 'Malcolm, you have done something to your face. And you too, Patrick. Please pass me the butter.' Patrick did so, with a smile.

The following afternoon, Keith Hepburn called on the Pencaitlands. Michael had first met him at Marjory's wedding the previous year. He had craggy, seamed features, very brown from the sun, and when he removed his hat, his receding hair, which he brushed backwards, was a gunmetal grey. He had dense, dark, thick eyebrows. His eyes however were a brilliant blue, and they sparkled with good humour. Michael felt instinctively drawn to him. The three men and Marjory, along with the two Equatoria Regiment Reservist officers, were sitting on the veranda, drinking tea. It took Patrick a while to tell Keith the full story of the *Wa Chui* ambush. Then he said to him, 'I propose we initiate a convoy system in future, for trips to Jiljil, with your meeting up with us where your farm track joins the road, and the two of us at least (and probably André Myburgh in his Land Rover, and perhaps Michael driving the Chevrolet while he's here) proceeding in convoy thereafter.'

'That sounds like a good idea,' Keith Hepburn agreed. 'What do you think, Anthony?' he asked, addressing the Equatoria Regiment Reservist Lieutenant by his Christian name, for he, like Patrick, knew his family.

'It is a very good idea, Mr. Hepburn,' the young man replied. 'Ideally, there should be military convoys, but there aren't enough military personnel.'

'How often do you normally visit Jiljil?' Patrick asked Keith Hepburn.

'It's been once a week up to now, but perhaps twice a month would be enough.'

'Right, once a fortnight then?'

'That sounds right,' Keith responded.

'Will you stay for a drink, Keith?' Patrick asked him.

Keith looked at his watch. It was half past four. 'Thanks,' he replied. 'But just the one, mind; I want to be back home before it grows dark.'

'What will you have? Beer – or something stronger?'

'A beer please, Patrick.'

'What about you, Mike? A beer?'

'Yes please, Pat,' Michael replied.

'And you, Marjory?'

'Nothing for me, thanks,' Marjory responded.

'How about a beer, Anthony – Jack?' Patrick asked the two Reservist officers. Both said yes, they would.

'Karim – *leta bia nne kwa bwanas, na whiskey kwa ajili yangu.*'

Karim, who was standing not far away, replied, '*Ndiyo, Bwana Mkubwa,*' and disappeared inside, returning shortly with four cold beers poured out in tall glasses, and a hefty scotch, all on a silver tray. It was, Michael thought, a little early for a neat whiskey, but Patrick seemed to have abandoned the five o' clock sun over the yardarm limitation.

Patrick raised his glass. 'Cheers!' he declared.

'Cheers,' Keith, Michael and the two young Reservists replied.

Chapter Ten

In July, Deirdre (the younger of Patrick's nieces) and Eleanor (the oldest), came home for the school holidays. At fourteen, Deirdre was still something of a mischievous tom boy, but Eleanor, at fifteen, had suddenly become a young lady, and was very conscious of her status as such. Consequently, Michael no longer found her company burdensome.

'I envy you, living in London,' she told him. 'How I would love to visit London!'

'I think you would enjoy it tremendously,' Michael responded. 'London is best enjoyed when you're young, though perhaps you should wait another year or two.'

'Of course, I hardly know anyone there,' Eleanor remarked. 'Just some distant cousins.'

Michael smiled at her. 'You would know me. I would enjoy taking you around London.'

Eleanor smiled back and lowered her lashes over her eyes. 'That would be nice,' she said.

André Myburgh was a competent estate manager. There was little that Patrick needed to do himself on the estate (that was the whole point of having an estate manager), but until fairly recently he had always liked to feel that he knew what was happening on his land. However, of late his diligence had begun to wane. Nonetheless, he would still occasionally take the Land Rover, or (as today) ride out on horseback, to tour the estate. Michael would invariably join him on horseback. Patrick rode well. He was at least Michael's equal as a rider, although neither man could match Marjory for her ability to become one with the horse. It was late July, and they were on their way back from the top pasture, where the barley was being harvested. Patrick had exchanged a few words with André Myburgh, who, because of the chronic lack of trained labour now available, was himself driving the tractor that towed the harvester. Patrick, who had otherwise said very little during their ride so far, seemed sunk in brooding, but now he remarked, 'Until recently this estate produced a huge financial surplus every year. I sometimes think those days are gone for good.'

'When the Emergency ends, labour will be plentiful again, and production costs will fall, if I understand you correctly, and Equatorian produce will become internationally competitive again, eh?'

'Will the Emergency ever end?' Patrick responded. 'Sometimes I fear that the *Wa Chui* cannot in fact be defeated, merely contained.'

'The Communist insurgents in Malaya were defeated,' Michael said. 'Surely the *Wa Chui* will be defeated eventually.' But Michael was not sure of that at all.

Patrick pressed his heels against his mount's sides, and urged it into a trot. Michael did likewise. The two men rode side by side. 'What worries me,' Patrick continued, 'is that no sooner will we have crushed the *Wa Chui* insurgency than we will be facing *Uhuru*. And with *Uhuru* will inevitably come land reform and the breaking up of the big estates like ours.'

Michael thought that Patrick was probably correct. The British government would abandon the European settler community as

Chapter Ten

soon as it could do so without losing face; as soon, in other words, as the insurgency was ended. The two men rode on through the long grass in silence once again. Of a sudden, a fan-tailed grassbird shot up out of the long grass just ahead of them, and Patrick's horse shied violently, and he was flung from the saddle. Michael reined in his horse. He could tell immediately that Patrick had hurt himself; he had landed very awkwardly indeed. Patrick groaned, and tried to stand up.

'God damn!' he exclaimed, his features twisted in pain, as, attempting to put his weight on his left leg, he fell to the ground again. 'I think I've broken it.'

'Let me look.' Patrick pulled up his trouser leg, very gingerly. Michael thought the leg did not look right. But really, he knew very little about it.

'It hurts like hell,' Patrick said.

'I'll go get help. I'll bring the Land Rover up here. OK?'

'Yah – please do that.'

Michael left Patrick sitting on the ground, and set his heels to his horse's flanks. At the big house, two miles away, he found Marjory, and the two of them drove the Land Rover back to Patrick.

'Oh – my poor Darling!' Marjory declared. 'Let me see your leg.'

Patrick had, thoughtlessly, pulled his trouser leg down again once Michael had left. Now, Marjory could barely get Patrick's corduroy trouser leg up over his injured lower limb, which had already begun to swell.

'We need to get Patrick to the doctor in Jiljil,' she said.

'I agree,' Michael responded. 'I'll drive him there in the Chevrolet.'

'I'm coming with you,' Marjory declared.

'It isn't safe,' Michael answered. But Marjory insisted.

'OK,' Michael said. 'You drive in front in the Chev with Pat – I'll follow behind you in the Land Rover.'

At the house, Patrick gulped down a hefty whiskey brought to him by Karim. Then the three of them set off, in two separate vehicles, for Jiljil, with a white faced Patrick sprawling in the roomy front seat of the Chevrolet alongside his wife. All three of them were armed. Michael felt for his friend. He himself had only ever broken a wrist as a child. He could only imagine how painful a broken leg was. In the Chevrolet, particularly when the car hit a bump in the road, Patrick would groan.

The journey was uneventful. In this, the dry season, they made fast progress, and they were at the doctor's surgery in Jiljil within less than two hours. Doctor Anstruther, a small, near-bald Englishman in his late fifties, who had arrived in the colony as a young man more than thirty years earlier, of course knew the Pencaitlands well. After examining the leg, eliciting groans from Patrick, he announced, 'I think we have a tibial plateau fracture, Lord Pencaitland; a break in the upper part of the shin bone. You will need an X-ray and a plaster cast. I think they should be able to do both today, at Naburu Hospital. I'll phone ahead.' It was now four o' clock. 'Can you drive your husband there, Lady Pencaitland?' the doctor asked Marjory.

'Yes. Michael and I will drive Patrick there.'

'Good. Let me make a telephone call first, then you can set off.'

It was about twenty-five miles along the main road to Naburu. The three of them arrived at Naburu Hospital just on five o' clock. They were expected.

'If you wish, we will keep your husband in overnight, Lady Pencaitland,' one of the doctors told her. 'It will be dark before we have finished. Do you have any of his things with you?'

Marjory had packed an overnight bag for Patrick. She might not have thought to do so, had not Michael (who was good at planning ahead) suggested it before they set off from *Mahali pa Kupumzika*. They said their goodbyes to Patrick and wished him

Chapter Ten

luck, and told him they would fetch him in the morning. Then they began the long journey home. They would be driving after dark for most of their journey. Michael wished Marjory was not with him.

'Are you OK following me in the dark?' he asked her.

'Oh Michael – of course I am,' Marjory replied impatiently.

Michael did not drive very often in England. A car was more bother than it was worth in London. He found this journey, along dirt roads all the way, especially taxing after the sun had dropped beneath the western horizon, and it grew dark almost instantly, as it does in the tropics. In addition, he was constantly aware of the threat from the *Wa Chui*. He kept glancing anxiously in the rear view mirror, to check that Marjory's headlights were there. She was keeping some distance behind him, to avoid driving in his dust. But the journey was completed without incident, and before he went in to dinner (having first changed out of his riding clothes, donning a pair of slacks, a clean shirt, a tie and a jacket) he had a very stiff whiskey. Karim asked him, 'Will the *Bwana Mkubwa* be well, *Bwana*?'

'Yes Karim. They will set his leg in plaster at the hospital. We will fetch him tomorrow morning.'

After dinner, Marjory used the radio telephone to get hold of André Myburgh at his small bungalow on the estate. She arranged that he would accompany them to Naburu in his Land Rover in the morning. (Marjory would travel with Michael in the Chevrolet). Karim would once again stay behind: neither Michael nor Marjory wished to leave Lady Fiona Pencaitland and Lady Catherine alone in the house, but for the Sikuyu servants.

'Very well, Lady Pencaitland,' the estate manager said. 'What time would you like me to be at the big house?'

'Just after breakfast. At eight-thirty, André,' she replied.

Patrick's lower left leg was in plaster when they fetched him the following morning, and he had a pair of crutches with him.

He had strapped his revolver to his waist again. Michael, Marjory and André were all three armed. 'I am very glad to see you,' Patrick addressed Michael and Marjory. Marjory kissed her husband. Patrick asked her, 'Have you got a cigarette?'

Patrick smoked only occasionally, with the exception of a cigar or two after a meal, but when he was feeling particularly stressed, he would have a cigarette. And right now, he was feeling very stressed: he was longing for a drink. André was waiting outside the hospital. Patrick greeted him, then they made their way to the Chevrolet, Patrick swinging between his pair of crutches.

'I'll be glad to get home,' he said.

Michael thought he was looking awful; pale and sweating. Every now and then he made strange, convulsive movements of his head. It occurred to Michael that perhaps Patrick needed a drink – he had been without one since yesterday afternoon. When at last they got home, Michael and Karim helped him up the stairs to the veranda. His mother was waiting for him there.

'Darling! How are you?'

'Fine, Mother, excuse me a minute, will you?' Patrick kissed her on the cheek, then he swung himself urgently on his pair of crutches towards the drawing room, where he made for the drinks cabinet. Karim came hurrying forward.

'Bwana Mkubwa! Naweza kukusaidia?'

'Ndiyo – whiskey kubwa, Karim,' Patrick replied.

Karim brought a large whiskey to Patrick, who had sat down in one of the armchairs.

'Asante sana,' Patrick thanked Karim, and gulped the whiskey down in one. 'Oh God,' he remarked. *'Mwingine!'* Karim brought him another large whiskey, which this time, Patrick drank with a little more restraint. Michael and Marjory, along with Lady Fiona Pencaitland, all of whom had followed Patrick into the drawing room, had gone out to the veranda again. When after some minutes Patrick joined them, he was looking more like his old self.

Chapter Ten

The doctors had told Patrick he was not to walk unaided on his leg for the next twelve weeks. He would be unable to drive the Land Rover, nor would he be able to ride. He could, however, drive the Chevrolet – if it was really necessary – which had an automatic gearbox, and required only the use of the right foot to operate the accelerator and footbrake, but he would not be able to keep an eye on the estate. For the next twelve weeks, until late October (by which time the short rains had set in), Marjory filled in for him, sometimes driving the Land Rover, but often, setting out on horseback. Michael, who felt that he could not return to England while Patrick was immobilised, would always join her then on her tours of the estate, and he realised that he was beginning to learn a great deal about farming in the Equatorian Highlands.

'Ten or twenty years ago,' he said to her one morning, as they were returning on horseback from a cattle dip (the dairy herd was driven by young *mchungajis* into a fenced paddock, from whence the cows were encouraged, using shrill shouts and long sticks, to enter the long narrow dip, where the pesticide solution freed them from parasites), 'with what I'm learning now, I might have been tempted to set up as a farmer in Equatoria.'

'But not anymore,' Marjory responded. 'So you do not think there is a future for us – for the Europeans – in Equatoria?'

Michael looked at Marjory, at the graceful carriage of her head on her slim neck, and her posture so straight atop the horse, she might have been riding with a spring steel rod pushed up her spine. Her face was brushed with gold from the sun, and her green eyes were the deep, intense colour of emeralds. How he wished he could believe that she – and her family, and of course, Patrick – could be certain of a future in the colony.

'I don't know. I certainly hope so,' Michael replied. 'For you and for all the European settlers in Equatoria.'

Patrick hated being a cripple. He spent much of the day sitting on the veranda, drinking cold beers in the morning and switching to Scotch by mid afternoon. The alcohol did not seem to calm him. His anger was always present, and it showed itself in his irritability and short temper. Above all, the anger and fear he felt was caused by concern for the unhappy future that probably awaited him – and all the big European landowners. Unable to move except with crutches, finding it difficult to leave the house (for he could neither drive the Land Rover nor ride a horse), he felt particularly powerless at this time. Occasionally two or three tough looking, unshaven young men wearing filthy, vaguely military bush fatigues would arrive in the late afternoon, and on the veranda they would almost always find Patrick, drinking Scotch, often with Michael and members of the family present.

'Jambo, Bwana Mkubwa, jambo Wanawake,' they would greet Patrick and the women, and Patrick would sit them down and give them a beer each, and only after downing their beers would they go upstairs to shave and have a bath and change their clothes for the very presentable civvies which they kept at the house. Then they would join the family for dinner that evening (and Patrick's spirits would be much improved by their company), and spend the night at *Mahali pa Kupumzika*, before gathering the loyal Sikuyu soldiers they commanded (who had been given hospitality round the back of the house, at the kitchen, and billeted for the night in the native compound), and disappearing at dawn the next morning. These young men were mostly farmers' sons, fluent in *Kiswahili* and adept in bushcraft, members of the special Equatoria Regiment units that patrolled the Nyahurari Forest and the western foothills of the Cairngorms Range, hunting down *Wa Chui* bands. (Similar units patrolled the eastern foothills of the Cairngorms Range, and the slopes of Mount Kirinjogu).

Since becoming housebound, Patrick had been spending many mornings talking on the radio telephone in his study. Several times, as Michael had passed the closed door of the study on his way to or from the library (and that in itself was unusual, that the door to Patrick's study should be closed), he had heard Patrick's voice on the radio telephone. But Michael had no idea who he might be talking to.

One afternoon in early August, soon after the girls had returned to school (Michael found that he rather missed Eleanor and her sweet, youthful vitality), Patrick and Michael were sitting together on the veranda. Patrick had been drinking Scotch for a while; Michael had yet to have his first beer of the day. Suddenly, apropos of nothing in particular, Patrick said, 'It would ruin me if the estate was broken up. Almost all my capital is sunk in this estate.'

'I see,' Michael replied. The fear – that *Mahali pa Kupumzika's* future might be threatened – was obviously weighing on Patrick's mind.

'When the Emergency ends,' Patrick continued, 'we will still be facing the spectre of black majority rule imposed on us by Westminster, and I very much doubt that a black majority government would stand for estates of this size being held by Europeans. More and more members of LegCo are coming round to the view that we would be better off going it alone than allowing black rule.'

'What do you mean, Patrick?'

'The talks in London with Harold Macmillan's government are not going well. The British government is adamant that black majority rule lies in store for Equatoria. LegCo has decided to recall the Equatorian government delegates to London. It seems very likely that we are going to declare our independence from Britain. Some of the members of LegCo are referring to it as UDI – a unilateral declaration of independence.'

Why did Michael feel such shock and surprise? Because (excepting only the American declaration of independence in 1776) such a thing had never been done before? Michael hoped that Patrick would not later regret confiding in him. He doubted

Patrick would have done so, had he been sober. But Patrick was rarely sober anymore after midday.

Michael said, 'My gosh, Patrick. You're talking revolution, aren't you? I wish you and Equatoria well of it. But try not to worry too much: for the present, Marjory is keeping an eye on things on the estate, and you have André Myburgh to actually run the show. And in another few months – maybe less – you will be on your feet again.'

Putting down his whiskey glass, Patrick smiled suddenly. In an instant, his mood had swung, and as he smiled, he looked ten years younger. Michael recognised for a moment the friend he had known of old, and he wished that Patrick would smile more often.

'Do you remember when Neil Bennett broke his ankle playing rugby?' Patrick asked Michael. 'He was such a tough, no one – least of all himself – realised he had done so until after the match. He thought it was just a sprain. His foot was in plaster for weeks. I wonder what he's doing now?'

Michael laughed. 'He's a bishop!' he declared. 'A muscular Christian if ever there was one!'

Patrick joined in the laughter. 'There's hope for us all,' he said. He looked at his watch. 'Come on Mike, its after four-thirty. Relax a little. You were always so upright at school. Join me in a beer at least.'

Is that how he used to see me? I never knew. 'Thanks, I shall,' he replied.

'Karim! *Leta bia kwa Bwana Michael, na whiskey kwa ajili yangu.*'

'*Ndiyo, Bwana Mkubwa.*'

Karim returned shortly with a tall, cold beer for Michael, and another Scotch for Patrick, who raised his glass. 'Cheers!' he said. 'To better outcomes.'

'To better outcomes!' Michael responded, raising his own glass, grateful for Patrick's sudden improvement in mood.

Chapter Eleven

In late August, the Postmaster at Jiljil contacted *Mahali pa Kupumzika* on the radio telephone soon after lunchtime. Karim, who had taken the call, told Michael, who was sitting on the veranda with the entire Hepburn family (excepting only the two girls, who were at school). Patrick, the Dowager Lady Pencaitland, Lady Catherine, and Marjory, were present. Kariuki, the new houseboy (all of sixteen years old), whom Karim was training up, stood silently and still against the wall. The three dogs lay on the red polished veranda floor.

'*Bwana* Michael,' Karim addressed him, 'the Jiljil Post Office will talk to you.'

Michael had no idea why Jiljil Post Office should want him. He looked at Patrick and Marjory. 'Better go see what they want,' Marjory advised. 'It may be important. I'll come with you – you haven't used the radio telephone before, have you?'

'No,' Michael replied. 'But I'm familiar with radio.'

Michael and Marjory entered the study. This was Patrick's sanctuary, and Michael rarely had cause to enter it. He saw a rack of rifles against the wall, and the glass topped case in which was arranged a collection of revolvers and automatic pistols. On the walls were framed English hunting prints and old, sometimes sepia toned, framed photographs of groups of men on hunting safaris wearing solar topis, with dead animals artfully arranged in front of or between them. Above the fireplace the fierce head of a lion shot by old Lord Pencaitland glared glassily down at them. On the other walls were mounted the horned skulls of various antelopes. A zebra skin hearthrug lay before the fireplace. The receiver-transmitter handset was lying to one side of the large radio unit. Marjory picked it up. She pressed the "press-to-talk" button on the side of the handset.

'Hullo. Lady Pencaitland speaking. Over.'

'Good afternoon, Lady Pencaitland. This is Jiljil Post Office. We have a telegram from England for Mr. Michael Hood. Over.'

'Hold on. Over.'

Marjory turned to Michael. 'They have a telegram for you from England. Do you want them to read it to you?'

'Yes. Yes – that would be best.'

'Here,' Marjory said. 'Take this receiver-transmitter. Press that little button to speak. When you have finished speaking, say "Over." They can then speak to you.'

Michael nodded, saying, 'I know. I've used radio transmitters during the War.' He took the instrument from Marjory and pressed the "press-to-talk" button. 'This is Michael Hood speaking. I believe you have a telegram for me. Would you please read it to me? Over.'

'Good afternoon Mr. Hood. The telegram reads, "YOUR MOTHER VERY ILL STOP ADVISE YOU RETURN SOONEST STOP CONTACT ME FOR FURTHER INFORMATION STOP RICHARD CARTER" Over.'

Richard Carter was the Hood family solicitor in Chipping Norton. Michael, who had felt the blood drain from his face as the telegram had been read to him, responded, 'I would like to send a telegram to Richard Carter immediately. Can that be done? Over.'

Chapter Eleven

'Yes Mr. Hood. We can do that. Over.'

'Are you ready? The telegram must read, "I WILL MAKE IMMEDIATE PLANS TO RETURN HOME STOP WHAT IS THE NATURE OF MY MOTHER'S ILLNESS STOP I WILL INFORM YOU OF ARRIVAL DATE STOP MICHAEL HOOD" Will you contact me at *Mahali pa Kupumzika* as soon as you have a reply? Thanks. Over.'

'We will do that, Mr. Hood. Let's see . . . please give me a minute . . . The telegram will cost you twenty-two East African Shillings – that's one Pound, two Shillings Sterling. You can pay for it next time you're in town. Over.'

'That's fine. I'll do that. Over and out.'

Marjory's face wore an anxious look.

'As you gather, my mother is seriously ill,' Michael told her. 'With what, I don't yet know. I need to book a flight back to London as soon as possible.'

'Oh Michael, I am sorry.' Marjory's fingers touched the back of his hand. 'I shall ask Patrick to phone his man in Namuri. He will handle the booking for you.'

Michael caught the train for Namuri at Jiljil on Wednesday 30th August. Patrick had insisted he come to see him off, with André Myburgh driving the Land Rover. (The men were loath to hazard Marjory's safety on what was proven to be a potentially dangerous journey, so Michael had said good bye to her at the house, wondering when he would next see her. Keith Hepburn had been following behind them in his Land Rover; both the Hepburns would pick up supplies while they were in town).

'I hope very much that things aren't as bad as you fear, Mike old man,' Patrick said on the platform, where he stood between his crutches, André Myburgh and Keith Hepburn either side of him. Michael had received a second telegram from the family solicitor: his mother had had a very serious stroke.

'Give your mother my love, and come back when you can,

Mike,' Patrick continued. 'You're always welcome. *Mahali pa Kupumzika* is your home too.' Patrick could remember the many occasions the Hoods had welcomed him into their home in the Cotswolds during school holidays. Welcoming Michael to stay as often and as long as he wished at *Mahali pa Kupumzika* afforded him an opportunity of repaying that kindness.

Despite his worries, Michael was touched. He felt closer to his friend than he had felt for a long time. 'Thank you, Pat. I shall.' And when the train pulled out with Michael aboard, he indeed felt as if he was leaving home behind him.

Michael spent the night at the New Cedric Hotel in Namuri, and took an Equatorian Airways flight the next day for London, via Frankfurt. He was not at all fond of air travel, but he had to confess that the Comet 4 in which he travelled was very comfortable, and he could hardly believe that he would be arriving at London Airport just the following day, Friday 1st September.

It was growing dark by the time Michael got off the train from London at Kingham Station. There were as usual no taxis at the tiny country halt, but Michael had left the bulk of his luggage at his flat in London, and he was now travelling with only a suitcase and a large shoulder bag, which he could manage fairly easily. His life at *Mahali pa Kupumzika* had not been entirely sedentary; the riding especially had kept him fit. After the brief dusk of Equatoria, he was delighted with the long, soft, gentle gathering of twilight as he walked the familiar lanes to the family home. Richard Carter had warned the family cook-housekeeper of Michael's arrival that evening. She had waited in, and a warm supper was being kept ready for Michael when he reached the old house.

'Mr. Michael,' the cook-housekeeper declared, 'I'm so pleased you're home! What a long journey you must have had.' Michael greeted her, then fondled his mother's red setter, which was thrilled to see him. Once he had reassured the dog that he was real, he reached into his bag and withdrew a small box of duty free chocolates which he gave to Mrs. Hughes.

Michael felt far from fully integrated. His consciousness of himself had not yet caught up with his sudden transfer from equatorial Africa to the familiar countryside of his childhood. He spent a restless night. He had to get up twice, and he dreamed he was back at *Mahali pa Kupumzika*. Consequently, he felt rather tired when he rose at seven o' clock the next morning, but the good breakfast that was served him at eight o' clock helped put him together again. His mother was being cared for at the Chipping Norton Community Hospital. Michael would be using her car, a Rover 90, while he was back home.

Michael had been at boarding school – first, preparatory school, then public school – since the age of seven. Most of his childhood illnesses – measles, mumps, chicken pox, colds and flu – had been spent in the school infirmary. The love he bore his mother was of that somewhat romanticized version common to men of his class; men who had grown up seeing their mother only during school holidays. This did not mean that it was any the less genuine than that of a day school boy for his mother, but it was not built on a steady daily relationship through the years. Michael usually addressed his mother as "Mother." Only as a little boy had he sometimes called her "Mummy." But the idea of a world in which she was not present appalled and scared him. Michael had no other close family. His father had died during his childhood. He feared the bleakness of a world without his mother in it, a powerful focus for his love.

But the prognosis for his mother's recovery was not good. The stroke had left her in a coma, and she was almost certain to die. This, a doctor explained to Michael, when he visited his mother in hospital the next day, a Saturday. He had brought flowers with him from her garden – roses and carnations – but these merely joined the other flowers in her room. Michael was shocked at seeing his mother lying there, her face fallen in and waxy, her breathing stertorous, her eyes closed. She was still in her sixties. Michael, when he thought about it at all, had imagined that his mother would be with him for a long time yet. Even had the doctor not explained, as gently as he could, that she was highly unlikely to recover, the sight of his mother, once so familiar, now hardly recognisable, lying in that bed, would have alarmed and distressed him. Michael had no great religious faith; he could find no comfort therein.

Michael sat with his mother for half an hour. He visited the next day also, and on Monday morning, as he was having his breakfast, the telephone rang. Mrs. Hughes answered it. She came through to the dining room. She looked distressed. 'Mr. Michael, it's the hospital, they want to talk with you.'

Michael knew immediately what he was going to hear. He felt a tightening of his throat and a shortness of breath. He picked the receiver up. 'Michael Hood speaking.'

'Mr. Hood. It's Doctor Hardiman. I'm afraid I have bad news for you.'

'Oh no . . .' Michael said softly.

'I'm afraid so. Your mother died early this morning.'

As if functioning in parallel with the self that was grieving, Michael spent the morning dealing with the undertakers, and with county bureaucracy. Just before one o' clock he thought to telephone the family solicitor, and tell him that his mother had died. Richard Carter had been a friend of Michael's father, and he had been the Hood family solicitor for a long time. He had known Michael's mother well; socially as well as professionally. Sharing in Michael's grief, he spent some minutes in commiseration with him. Then he said, 'You know your mother had her will lodged with me, and that she had appointed me as executor. I do not think you will find any surprises in the will. You are your mother's primary beneficiary. Whenever you wish, I can summarise the will's main provisions. Is there anything I can do to help you with your mother's funeral arrangements?'

'I have that in hand,' Michael replied. 'As soon as I have a date for the funeral, I shall let you know. I think I shall return to London after the funeral.'

The funeral was held a week later, on Monday 11th September. It had been an unhappy week for Michael. He had been alone but for Mrs. Hughes and the dog, although he had received many letters and quite a few telephone calls from family friends expressing their condolences, and asking whether there was anything they could do for him. There was not. Michael's mother was buried in the churchyard of Saint Andrew's Church in Kingham, alongside his father's grave. Throughout the service, Michael felt to some degree removed from the proceedings, as if he – the real Michael – were not present at this sad occasion. The reception afterwards was held at his mother's – now his – house. There were upwards of fifty people at the funeral service, and at least thirty came to the reception, where Mrs. Hughes (with the help of a village girl in the kitchen, hired for the occasion) served a buffet lunch. Michael said and did what was required of him. He longed right now to head for London, for his home in Soho, where he had routines, habits, friends, amidst which and with whom he could re-establish what he felt was missing from his life at the moment: a sense of identity.

But Michael no longer seemed to respond to London as he once had. He found that his concentration was impaired; he could not focus his mind. Completing the novel he had begun in September the previous year, which he had thought he might do, was, he found, out of the question. To what extent this failure to concentrate his mind was due to grief (neither Michael nor his parents had had siblings; Michael had neither aunts, uncles, nor first cousins; his mother had been his entire family), and to what extent due to the restlessness his visits to Equatoria had given rise to, remained unclear.

After a few days in London, Michael realised that he was missing *Mahali pa Kupumzika*. It was the vivid colours of Equatoria that he yearned to see again; the wide horizons and vast sky of an intense, shimmering blue; it was Patrick and Marjory with whom he longed to be, for they were now the closest he had to family. He felt his life in London was idle and without value. The bustle and crush of humanity oppressed him as London had never oppressed him before.

Michael telephoned Richard Carter. 'Am I needed here – in England – while we await a grant of probate?' he asked.

'No, not really,' the solicitor answered.

'I want to return to Equatoria,' Michael told him.

'There's no reason why you should not, Michael.'

'Good! That's what I'm going to do. You know how to get hold of me.'

He pondered for some time over the wording of a telegram to Patrick and Marjory. Eventually, he decided that a plain and simple communication was best. So he sent them a telegram reading, "I WISH TO RETURN EQUATORIA AS SOON AS POSSIBLE STOP MAY I STAY WITH YOU AGAIN STOP MICHAEL"

A day later Michael received a telegraphic reply, which read, "ALWAYS WELCOME STOP PLS NOTIFY ARRIVAL DATE STOP PATRICK"

Michael felt as if a weight had been lifted from him. At the travel agency in Oxford Street he booked a BOAC flight to Namuri via Rome and Khartoum, leaving in three days' time, on the afternoon of Friday 22nd September.

Kept a secret from the world, Patrick was afraid. He knew that the drink had got a terrible grip on him, as it had with many of his bloodline, and that he was unable to break that grip. He recognized that these were dangerous times. For *Mahali pa Kupumzika* especially, with its proximity to the Nyahurari Forest and the foothills of the Cairngorms Range, these were particularly dangerous times. Patrick was glad of the presence of a friend whom he could trust; a sober, responsible friend who would do his best by the family and the estate – and ease the pressure on Patrick. And so he was glad of Michael's imminent return.

Chapter Twelve

In order to make the flight as tolerable as possible, Michael travelled first class, so his seat was not particularly cramped, but he preferred the Comet 4 of Equatorian Airways in which he had flown the last time, to the Boeing 707 in which he was now flying. The Comet had been quieter, with less vibration. But as the plane descended over the Mvong Hills, coming in to land at Namuri Airport in the morning, Michael felt excitement and – for the first time since his mother had died – a momentary happiness. The rains had not yet arrived and the long grass was a golden brown. There were no clouds in the sky, whose colour shaded from powder blue directly above the horizon to azure; a deep, radiant blue rarely seen in the skies of England. The sun was nearing its zenith, and Michael's shadow was a mere pool of shade at his feet as he walked from the aircraft to the airport terminal. The air was warm and very dry.

Once through Customs, Michael took the BOAC courtesy shuttle to the New Cedric Hotel. He would be spending two nights here, catching the train to Jiljil on Monday morning. He had already missed the up train that day, and there was no train the following day, a Sunday. He shaved and washed in his

Chapter Twelve

room upstairs, then went directly to the Thorn Tree Boma, where he ordered a very cold Tusker lager which arrived in a tall glass bedewed with moisture.

Michael had picked up a *Namuri Times* in the hotel lobby, hoping to bring himself up to date with the current situation in the colony. He read that the government was planning to extend military call-up to all male European permanent residents between the ages of eighteen and thirty-eight (why thirty-eight, he wondered, and not thirty-nine, or forty?) He also learned that not only were passenger trains headed and tailed with Equatoria Regiment or British Army machine gun detachments in open wagons, but since a coast bound passenger train had been derailed by explosives on the track near Naburu earlier that month, and four passengers killed in the subsequent exchange of gunfire with the *Wa Chui*, the Port Hardinge – Port Caroline railway line was now the subject of regular Army patrols between MacKay Road and Port Caroline, with less frequent patrols on the branch line between Jiljil and Jackson Falls. Michael read also of landmines being placed on the main road between Namuri and Port Caroline. In a particularly gruesome report, he read that only two days ago a farm lorry transporting sheep headed for slaughter at Naburu had been blown up by landmines, and the two men in the cab had died, along with most of the sheep, the carcasses of the latter strewn indiscriminately across the road together with the bodies of the driver and his mate. Regular military patrols of the main road between Namuri and Port Caroline, and setting up checkpoints along the road, were shortly to be instituted. (Michael remembered, during a conversation he had had at *Mahali pa Kupumzika* one evening in June, conjecturing that the *Wa Chui* would next be seeking to obtain landmines from their Chinese allies).

Michael read also of a growing shortage of goods in the shops upcountry. What were termed strategic goods – diesel and petrol, and farm supplies such as animal feed and spares for farm machinery – were being granted transport priority over less vital goods by the recently instituted district strategic transport boards. The transport of agricultural produce destined for export was also prioritised. Michael read of a dearth of dairy products in Namuri and Port Hardinge. Dairy farmers who were unwilling or unable to make the daily run to the nearest town themselves with their milk were going out of business, with dairy herds being turned into beef. Commercial road transport had become patchy up country, and due to the necessity to patrol and check the railway line, goods trains were running slower and less frequently than before. However, Michael noticed no shortage of goods displayed in the shop windows in Namuri when he went for a walk in the city later that afternoon. He supposed that road and rail transport between the coast and Namuri was barely disrupted. The *Wa Chui* insurrection was confined largely to the Sikuyu tribal region – the Highlands – and to the country reaching as far as the shores of the Lake. The scarcity of commercial transport began to make itself felt inland, beyond Namuri.

Michael was shocked and distressed at how much, in the mere month that he had been away, the situation in the colony seemed to have deteriorated. He worried for his friends at *Mahali pa Kupumzika*.

On Monday the train Michael had boarded at Namuri arrived at Jiljil later than had been usual in the past. The journey had been slower. It was after four o' clock before the train pulled in at Jiljil Station. But Patrick (still using crutches), André Myburgh, and Keith Hepburn were waiting for Michael on the platform.

'Jambo Michael! Karibu!' Patrick declared, holding out his hand.

'Jambo Patrick. Habari?' Michael responded, seizing the proffered hand.

'Nzuri sana,' Patrick answered. But Michael did not think

Chapter Twelve

his friend looked well at all. He noticed how bulky Patrick had become; how his high colour, and the broken veins around his nose, showed evidence of heavy drinking.

They made their way to the two cars. (André Myburgh had been driving the Chevrolet on the way in, with Patrick by his side. Keith Hepburn had followed in his Land Rover). Keith Hepburn's Land Rover was loaded with supplies, as was the Chevrolet (Michael wondered how they would squeeze his luggage in), for the men had gone shopping in town before meeting Michael. The estate manager and Keith Hepburn carried Michael's luggage, refusing his help. They piled it onto the Chevrolet's wide rear seat, having shifted the rifle that was there to the front seat, for even with three men in front, there was plenty of room for it.

André, then Patrick, managed to get into the front passenger side of the Chevrolet.

'Do you mind driving?' Patrick asked Michael, handing him the ignition key.

So Michael started the big car's engine, and eased the column shift into "Drive," following Keith Hepburn out of the station car park.

Patrick reached forward and opened the glove pocket in the dashboard in front of him. He extracted Michael's Colt revolver and passed it to him.

'I brought this with me. I hope we won't need it on this trip.' He laughed.

Patrick, the estate manager, and Marjory's father were of course already armed.

Michael asked, 'How is the family?'

'They're all well,' Patrick replied.

'And how are things on the estate?' There was genuine interest in Michael's tone.

Patrick did not answer immediately. He was looking out of his window. Then, ignoring the estate manager's presence, he turned his head, and said, 'It's a daily struggle now with the problems we face in the Highlands. The labour force is right down now. So many estate workers have simply walked away – into the forest, perhaps? We had to bring in the harvest with half the usual number of workers. And Mwara's replacement has also disappeared, gone to join the *Wa Chui* no doubt, like Mwara. So Karim is alone now. I left him with the women. He knows how to use a gun. I don't like leaving the women alone.'

'But you still have the cooks, I hope?' Michael asked, laughing.

'*Mpishi Moja* is still with us. *Mpishi Mbili* has gone – disappeared like the others. Perhaps that's for the best. He might have tried to poison us had he stayed. I imagine we still have a kitchen *toto* or two.'

They arrived at *Mahali pa Kupumzika* almost an hour after sunset. Michael experienced a powerful sense of relief. Driving on these roads was difficult enough in the dark, without having to worry about a possible *Wa Chui* attack. There was the usual excitement with the three dogs as the Chevrolet drew to a halt at the foot of the steps. The two Rhodesian ridgebacks gambolled about Patrick's feet, threatening to knock him off his crutches, but the Alsatian, after sniffing Michael's trouser legs, and permitting Patrick to pat it on the head, shortly went back inside the house. Michael helped Patrick up the veranda stairs. Michael wondered where Karim was. As they reached the veranda, Marjory appeared from inside the house. She came forward, smiling.

'How are you, Michael? I thought about you, and your sad loss, while you were away. I'm glad you are back.' Marjory turned a cheek towards him, and Michael kissed it, saying, 'I'm very glad to be back. It feels like coming home.'

As Michael entered the drawing room, Karim appeared, looking (if such were possible) a little flustered. There had been some upset in the kitchen which he had had to attend to.

'*Jambo* Karim,' Michael greeted him, smiling.

Chapter Twelve

'*Jambo Bwana* Michael. *Habari?*'

'*Nzuri sana,*' Michael replied.

The two older Hepburn women, one a Hepburn by marriage, the other (about fifteen years her senior), a Hepburn born, were seated, drinks by their sides. Michael greeted them both. Lady Fiona Pencaitland offered her hand and smiled. 'Welcome,' she said. Lady Catherine looked at him uncertainly, and remained silent.

'We'll have an early supper,' Marjory told Michael. 'We have become very informal – you know, with Patrick's leg; he cannot change outfits easily with that plaster cast. I don't suppose you will have had any lunch.'

'No, I haven't,' Michael replied. 'The journey was full of delays, the train kept stopping for unaccountable reasons, and when it moved, it moved more slowly than I remember. And lunch was not served.'

'Poor Michael,' Marjory smiled at him, a sudden spark of wicked humour in her eyes. 'It's rough in Africa, isn't it? Never mind, we'll have something to drink now, and it will soon be time for supper.' Patrick had already ordered a whiskey from Karim. Michael, once he had sat down, did likewise.

Thoughtfully, Michael had not brought Patrick a gift of MacAllan whiskey this time, or any other alcoholic beverage. Instead, having presented both the older women with beautifully scented handmade soaps (Michael struggled, and often failed, to be original in his gift giving), and Marjory with a Hermès scarf of silk, light as gossamer (which was very well received), he gave Patrick a box of Montecristo Cuban cigars.

'I'm going to enjoy these, old chap!' Patrick exclaimed. '*Asante sana!* Luxuries like this are simply unattainable outside Namuri – and I've not been to Namuri since I broke my leg. This damn leg! You know I've been unable to attend the final one and a half months of LegCo's sessions. There's been a lot going on at LegCo behind the scenes right now. The Council was sitting from the start of June through to the end of August, you know.'

Patrick extracted a cigar from the box and removed the cellophane wrapper. Looking around, he could not see Karim. He raised his voice. 'Karim! Karim! *Kuja hapa!*'

Karim reappeared. He had been laying the table in the dining room. He had too much to do.

'Karim, my cigar cutter is in the study.' Michael addressed the manservant in English, perhaps because the *Kiswahili* translation for "cigar cutter" would have been awkward. 'Please bring it to me.' Then he switched to *Kiswahili*. *'Na pia whiskey,'* he told him.

'Ndiyo Bwana,' Karim replied, and left the room.

'Karim has too much on his plate now,' thought Michael, but he kept the thought to himself. Karim returned with the cigar cutter. At the drinks cabinet he poured Patrick a double Scotch, and bore both the cigar cutter and the whiskey to Patrick on a small round silver tray.

'*Asante,*' Patrick thanked him. With the cigar cutter he performed an operation on one of the Montecristo cigars Michael had given him. He offered a cigar to Michael, which was accepted. Both men lighted their cigars, and the rich aroma enveloped them. The air was heavy and still that night, and Michael felt that the countryside was waiting, breathless, for the coming of the rains. The air of anticipation, indeed, of atmospheric tension, rose day by day after Michael's return; the clouds over the Cairngorms growing heavier and darker with each passing day, and at night, lightning played on the eastern horizon and distant thunder was heard. Then, on Sunday the 1st of October, the rains began to fall – a deluge, an elemental assault – and it became very difficult to pursue any business at all outdoors. But, as best they could, given the reduced number of farm workers available, the estate had been made ready for what were known in the colony as the "short rains."

Michael found a particular pleasure in standing in the shelter of the veranda and watching and listening to the rain falling. But he did not stay long on the veranda, for it felt cool outdoors, and Karim had lighted a fire in the drawing room, which is where the family now spent much of the day. Karim was fighting a losing battle, single handed now, to keep abreast of the housekeeping. Michael could not help but notice that in the other public rooms – the dining room, the library, the small parlour between the library and the drawing room – neither the silver and brass nor the furniture was being polished anymore, and the rooms smelled of dust. Only the drawing room still showed evidence of daily cleaning and polishing. Patrick however had Karim light a fire in his study most mornings, for he retreated to his study for entire mornings at a time. Michael guessed that he was probably engaged, at least some of the time, in using the radio telephone in pursuit of LegCo's plans for the colony's forthcoming declaration of independence. This would be nothing like the eventual black majority independence that Westminster envisaged, but independence under European minority rule.

For the next two months, with heavy rains an almost daily occurrence, *Wa Chui* activity all but ceased. Then, in very early December, the rains ended, so abruptly it was as if a giant tap had been turned off in the Heavens. Over dinner one evening Patrick said to Michael, 'The *Wa Chui* are going to begin their wickedness again now that the rains are over.'

The leading men of the colony (among whom Patrick occupied an important symbolic position, for he was the son of old Lord Pencaitland, who had done so much to help establish the colony in the early years of the century) planned to declare independence on the 9th December, the same day as a neighbouring colony, Tanganyika, gained full independence from Britain. However, where black rule would be established in Tanganyika, the Equatorian government was determined to maintain European control.

Chapter Thirteen

On the night of the 7th December, the household at *Mahali pa Kupumzika* was awoken in the early hours by bursts of automatic gunfire not at all far away.

'The *Wa Chui!*' declared Patrick, looking around wildly, as he tumbled groggily out of bed, having been shaken into wakefulness by Marjory. He reached for his revolver, which he kept underneath his pillows. His head felt thick, for he had drunk a generous amount of wine at dinner the evening before, and a fair number of whiskeys after dinner. Marjory was already donning a dressing gown, over which she strapped her revolver around her slim waist. There was a knock at their bedroom door.

'It is I, Karim, *Bwana Mkubwa*,' they heard from the other side of the door. Karim had a room on the first floor at the end of one of the two wings that reached out from the back of the house.

Patrick opened the door to the bedroom. 'Are the shutters closed?' he asked Karim.

'Always I close them before I go to my room, *Bwana Mkubwa*,' the Somali manservant replied.

'Come downstairs with me, Karim,' Patrick continued. 'I am going to try to raise *Bwana* André on the radio telephone, and then the Reservists at the native compound.'

Chapter Thirteen

'Patrick,' Marjory said, 'Can Karim come back upstairs afterwards, with a couple of rifles – one for Michael, one for me – and anyway, where is Michael?'

'Have you seen *Bwana* Michael?' Patrick asked Karim.

'Hapana, Bwana.'

At that moment Michael, tousle haired and wearing a dressing gown, his revolver in one hand, appeared behind Karim. 'What would you like me to do, Patrick?' he asked.

Patrick wished he did not have such a headache. 'Marjory, please bring me a glass of water and some aspirin.' She went to their bathroom. Patrick turned to Michael again. 'It's better you stay up here and guard the women. Will you do that? I am going to try to raise André, and the unit guarding the native compound, on the radio telephone. I will try and raise the Police in Jiljil as well.'

'Right,' Michael replied.

'Karim will bring a couple of rifles up to you,' Patrick added.

The gunfire, which had been coming from the direction of the native compound, could now also be heard from the direction of André Myburgh's bungalow. There were bursts of automatic fire and several single shots, as from a rifle.

'I think André is under attack,' Marjory commented, after Patrick and Karim had left them.

Michael thought Marjory was looking extremely attractive. Her hair, normally arranged in a high chignon off her neck, was unbound, and hanging loose across her shoulders. There were highlights of gold in her hair in the electric light. With her hair down, she looked very much younger.

'Marjory,' Michael said, 'we must turn all the lights off. Would you mind checking that the lights are off in Lady Pencaitland's and Lady Catherine's rooms? Light will only offer the *Wa Chui* a target. And bring the two ladies back here. We must stay together.'

Marjory nodded and disappeared down the corridor, carrying

her revolver in one hand. Michael flicked the wall switch at the door to douse the lights in the bedroom. Although Michael could not see it, for it hung low in the west, behind the house, there was a three quarters moon in the sky, and once his eyes had become accustomed to the dark, the moon cast sufficient illumination to see by, a thin, silvery light. Was it a good sign that the gunfire had ceased? Had André and the Reservists driven the *Wa Chui* off?

Marjory reappeared with the two older women. Both these latter were calm, but Lady Catherine (whose unbound, long white hair hung halfway down her back) looked bewildered. The Dowager Lady Pencaitland (whose hair was also unbound, and was spread across her shoulders) had strapped a revolver around her waist. The Alsatian dog was with her. Lady Fiona Pencaitland led Lady Catherine to a chair in front of the fireplace, and sat her down. 'I'm sure you will be able to go back to bed soon, Aunt,' she said.

When it comes to the crunch, thought Marjory, Fiona has all her wits about her. But Lady Catherine asked, 'What are we doing here? What is the reason for all the commotion?' No one answered her.

Then Karim returned, with a rifle in one hand and another slung over his shoulder. Both were bolt action .30-06 sporting rifles.

'*Bwana*, I must go back downstairs to the *Bwana Mkubwa*,' Karim said.

'OK Karim,' Michael answered, taking the rifles from him, and handing one to Marjory. 'Are they loaded?'

'*Ndiyo Bwana.*' Michael worked the bolt of his rifle to be sure. Karim gave him a box of ammunition. Karim left them again, leaving Michael, Marjory and the two older women together in the room.

Michael went to look out the window again, but he could still see nothing but the garden with its backdrop of trees, bathed in

Chapter Thirteen

the silvery wash of moonlight. Beyond, to the east, a long, low, dark shadow loomed, stretching across the entire horizon; it was the Nyahurari Forest and the foothills of the Cairngorms. Michael would have liked to have gone to one of the rooms in the north wing, from which he thought he might gain a sight of André Myburgh's bungalow, but he did not want to split the party up, so he stayed with the others. He was feeling tense, alert, but not in the least fearful. On the contrary, he felt preternaturally alive. This night's events took him back to the War, where his cool headed, quick thinking abilities to act decisively in a crisis had very quickly been rewarded with promotion to the rank of major. Admirably, the women (including, in her fashion, Lady Catherine, although she did not understand enough to feel fearful) were equally cool headed so far.

Michael was still looking out the window, and thus he was able to see the shadowed forms of a small group of armed men, no more than eight in number, spread across a broad front, as they appeared individually in the garden from between the scattered trees. With a start of relief he recognised them as the Reservist unit that guarded the native compound. So they had survived the *Wa Chui* attack.

'Lieutenant MacDonald!' he called, through the open window.

'Sir!' the young Lieutenant answered, stepping forward.

'What is the situation?'

'We came under attack. We drove them off. But we heard gunfire some distance away also. We came to check that you were alright,' Lieutenant MacDonald replied, his voice raised.

'The gunfire you heard would have been André Myburgh's bungalow under attack. Do you know what's going on there?'

'Negative. We came straight here.'

'Send some men to see what's happening at André Myburgh's bungalow,' Michael ordered the young man. 'You can bring the other men onto the veranda.'

'Yes Sir,' the Reservist Lieutenant replied. He detailed Sergeant Cunningham to take three men with him, and the Sergeant and his men set off for André Myburgh's bungalow. Lieutenant MacDonald, with the remaining men, took up a position on the veranda, kneeling behind the low wall as they looked out across the garden. All was quiet but for the usual night sounds. Michael dared to hope that the *Wa Chui*, those that may have survived, were in retreat. He turned to Marjory, 'I must bring Patrick up to date. I'll be back.'

Michael found Karim and the two Rhodesian ridgebacks in the hall. Karim told him that Patrick was in the study. When Michael got there, Patrick had just given up trying to get hold of André Myburgh on the radio telephone.

'I've had no luck raising the soldiers at the native compound, nor André. I am going to call the Police now,' Patrick told Michael. 'Are things OK upstairs?'

'Patrick, the Army unit have seen their attackers off. Four men have been detailed to find out what's happened at André Myburgh's bungalow. The remaining men, plus Lieutenant MacDonald, are on the veranda. I think we should wait for a sit rep before contacting the Police.'

'Yes, of course, you're right,' Patrick responded. The two men joined Karim in the hall. Patrick said to Michael, 'I need to be able to communicate with the Army unit. I think I'll stay down here.'

Michael had told the women he would not be away for long, but he wanted to find out what had happened at André Myburgh's bungalow. He joined Patrick at the front door, which Karim now unbarred. Opening the front door, Michael called out, 'Lieutenant! We're coming to join you!'

The estate manager was dead. Sergeant Cunningham, returning with his three Sikuyu *askaris*, reported to Lieutenant MacDonald, 'We found Mr. Myburgh's body inside his bungalow, Sir. He had been shot – many times. It seems like the *Wa Chui* managed to force their way inside the house.'

Michael felt little surprise. Anger, rather than distress, was Patrick's immediate response. 'The swine!' he declared. 'Did you notice – were there any weapons still in the house, Jack?' he asked the Reservist Sergeant. 'André had a collection of firearms.'

'No Sir, I don't think there were.'

'So the *Wa Chui* have got away with André's guns. That's bad.'

Another half hour passed with neither sight nor sound of the *Wa Chui*. There were still several hours to go before the dawn. The young Reservist Lieutenant said to Patrick, 'I think the *Wa Chui* have pulled out, Sir. We must have hit at least half a dozen during their attack on us – possibly more. But I think I should return to the men I left at the native compound.'

'Right-O, Anthony. I would be grateful though if you would leave three or four men with us until dawn. The women would feel happier.'

'I will leave Sergeant Cunningham here with three men, Sir. I'm sorry about Mr. Myburgh.'

'So am I. But well done, seeing the *Wa Chui* off like you did.'

'Good night, Lord Pencaitland.'

'Good night, Lieutenant MacDonald.'

Patrick sent Karim upstairs to tell the women that they were standing down now, but that four of the soldiers would be remaining until the dawn.

'Can you make us all a coffee, Karim?' Michael asked the Somali servant, when he came back downstairs with Marjory. 'Marjory, would you like a coffee – or a tea?'

Marjory said she would have a coffee. After a while, Patrick joined them in the drawing room, where Karim brought them some coffee. Patrick poured a large measure of whiskey into his coffee.

'I got hold of the Police in Jiljil,' he told them. 'They will radio the nearest Army unit patrolling the fringes of the Nyahurari

Forest. Perhaps they will pick up the *Wa Chui* band on their way back. We're presuming they will make for the Forest. The Police will send someone to us later this morning.' Patrick turned to Karim. 'Karim, please take some coffee to the soldiers outside.'

'*Ndiyo Bwana.*'

The three of them remained in the drawing room for a while, talking, smoking, and drinking their coffee. Slowly the high degree of nervous tension ebbed. Then Michael said, 'I'm going to try and get some sleep.'

'Good idea,' said Marjory.

'I'll stay down here for a while,' Patrick told them. He reached for the bottle of Scotch again. Marjory and Michael climbed the stairs. At the top of the stairs, where there was a light shining, Marjory turned to Michael.

'Tonight's events seem somehow unreal. I should be – I don't know – I should be feeling something more than I am.'

'That's a fairly typical reaction, Marjory. I think you did very well.'

At no stage had Marjory shown either fear or panic. Michael admired her tremendously. He longed to brush aside the tendril of loose hair at the side of her face, and kiss her. Marjory was staring at him. Michael looked away, lest she read the longing in his eyes.

'Good night, Michael,' Marjory said.

'Good night Marjory,' he replied, and he turned the other way down the corridor, to his bedroom. He got into bed, but he was still awake after half an hour, so he got up again and sat in the armchair, where at last he fell into a doze. His Colt revolver lay on his lap.

PART TWO

Chapter Fourteen

On Saturday 9th December 1961, two days after the attack on the Hepburn estate, the neighbouring British colony, Tanganyika, gained full independence from Britain, and the Equatorian Council of Executive Members (henceforth to be known as the Cabinet) proclaimed Equatoria's unilateral independence. At dawn that day, Equatorian troops had disarmed the British Army contingents in the colony, and placed them under detention, prior to their embarkation for Britain from Port Hardinge. There were three injuries – two Equatoria Regiment troopers and one British Army soldier – but no fatalities. Radio Equatoria (the colony had no public television service) announced Equatorian independence every half hour throughout the day, and that morning's edition of the *Namuri Times* had banner headlines, "EQUATORIA GOES IT ALONE." The British Governor was flown to Port Hardinge directly (his baggage to follow by train), there to await a steamer for Britain, and at noon, a small ceremony saw the British Union flag lowered on the roof of the Governor's residence (at the same time, but without any ceremony, the Union flag was lowered above the Equatorian government buildings, and outside Namuri Post Office), and the brand new

Equatorian flag was raised (an horizontal band of gold, or in this case, yellow, representing Equatoria's savanna grasslands, above a band of green, for her farmlands, with a small British Union flag at the top inner corner).

Patrick, wearing his wartime medals, a sober suit and a fedora hat, was present for the noontide ceremony outside the Governor's residence (now the residence of the new republic's President, who occupied a purely ceremonial role, and possessed no executive powers). Patrick had driven to Namuri that morning, setting off before dawn, leaving *Mahali pa Kupumzika* in the care of his wife, Michael, and Karim. He would spend the night at the Musaiga Club in Namuri, returning the next afternoon. Patrick had been asked by the First Councillor (one Ian Blackfell, who was now the republic's Prime Minister) to assume the position of State President, but he had declined.

'I do not wish to leave *Mahali pa Kupumzika*. Nor would I wish to leave the women alone in the house for long periods of time. But I am deeply conscious of the honour, Ian.'

In truth, Patrick was in no fit state now to have taken on such a commitment. On the day following the *Wa Chui* night attack on the *Mahali pa Kupumzika* estate, his mood had been febrile, and both Marjory and Michael had been concerned (although neither had said anything to the other) at how much he was drinking. It crossed Michael's mind that Patrick may have been acutely afraid, but he did not wish to think that his old friend was a coward, so he rejected that thought.

Patrick was, however, determined to drive to Namuri for the independence ceremonies the following day. Quite aside from the dangers of driving anywhere in the Highlands now, Michael wondered how a man who was drinking so much could safely tackle the long drive to Namuri and back. When Michael offered to accompany him, Patrick responded angrily, 'God damn it, Michael! I'm not a child. I don't need minding!'

Then Patrick had spent an hour shooting with his revolver at a target he had set up on the front lawn. The target practice session seemed to calm him, and later, he said to Michael, 'I will feel happier if I know that you are looking after *Mahali pa Kupumzika* and the women while I'm away, Mike old boy.'

In the days following André Myburgh's death, Patrick made no attempt to assume the practical responsibilities for overseeing the estate which were now his. Had Marjory, with Michael's help, not shouldered this burden, there would have been no one at all in charge of running the estate. At times, Michael and Marjory would take a sidelong glance at each other, each about to confess their concerns for Patrick, but each time failing to do so.

Britain's reaction to Equatoria's unilateral declaration of independence was one of outrage. Over the next few months, the Republic of Equatoria remained unrecognised by any other country, excepting only the new Republic of South Africa, and Nicaragua, Panama and Taiwan. But the Equatorian government remained optimistic for the republic's future, and it showed a new energy and determination in the fight against the *Wa Chui*. In reaction to shocking cases of the torture of European farmers taken alive by the *Wa Chui* during attacks on isolated farmsteads, the death penalty was applied with increasing frequency against *Wa Chui* guerrillas captured under arms. Reports of the use of torture by the Equatorian armed forces against captured *Wa Chui* guerillas began to appear in the British press. Some of these stories may have been true, for this had become a loathsome, brutal struggle. The *Wa Chui* stepped up both the frequency and the brutality of its attacks, and by late May 1962, the *Wa Chui* were operating outside the Highlands region also, and the road and railway, as they passed through the wide belt of thick bush and game country between Port Hardinge and Namuri, became as dangerous to travel as the road from Namuri to Port Caroline, the lakeside port in the interior.

In late February 1962, Michael realised that his passport was due to expire in early April. With no diplomatic relations existing between Equatoria and Britain, Michael could not get his passport renewed in Equatoria. He discussed the problem with Patrick and Marjory.

'I do not want to go home yet, but I may have to, to get my passport renewed,' Michael told them.

'I'm not certain,' Patrick responded, 'but I think you could have your passport renewed in Tanganyika. And there's always South Africa.'

'Pat,' Marjory interjected, 'South Africa is such a long way away.'

But Michael thought it might be interesting to visit South Africa. 'You see,' he said, 'I don't want to find the border closed against my return, if I visit Tanganyika to get my passport renewed. The situation is so volatile, that's a possibility.'

'You may be right,' Patrick agreed. 'If you don't want to go home yet, South Africa would certainly be an altogether safer bet.'

Michael did not wish to return to England yet. Not only was there no one there whom he longed to see, but to his surprise, he found that his sympathies lay wholly with Equatoria, now that the country had declared its independence from Britain. He was angry with the British government, which he thought was behaving like a bully towards the new republic. His sense of fair play was outraged, and he found himself siding with the underdog – in this instance, Equatoria. However, he certainly did not wish to find himself with an out of date British passport, unable to travel again.

'I could fly direct to South Africa, I expect.'

'Yah. I think South African Airways operates a flight between Namuri and Johannesburg,' Patrick said.

'Patrick – would you do me a favour and ask your man in Namuri to check on that for me?'

'Of course, Michael.'

A week or so after the *Wa Chui* attack on the estate, Patrick began to make an effort to assume the duties which were now his. His attempts to discharge his responsibilities to *Mahali pa Kupumzika* were, however, erratic. He would disappear for hours to his study in the morning, and sit drinking on the veranda in the afternoon, and it was Marjory, with Michael accompanying her, who went out regularly every day (either on horseback, or in the Land Rover) to inspect and oversee operations on the estate. The farm was being made ready for the coming of the long rains, and for the planting of the new maize. Then it was time for Michael to fly to Johannesburg.

Patrick offered to drive Michael to Namuri, but Michael did not think this was wise. Patrick was drinking every morning now. However, Patrick, and Keith Hepburn, travelling in separate vehicles, drove Michael to Jiljil Station. (Afterwards the two Hepburn men would shop for supplies in the town). The casual observer may not have guessed, from the scene at the railway station that Monday, at the unrest afflicting Equatoria, except for the presence of a dozen native *Askaris*, now armed with rifles, and their two European officers. The station platform was almost as busy as Michael had ever seen it, thronged with a cross section of Equatoria's population. There were, despite the restrictions on travel by the natives, a few black travellers (presumably carrying travel passes issued by the local district officer) on their way to the city. Some were wearing tribal dress. There were black city dwellers (also carrying travel passes) dressed in European outfits, who had been visiting family in the country. There were several Europeans (the only travellers not making a good deal of noise), some of the men travelling in their safari suit country outfits, others already dressed for Namuri in jackets and ties. The women tended towards floral prints, gloves and hats. One elderly man was wearing a solar topi, a style of hat uncommon since the 1940s. The large groups of

Indians, all talking at once, made up a colourful contingent on the platform, the costumes of their womenfolk in particular indicating their religious affiliation. (The Hindu women wore very bright saris, the ends of which were flung over their heads, while the Muslim women, their heads covered by headscarves, wore equally colourful tunics and pantaloons). The Native travellers were often accompanied by goats and chickens, the goats led by plaited leather halters, and the chickens either with their feet bound and carried loose, or stuffed inside loosely woven baskets.

When the down train drew in, the engine's whistle emitting piercing blasts of sound, Michael noticed the Equatorian Army machine gun detachment travelling in the open wagon in front of the engine. The Equatorian Army had expanded in size, with compulsory military service having been extended from age eighteen right through to thirty-eight. The original colonial Equatoria Regiment had been reconstituted as a battalion of twice its original strength, and two new battalions had been formed. There was also a recruitment drive among the non-Sikuyu tribes. The number of reservists had also increased, with male European permanent residents up to the age of fifty-five, rather than forty-five, now eligible to serve in the Equatorian Army Reserve.

It was late afternoon, not long before sunset, before the train pulled in at Namuri Station. Michael had made a booking for the next two nights at the New Cedric Hotel. He would be flying early on Wednesday morning, for tomorrow he would have to find a photographic studio where he could obtain some passport photographs. He had felt some concern at leaving *Mahali pa Kupumzika* right now, for he was far from certain that Patrick was up to dealing with a crisis. He told himself however that Marjory was bold, cool and competent, and would do whatever needed doing should an emergency arise during his absence. And Karim had shown several times already that he had a cool head. So Michael ate a good dinner at the hotel, and slept well.

Chapter Fourteen

As the aircraft made a wide circle above Johannesburg two days later, Michael was struck at how American the city looked. Laid out on a grid pattern, with the towering high-rises of Hillbrow built on top of the ridge to the north of the city centre, there was little from this perspective which marked it as an African city. But the vast yellow mine dumps to the south, west and east of the city (one of which had a drive-in cinema located on top of it) left one in no doubt that this was a gold mining city. Jan Smuts Airport lay some miles to the east of the city, and Michael took a taxi to the Sunnyside Hotel in the leafy old suburb of Parktown. The Sunnyside was a rambling Edwardian building more like a large country house than a hotel, set in extensive gardens, once home to Lord Alfred Milner, the post-Boer War British Administrator. Michael had made a booking for the next three nights. As he ate dinner, he mulled over the tasks that lay ahead of him the next day. Sitting alone at his table, he was already missing *Mahali pa Kupumzika*. He had lost the knack of solitariness.

The next morning Michael took a taxi into the city centre, where he visited the Standard Bank. Here he opened a current account. He had come to the realisation that if he was to manage to evade the recent prohibition on funds from Britain being invested in Equatoria, he would need a bank account in South Africa to which he could direct funds from England – and from which, in turn, he could transfer funds to an account he had recently opened at the Standard Bank branch in Jiljil.

Sitting after lunch with a cold Castle lager on the terrace overlooking the gardens later that day, Michael was approached by a man in his thirties wearing a somewhat rumpled fawn coloured suit. The man held out his hand.

'Mr. Hood? May I introduce myself: Terry Hapgood from the Johannesburg daily, the *Star*.' His accent was South African, and his features were mobile and engaging. Michael, somewhat nonplussed, shook the man's hand.

The journalist smiled. 'We heard that the acclaimed British historical novelist Michael Hood was in town. Would you mind very much if I asked you a few questions?'

'I don't suppose so,' Michael replied. 'Go ahead.' Michael was not accustomed to chance interviews by newspaper journalists. In England he was not so well known that he had to participate in a great many interviews, and those few he took part in were carefully planned by his agent.

Terry Hapgood asked the usual sort of questions about Michael's writing. He had done a little homework, and he knew the titles of Michael's novels. When asked what he was working on now, Michael replied, 'Nothing.'

'You are not here doing research for a novel, Mr. Hood?'

'No, this is a private visit.'

Terry Hapgood gave his disarming smile again. 'May I ask why you are in South Africa, then?'

'As I say, a private visit, but I shall also be taking in a game tour of the Kruger National Park.'

The journalist changed the subject. 'I understand you have arrived from Namuri. What are your views on UDI?'

'I have no views – at least, none that I wish to share with the public.'

'Will you be returning to Namuri, or travelling to England after your visit to South Africa?' the journalist asked, smiling.

'I have friends I'm staying with in Equatoria,' Michael answered. 'I shall return to Equatoria after I have concluded my business in South Africa.'

'I don't suppose you would tell me what that business might be?' Terry Hapgood asked, his persistence overlaid by another smile.

Michael smiled back. 'Just a small matter which has to be attended to. I hope it wont take me long to deal with.'

'And one final question, Mr. Hood: which one of your novels do you like the most?'

Chapter Fourteen

Michael laughed. Terry Hapgood was an engaging fellow. 'I like the quartet of which the first title was *"Rajas and Ruffians."* When I wrote *"Rajas and Ruffians,"* I had little idea that it would give birth to a quartet. India has always fascinated me – particularly, the British in India. I myself had family in India a few generations back.'

The journalist was scribbling rapidly in a notebook. When he had finished, he looked up and said, 'My wife and I would be honoured if you would have dinner with us this evening – unless you have a prior engagement?'

And so it was that Terry Hapgood collected Michael at seven o' clock that evening, and drove him to his home in Orange Grove. On the understanding that this was an entirely social engagement, Michael was able to relax. It did him good, being able to chat with people for whom Equatoria and its problems were merely foreign news. Terry Hapgood's wife was a delightful woman, and the meal she served was excellent. She proved to be a sympathetic listener, moreover, skilled at drawing Michael out, and to his surprise he found himself talking about the loss of his mother, and the sense that his ties in Africa had grown all the stronger for it. 'I have no family, you see,' he told June Hapgood. 'My friends in Equatoria are the closest I have to family now, and I seem to be spending a great deal of time with them.'

While the Hapgoods' servant was clearing the table after dinner, the three Europeans moved outside onto the veranda (which June Hapgood called the *"stoep"*) with their coffees. The night air at this time of year on the Highveld (it was mid March) was cool enough to be refreshing after the warmth of the dining room, and Michael enjoyed his cigar. It was almost eleven o' clock when Terry Hapgood drove him back to the Sunnyside Hotel. Michael had an appointment at the British Consulate in Pretoria the next morning.

Chapter Fifteen

Michael, with the help of the concierge, had arranged for a hired car to be delivered to him at the hotel in the morning. Armed with maps both of Johannesburg and Pretoria, and possessed of some degree of trepidation (he drove rarely enough as it was, and almost never in unfamiliar territory), Michael managed to find the Pretoria road to the north of Johannesburg. It was a two lane highway set between rows of eucalyptus trees growing from wide, dusty verges, and it was very busy that Friday morning, with almost as many commercial vehicles as private cars. In South Africa, rail transport took a poor second place to road transport. Michael did, however, possess a good sense of direction and of locality, and he could read a map and translate the symbols into three dimensional physical features in his mind's eye. What was more, he had learned, when in the Army, how to memorise a route and fix it in his mind. He was able therefore to find the British Consulate in Pretorius Street in Pretoria without losing his way.

On his way there he made a small diversion (on the advice of Terry Hapgood, on the latter learning that Michael would be visiting Pretoria), to take in the classic view of the magnificent Union Buildings, high above the city on Meintjieskop. This

Chapter Fifteen

strikingly dramatic structure, the executive seat of government in South Africa, was designed by the English architect, Sir Herbert Baker, who, in the late nineteenth and early years of the twentieth centuries had designed so many of South Africa's most glorious and dramatic buildings.

At the Consulate Michael met an official to whom he gave his passport, along with the two passport photographs he had had taken in Namuri. This man informed Michael that a new passport would be ready within three days. This suited Michael, for he had a tour of the Kruger National Park booked for the following three days.

Not very far from the Consulate was an Italian restaurant, La Cantina, recommended by Terry Hapgood over dinner the evening before. Michael was partial to Italian cuisine, with which, living in Soho, he was familiar, and at the restaurant he enjoyed a Spaghetti Carbonara with a glass of wine. That evening, sitting in his hotel room after dinner, trying to read one of his favourite Graham Greene novels, *The Quiet American* (whose story seemed so much more relevant to him now that he had come to witness the end of British rule in an Equatoria blighted by bloody insurrection and collapse), Michael found a gathering loneliness creeping up on him. Until his mother's death, loneliness had gone largely unrecognised by Michael, and it took him a while to recognise it now. Once he recognised that what he was feeling – this uncomfortable emotion – was loneliness, he went downstairs to the hotel bar, which, at half past nine that Friday night, was very busy. It seemed to be frequented as much by groups of non-resident visitors as by hotel guests (the latter, Michael assumed, were, like himself, the solitary drinkers). The bar was clearly a popular Johannesburg watering hole. Michael found the loud chatter and bustle a welcome antidote to his *tristesse*. He spoke with no one, but was content to sit at the bar counter for almost an hour, during which time he drank two large whiskeys and nibbled at a bowl of peanuts. The two large whiskeys helped Michael fall asleep almost immediately he went to bed, around eleven o' clock.

On Saturday morning Michael awoke to birdsong in the trees outside, and when he drew back the curtains and looked out the window, he saw a clear blue sky. What a wonderful, benign climate the Highveld has, he thought. He left the keys to the hired car, which he had parked the afternoon before not far from the entrance to the hotel, at the concierge's desk downstairs. Breakfast was served from half past seven, and Michael had managed to finish his breakfast by eight o' clock, and was waiting outside, when a young man with short blonde hair and cheerful features, wearing khaki shorts, open sandals and a khaki bush shirt, with an official field guide's badge pinned to his shirt, arrived in a Volkswagen T1 Kombi bus to collect him.

'Mr. Hood? Good morning. I'm Mark Davies, your tour guide,' he greeted Michael, who shook his hand. Michael had understood there would be three or four other passengers on the tour with him, one of whom was already sitting in the Kombi bus. Michael glanced at her as he entered the vehicle. She looked to be in her early fifties, an attractive woman with auburn hair cut short, black slacks, and a cream coloured blouse. She had a fine woollen cardigan, a pale green in colour, draped over her shoulders. She introduced herself as Audrey Howes, a South African, but her accent was an educated one, not far removed from Michael's own. In short order, Michael learned from her that she had been widowed a year ago, and this tour was by way of a determined effort to begin living her life again.

'And what about you?' she asked Michael, smiling. 'You are obviously English, but what else can you tell me about yourself?'

Michael smiled in response to her cheerful, friendly curiosity. 'Well, I'm currently staying with friends on a large farm in Equatoria, but I had to visit South Africa to get my British passport renewed.'

Chapter Fifteen

'Oh – yes – I don't suppose that's possible in Equatoria anymore.'

'That's right, it isn't. So I flew from Namuri, and I visited the British Consulate in Pretoria yesterday.'

'Will it take long to renew?' Audrey asked.

'I don't think so. The official I saw there told me a replacement would be ready to collect within three days.'

'So you're filling in time – is that it?'

Michael laughed. 'Sort of. But I had intended doing a game tour anyway. I haven't been able to tour Equatoria's game regions. It's too dangerous right now.'

'And what do you do; I mean, how do you earn a living, Michael?'

'I'm a novelist.' Michael smiled ruefully. 'Although I haven't written a novel for a while.'

'Oh – how wonderful!' Audrey exclaimed. 'I love reading. Would I know anything you have written?'

But at this point the Kombi bus pulled in at the Carlton Hotel in the city centre, where two more passengers were to be collected. This couple, Gunther and Angela, proved to be German; perfectly pleasant people, but with little English. Mark Davies, the tour guide, was speaking to them in what sounded to Michael like fluent German. The Kombi bus then headed eastward out of the city, the sun climbing rapidly in a cloudless, cerulean sky ahead of them.

The route at first was somewhat dull: the countryside was flat, and they passed vast fields of maize, and the occasional coal mine and adjacent power station, the huge cooling towers emitting white wisps of steam. They left the main road at Belfast, and soon found themselves in a more varied landscape of low hills and fields of maize and sunflowers. They were gradually losing altitude, descending slowly as the land fell away before them. In the valleys were clear, narrow, fast flowing streams. Their young guide told his passengers that this region was the heartland of the original Trekkers' settlement of what later became the Transvaal.

They drove slowly through the small town of Lydenburg, established, so Mark Davies told them, in 1849 by Andries Potgieter, one of the original Trek leaders, when Ohrigstadt, an earlier settlement to the north, was abandoned due to a malaria outbreak. Lydenburg, Mark Davies told them, became the capital of the Lydenburg Republic, which, in 1860, joined the South African Republic (known to the British as the Transvaal).

'Lydenburg was on the wagon trail to the Portuguese settlement at Delagoa Bay, you see,' their guide told them. 'That's modern day Lourenço Marques.' This provided the Boer republic with an outlet to the sea that was not British controlled. 'Today,' Mark continued, 'Lydenburg is the centre of fly fishing in South Africa. But Lydenburg was once the site of South Africa's earliest gold finds. This alluvial gold – that is, gold that you pan for in rivers and streams – was discovered in 1873.' Mark Davies then switched to German, presumably to repeat what he had just said for Gunther's and Angela's benefit.

Heading east, they exited Lydenburg, and their guide told them they would be climbing, and then descending, the Long Tom Pass. 'The pass is named after the Boers' one hundred and fifty-five millimetre field guns, made by the French firm, Creusot, that saw action here during the Second Anglo-Boer War of 1899 – 1902,' he said. 'There is a replica of the gun the far side of the pass. The pass takes us to Sabie, which lies one thousand two hundred and fifty feet lower than Lydenburg. We will then have left the Highveld behind and we'll find ourselves in the Lowveld, which will be much warmer. It's *"Jock of the Bushveld"* country.' Mark grinned at his passengers over his left shoulder. Michael thought he was doing his best to make a long journey interesting. The young man again repeated what he had said, in German. Gunther asked him a couple of questions, to which their guide replied fluently.

Chapter Fifteen

'Mark, where did you learn to speak German?' Michael asked him.

'I studied German for Matric at school.'

'It must make you sought after as a guide,' Michael remarked.

'*Ja* – it is useful.'

'Mark,' said Audrey, 'remind me, what was the story behind "*Jock of the Bushveld*?" '

'During the 1880s Percy FitzPatrick, who was born in the Cape Colony, worked as a transport rider in the Lowveld region,' Mark Davies replied, 'and Jock was the name of his dog, a Staffordshire-Bull Terrier cross. FitzPatrick – later Sir Percy FitzPatrick – wrote about his and the dog's adventures in the bushveld country, and published the stories under the title "*Jock of the Bushveld*." '

Mark Davies halted the Kombi bus some miles beyond the crest of the pass, with a superb view of the surrounding countryside; rolling hills stretching to the far horizon, where a pastel blue sky met a landscape almost lost in haze. Here, Michael and Gunther admired the replica of the Creusot gun. The route had been a steep climb, and the rear-engined Volkswagen bus had made heavy weather of it, and the descent, the road twisting and winding back and forth on itself, was a welcome relief. The country was heavily forested, almost all of it given over to plantation forestry – conifers and eucalyptus – which their young guide told them was used for the production of timber, paper, mine props and wood pulp.

'It looks pretty, this forested landscape,' the young man commented, 'but it is a near desert in ecological terms. There is little indigenous animal or bird life adapted to living in the plantation forest.'

'Are there no tracts of indigenous forest left?' Michael asked.

'Yes, there are some,' Mark replied. 'Did you notice a turnoff to the right some way back, signposted the "Sterkspruit Nature Reserve?" In the kloofs are indigenous forests. You can find the Cape clawless otter in the kloofs hereabouts.'

What a knowledgeable guide this young man was, thought Michael.

Before stopping for a late lunch at Sabie (a forestry centre and tourist town whose main street was very broad, lined with two story buildings which had sloping corrugated iron roofs sheltering the pavement from the sun), the group visited the Lone Creek falls, an impressive waterfall falling almost three hundred feet in an unbroken drop. The German couple took more photographs. Michael did not have a camera with him, but Audrey took a photograph of him standing with the falls as a backdrop. Audrey had continued her cheerful chatter throughout the drive, and Michael had to confess that she was a good looking woman, if a little too talkative. But in the rare periods of silence, Michael's thoughts would invariably return to *Mahali pa Kupumzika*, and to Marjory, both of whom he was missing a great deal.

'If you give me an address to which I can send it, I'll post you a copy of the photo, Michael,' Audrey told him. 'And would you mind taking one of me?' she asked him, handing him her camera. 'If you stand here, the focus is right. All you need do is frame the picture and click the shutter.'

Michael took a photograph of her.

On Mark Davies's recommendation, Michael ordered trout for lunch, with a garlic and lemon butter herb sauce (how popular was he going to be in the Kombi bus now, he wondered), the trout caught locally that morning. It was, he found, delicious. He shared a half bottle of delicate South African white wine with Audrey. On their way to Hazyview after lunch, Michael found himself dropping off once or twice. Audrey too was silent at last, and appeared to be dozing. The countryside was intensively cultivated, and there were extensive banana and macadamia nut plantations. It was warm, far warmer than it had been on the Highveld.

They entered the Kruger National Park via the Paul Kruger

Chapter Fifteen

Gate, not far beyond Hazyview. Michael sat up straight again, and began to pay attention to his surroundings. He was mildly rewarded with views of zebra and impala, and then a group of giraffes, very stately as they moved in what seemed to Michael to be slow motion. Then their guide stopped the Kombi bus and pointed to their right.

'There – about one hundred feet away – some white rhinos, there are five of them, beneath the maroela tree. Do you see them?'

Gunther clicked away, his expensive looking camera armed with a massive lens which Michael imagined brought the animals very close. Michael was happy just to gaze at the creatures. They were the first rhinos he had seen outside of a zoo. They looked, he thought, as placid as cattle.

'White rhinos are grazers,' Mark Davies told the group. 'They are generally fairly even tempered. I have walked among a group of white rhinos and they were not bothered.'

'How do you tell white rhinos from black rhinos?' Audrey asked. 'It's not their colour, is it?'

'You are quite right,' their guide replied. 'Their colouring is the same. One of the most obvious differences is that white rhinos have wide straight lips – thus *"wyd"* in Afrikaans, which became "white" in English. The black rhino is a browser, and has a prehensile, hooked upper lip, for plucking leaves from bushes and trees. It is smaller than the white rhino, and more compact. And it has an altogether meaner temper. You wouldn't go walking among black rhinos!' Mark then switched to German, for the benefit of Gunther and Angela.

Skukuza Camp, not very much further along the well made road, surprised Michael. He was not sure what he had been expecting; certainly not this charming camp made up of individual thatch roofed *rondavels* with a veranda each, set amidst green lawns and mature shade trees. The windows and the doors of the *rondavels* had close meshed flyscreens to keep insects out, and the *rondavel* to which Michael was shown felt pleasantly cool, beneath its thick thatched roof, after the afternoon heat outside.

Audrey had arranged that they go exploring together after they had deposited their bags, and the two of them wandered through the camp, eventually arriving at a wooden viewing deck on the banks of a broad, slow moving, greenish-brown river, overhung with enormous trees from which loud birdsong emanated. The lawns ran right down to the trees.

'This is the Sabie River,' Audrey told Michael. 'Aren't the trees wonderful? That's a sycamore fig – it's magnificent, isn't it?'

'It's my first big river in Africa,' Michael remarked. 'It puts me in mind of the scene from Rudyard Kipling's *"Just So Stories,"* do you know the one, *"The Elephants' Child,"* where the baby elephant comes up alongside the banks of the "great green greasy Limpopo River."'

'Oh – so you know the *"Just So Stories!"* I loved them as a child.'

'So did I,' Michael responded, smiling at Audrey. 'My mother used to read them to me when I was very young.'

The service in the camp's restaurant – a large room beneath a high, thatched roof – was very good, and the dinner the group ate that evening was excellent. Crocodile steaks were on the menu, among a variety of game and conventional dishes. Michael felt that crocodile was unclean meat, and he chose a dish he had enjoyed several times already at *Mahali pa Kupumzika*; roast sirloin of impala. Playing safe with the fish course (they were after all located several hundred miles from the coast), he declined ordering the shellfish on the menu, opting for pan fried trout, which he knew would have been caught not very far away. With his roast impala, he drank a Constantia Cabernet Sauvignon, which he shared with Mark Davies. The young guide, who had changed into fawn slacks and a long sleeved white shirt, was happy to enter into (and even at times to lead) the conversation, which ranged over a wide number of topics. Mark switched easily to German every now and then, although Gunther and Angela both made an effort to speak some English.

After the meal, Michael and Audrey walked back together through the dark towards their *rondavels*. Widely spaced lampposts cast some small amount of light. The air had a warm, silky softness to it. The night calls were much like those Michael heard at *Mahali pa Kupumzika*. They could hear hyena giggling maniacally not so very far away – Michael hoped, on the far side of the fence that he had been told surrounded the camp. After they had reached Audrey's round thatched hut, Michael said, 'Goodnight Audrey.'

A look of momentary disappointment crossed Audrey's face. Then she said, 'I have enjoyed today. Have you?'

'Yes, I have. It's all very new to me.'

'Goodnight then. Sleep well, Michael,' and Audrey went inside her *rondavel*, alone. Michael wondered whether he had been expected to accompany her. He was not very practiced at reading the signals in situations like this one (which was, perhaps, why he remained unmarried), and anyway, his mind was focused on one woman only, and that was Marjory, the wife of his best friend from schooldays.

The next morning, a Sunday, after a huge breakfast in the restaurant, which included Michael's favourite breakfast dish, smoked kippers, the group headed northwards through the Park. The weather continued warm and sunny. They were fortunate in their game sightings. Had Mark Davies not been driving at only fifteen to twenty miles an hour, and scanning the countryside as he drove, they might have missed the acme of sightings: a pride of lions resting beneath an umbrella thorn acacia, a few miles this side of Satara Camp. Their guide halted the vehicle suddenly, and all four passengers were immediately alert and looking around them, but until Mark Davies pointed and said, 'There! Under that big tree sixty feet away – the umbrella thorn – a pride of lions,' no one had spotted them, for their tawny golden hides blended in with the sandy soil and the sparse, golden grass surrounding the base of the tree.

Michael was delighted with this sighting. He had now seen both elephants and lions in Africa, and a good deal in between. Gunther had his big camera up and pointing at the pride, which consisted of a male with a splendid dark mane, and four females (the big cats were lying at their ease, couched, or on their sides). There were five cubs also, rolling, wrestling and mock fighting.

'Oh, how sweet!' Audrey declared.

Michael did not regret that he had no camera with him. Who would he have shown the photographs to? It was enough to know that some country such as this, existed. It seemed to speak to a part of Michael of which he had so far been unaware. There had only been one person he would have taken pleasure in sharing such photographs with, and that had been his mother. His friends in London were not much more than mere frequently seen acquaintances, whom he met usually in the pub, and none, not even Maurice Grainger, was truly close enough to him to admire any holiday snaps he might have taken. (As for his friends at *Mahali pa Kupumzika*, Michael rather suspected that Marjory was not the sort of person you sat down with and showed your holiday photographs to). Michael was essentially a somewhat lonely man, and while he had not recognised this fact while his mother was alive, he knew it for the truth now.

The group had lunch at Satara Camp's restaurant. They then continued on their way, driving slowly northwards, and in due course they crossed the Olifants River, a much broader, far more impressive river than the Sabie River. They followed the road in a wide arc, and arrived at Olifants Camp, located on the banks of the river. It was about four o' clock. Michael retired to his *rondavel* (near enough identical to the one he had had at Skukuza Camp) for a nap.

Chapter Fifteen

On Monday they exited the Park, and drove all day, taking a slightly different return route, for they passed by the Blyde River Canyon, and Graskop (where they admired the splendid waterfall). Standing on the edge of the Blyde River Canyon, the sensation of a god-like perspective was pronounced. The view inspired awe in Michael. Far, far below, he could make out the Blyde River. On the far side of the vast canyon the *Drie Rondavels* stood out against the blue sky; three peaks with near vertical sides and conical caps, and Michael could see how they had acquired their name. He found himself regretting that the Emergency in Equatoria prevented him from touring that country, where surely there must be scenery just as magnificent, just as impressive. He could imagine such an outlook as this inspiring one of his favourite authors from his boyhood, H. Rider Haggard, to write one of his wonderful adventure stories.

It was near sunset before Mark Davies dropped Michael off at the Sunnyside Hotel. Michael took his leave of Audrey, who insisted that they exchange addresses. Michael gave her one of his London cards. She leant across and kissed him on the cheek as he was about to get out. It occurred suddenly to Michael that had he been another sort of a man, he could easily have seized the opportunity that Audrey had offered him. But Michael had thoughts only for Marjory. He shook their young guide's hand and tipped him twenty Rand. 'You are an excellent guide, Mark. Thanks for the tour,' he said.

Dinner would shortly be served in the hotel dining room. Michael ate, alone once more. Tomorrow he would take delivery of another hired car, and he hoped to collect his new passport at the British Consulate in Pretoria. But he would telephone the Consulate before he set off. And, new passport in hand, he could then return to Equatoria; to *Mahali pa Kupumzika* – and to his hopeless infatuation with Marjory.

Chapter Sixteen

Early on Tuesday afternoon, having obtained his new passport that morning, Michael gave his air ticket, which had an open return date, to the hotel concierge, and asked him to find out when soonest he could book him on a flight to Namuri. 'I will be on the terrace,' Michael told him.

The concierge found him there twenty minutes later. Michael was drinking a Castle lager, reading the Johannesburg daily, the *Star*. 'Mr. Hood,' the concierge said, 'I can get you a seat on the flight for Namuri tomorrow morning. Would you like me to book the seat?'

There was, Michael felt, no purpose in staying in South Africa any longer. 'Yes, that would suit me. Please go ahead and make the booking. Tell me, can you arrange for a telegram to be sent to Equatoria before the end of the day?'

'Yes Sir. I have telegram forms at my desk.'

A few minutes later, leaving the last couple of inches of his beer unfinished, Michael headed for the concierge's desk, where the concierge was busy confirming his flight for tomorrow. On a telegram form, Michael wrote: "PLEASE MEET ME JILJIL STATION THURSDAY 15TH STOP REPLY NEW CEDRIC HOTEL STOP MICHAEL"

Chapter Sixteen

He addressed the telegram thus: "Lord and Lady Pencaitland, *Mahali pa Kupumzika,* C/O Jiljil Post Office, Equatoria." Michael waited until the concierge had confirmed his flight for the morrow, took back his air ticket, thanked the man and tipped him. He returned to the concierge's desk just before dinner, and the concierge confirmed that his telegram had been sent.

'You can collect your boarding pass at the South African Airways desk at Jan Smuts Airport just before departure, Mr. Hood,' the concierge told him. 'Would you like me to book you a taxi? Your flight departs eight-thirty in the morning. You should check in no later than seven-thirty. You will need a taxi for a quarter to seven tomorrow morning.'

Michael said yes to the offer of a taxi.

As he sat waiting in the foyer the next morning, he had not had any breakfast; that had proved impossible to arrange so early, but he had drunk two cups of strong coffee. Even so, he felt as if he was not entirely grounded, and he experienced that frisson of nervous excitement he associated with very early departures, an excitement engendered in part by an empty stomach, and emphasised by the rising sun hardly above the horizon, and the slight chill to the air.

As Michael checked into the New Cedric Hotel in the late afternoon of Wednesday the 14th March, the skies were heavy with low, dark cloud. The streets of Namuri had been glistening with a recent downpour, and it now began to rain again. Michael hoped the maize planting at *Mahali pa Kupumzika* was well in hand. He had left *Mahali pa Kupumzika* eleven days earlier.

'Are there any messages for me?' he asked.

'A moment Mr. Hood . . .' the young man at reception replied. 'Yes,' he continued, 'There is one. Lady Pencaitland telephoned this morning. She will meet you at Jiljil Station tomorrow.'

Michael felt a momentary disquiet. Why was the message from Marjory, and not from Patrick?

It was cool at night during the rains, so Michael had dinner in the hotel dining room that evening, rather than at the open sided Thorn Tree Boma restaurant. After dinner, he glanced through the *Namuri Times* as he sat in the lounge. There had been another landmine incident on the Namuri – Port Caroline road. In the Highlands, a European farmer, his wife, and their two small children had been murdered by the *Wa Chui* in a night attack. There were the beginnings of fuel shortages reported in the country now, as the economic sanctions imposed by Britain and other countries began to make themselves felt. Perhaps the most dramatic news was the imposition of a country-wide travel curfew (excluding only the Coastal province) between eight o' clock in the evening and five in the morning. And – rather worryingly, in view of their history – there had been some incidents reported of unrest on the Amai reserves. The Amai, a pastoral tribe with a fierce, warlike past, were traditional enemies of the Sikuyu, and had so far played no part in the uprising.

Michael found the news depressing. He left the lounge and went to the small residents' bar on the first floor, where he ordered a double scotch and lighted one of the duty free Romeo y Julieta Corona cigars he had bought at Jan Smuts Airport. (He had a box of these for Patrick too). He was rereading another of Graham Greene's novels, *"The Power and the Glory,"* which he had found in the library at *Mahali pa Kupumzika*. When he had finished smoking his cigar (he had had a second scotch with it), he went up to his room, and by ten o' clock he was in bed. It had been a tiring day (how he disliked air travel!) and he had been up so early at the start of it.

Michael felt as if he was coming home, as the train pulled into Jiljil Station at about four o' clock in the afternoon the next day. Trains and home coming were closely linked in his consciousness. There were the almost ritualised journeys home by train from school at the start of school holidays, almost always with his friend

Chapter Sixteen

Patrick travelling with him, and the many, many times he had caught the train to Kingham from London as an adult, on visits to that same childhood home in the Cotswolds; and he seemed to have made this journey by train to Jiljil, on his way to *Mahali pa Kupumzika* (which now felt like home to Michael), several times already. From the window of his compartment, Michael could see Marjory and Keith Hepburn, standing side by side on the station platform. They both wore sidearms. But where was Patrick?

'Michael – *Karibu*,' Marjory greeted him, as Michael leant out his compartment window.

'*Jambo* Marjory,' he responded.

'*Jambo Michael*,' Keith Hepburn declared, reaching up for the first of Michael's suitcases to be passed through the window. Once the luggage was on the platform, Michael left the carriage, and he and Marjory kissed each other on the cheek. Michael was smiling broadly. Marjory too was smiling, but her smile lacked the vigour and openness that Michael had come to expect.

'How are you, Marjory?' Michael asked her.

'I'm alright, thanks. What about you?'

'Oh, I'm doing OK,' Michael replied. 'Glad to be back. Where is Patrick?' he asked.

A shadow passed across Marjory's face. 'Later,' she replied. 'I'll talk later.'

Michael turned and shook hands with Keith Hepburn, who said, 'Michael, *habari?*'

'*Nzuri sana*,' Michael replied. They walked to the car park, the two men each carrying a suitcase. Michael's large bag was slung over his shoulder. They loaded the luggage into the back of the Land Rover, and Marjory's father climbed into his own Land Rover. Marjory got in behind the wheel, and Michael sat in the seat on the left.

'You don't mind driving?' he asked her. 'I can drive if you want.'

'I don't mind driving,' she replied. 'You will find your Colt revolver in front of you, Michael. It's loaded.' Marjory pulled out of the car park, her father following her in his own Land Rover. The countryside lay in the grip of the long rains, and the roads could only be navigated by four wheel drive vehicles.

Michael reached for his holstered Colt revolver, which was on the small parcels shelf in front of him, and placed it on his lap. After a while, Marjory concentrating on her driving, for the surface of the road was slick in places, and the heavy car slithered and skidded not infrequently, Michael asked, 'How is Patrick?'

'Ohhh . . . I don't know,' Marjory answered him, a note of despair in her voice. 'He's not himself anymore. He did not want to leave the house when I set off for Jiljil.'

'What do you think is wrong with him?'

Marjory glanced at Michael before facing front again. 'You and I have both known for some time that he's drinking far too much,' she said. 'That is part of it, I think. But he's given to wild mood swings, and he has very little to do with managing the estate anymore.'

'I think I really began to notice a marked change in Patrick after the *Wa Chui* attack in which André Myburgh was killed,' Michael responded. 'But really, it's drink that is almost the whole problem. You know, I've been wishing to mention my concerns for Patrick for a long time, Marjory, but the timing never seemed right. I'm pleased we are talking about it now.'

'I wish we didn't have to,' Marjory responded unhappily. 'But I'm very glad you are back. Perhaps it will do Patrick good, seeing you again. And I value your company when I do my rounds on the estate every morning.' Marjory glanced briefly at Michael again. 'It's not really safe going out alone anymore, you know – especially for a woman. You just don't know which of the workers has taken the oath.'

'I've missed *Mahali pa Kupumzika*. It's been less than two

weeks, but I feel as if I've been away longer. I was looking through the *Namuri Times* last night. I do not think this is a good time to be away for too long.'

'God knows how it's all going to end!' Marjory exclaimed. 'Probably not very well.'

Neither Michael nor Marjory spoke for the next five miles or more. Michael was remembering his schooldays, and his school friend, Patrick. He was slowly coming to understand that something would have to be done for Patrick. Marjory was concentrating on her driving. They had not yet reached the big house before the western horizon was showing only a thin strip of light – a narrow band of glowing orange, topped by cyan yellow – beneath low, purple-grey cloud. Keith Hepburn had turned off the road for his farm some distance back. They were alone on the road now, and Michael felt some relief when at last they saw the dark loom of the house ahead of them.

There was a paraffin lamp burning on the veranda, and Karim came down the steps as they drew in. The two Rhodesian ridgebacks came bounding down the steps ahead of him, barking happily, and gambolling around the Land Rover. They pressed up against both Marjory and Michael (for they accepted him as a member of the family by now).

Karim greeted Marjory – '*Habari ya jioni Memsaab*' – then Michael, '*Habari ya jioni, Bwana.*'

'Good evening, Karim,' Michael responded. 'I hope you are well.'

'*Nzuri sana, Bwana.*'

Michael and Marjory left Karim seeing to the luggage, and went inside the house as it began to rain again, a heavy, cold rain. They found the Alsatian dog with her mistress in the drawing room (which was lighted by two paraffin lamps, and by the flicker of the fire in the fireplace). Lady Pencaitland had a pink gin on the little table next to her chair. The room was scented with burning cedar logs. Lady Catherine was sitting close to the fire, with a glass of sherry alongside her. Lady Pencaitland smiled at Michael.

'Good evening, Michael. Did you have a good journey?' she asked.

'It was without untoward incident, Lady Pencaitland,' Michael replied (wondering why he was talking like a character out of Jane Austen), and taking the hand she extended in his for a moment. 'I hope you are well. Good evening Lady Catherine,' he greeted Patrick's aunt, who asked, 'Have you been away again, Malcolm? How are the girls?'

'I believe they're well,' Michael told the old lady.

'I'll have a brandy please, Karim,' Marjory said, when the manservant, who had taken Michael's luggage up to his room, returned.

'Ndiyo Memsaab.'

'I could do with something to warm me,' Marjory told Michael, smiling.

'That makes two of us. Please get me a large whiskey, Karim,' Michael called to the manservant, who had gone to the drinks cabinet to pour Marjory's brandy.

'Ndiyo Bwana,' and Karim brought the drinks on a small silver tray, a brandy for Marjory, who had sat down, and a generous neat Scotch for Michael, who now sat down and lighted a cigarette. Michael was wondering why Patrick was not there to greet him. As if reading his mind, Marjory asked her mother in law whether Patrick was still in his study.

'I think so,' she replied. 'He has a lot of work to do, Marjory. I expect he will join us for dinner.'

Marjory wondered what work (if any) her husband was busy with. She felt that he could have made the effort to be there to greet his friend. But Patrick appeared at dinnertime, wearing an evening jacket. Michael had changed before dinner, and, forewarned by Marjory (who was wearing a gown with a little, tight waisted jacket in matching blue silk, against the cool weather), had donned his own evening jacket. The gathering had been about to give up on Patrick – Karim had sounded the dinner gong in the hallway more than ten minutes ago – and they had now sat down at the table (which was lighted by a paraffin lamp hanging from the light fitting in the middle of the ceiling, and by two triple branched candelabras of silver on the table. Diesel fuel was becoming difficult to obtain, and had to be saved for the farm machinery, so the electricity generator was not running).

Patrick greeted Michael as if he had seen him just that morning. 'Michael old chap!' he exclaimed, as he sat down, without having offered his hand for Michael to shake. 'What do you think about the curfew?'

'I suppose it's a sensible move, Patrick,' Michael responded. 'If the government had more troops to spare, there could be more Army road patrols, but there isn't the manpower.'

'I think it's outrageous,' Patrick declared, his florid features adopting an angry frown. He pulled his chair back abruptly, and the legs scraped loudly on the polished floor. 'The *Wa Chui* will think that they're winning the war.'

Michael realised with a sudden shock that his old school friend was beginning to irritate him. His bright red features irritated him; his loud voice irritated him; his abdication of his responsibilities for running the estate irritated him.

'But does it actually affect us, Patrick?' Michael asked. 'We're not going to be going anywhere at night, eh?'

Karim had already reached across and poured Patrick his first glass of wine. Patrick picked the glass up and drank deeply, then put the wine glass down rather hard. Some wine slopped over the rim of the glass. Michael was afraid Patrick would break the glass. It was obvious that Patrick had been drinking at least the entire afternoon.

'It's the principle of the thing, don't you see?' Patrick retorted. 'We're being made prisoners in our own country.' He turned to the manservant. 'Karim – why do we never have fish anymore? We move from the soup straight to the main course.'

'It's difficult getting hold of fresh fish now, Darling, you know that,' Marjory interjected. 'Hari Patel wont make deliveries to us anymore. He's afraid of running into the *Wa Chui* along the road.'

'That's the trouble with these people: they're so timid; afraid of their own shadow,' remarked Patrick. Then the meal proceeded in silence but for the clink of cutlery on the china, until Marjory began to ask Michael questions about his South African visit. Patrick glowered silently as the two of them were speaking together, then he loudly interrupted Michael, who was about to answer a question Marjory had put to him, and said, 'The British government doesn't seem to have any problems about European rule in South Africa. What's their gripe about European rule in Equatoria – eh? Can anyone tell me that?'

Michael had sometimes wondered the same thing. 'I don't know, Patrick,' he responded. 'It makes no sense to me either.'

In June, Patrick had to attend an Equatorian Army Reserve training camp at Naburu. He had a Reservist rank of Major. He was away for two weeks. He had taken a dozen bottles of Scotch with him, but he returned with four untouched bottles, which for Patrick represented a considerable reduction in his alcohol intake over fourteen days. He quickly made up for lost ground after his return.

Chapter Seventeen

Michael no longer felt he could leave *Mahali pa Kupumzika*. Patrick was not competent anymore. How could he leave Marjory alone to shoulder the burden of running the estate during such difficult times? So he no longer thought seriously of returning to London, or to his family home in the Cotswolds. He hoped his mother's elderly dog was happy with Mrs. Hughes (the cook-housekeeper was staying on at the old house, and she was looking after the dog). Sometimes he felt a twinge of guilt at being away so long. He wondered how long a dog pined for someone. Michael's mother had died only a little over nine months ago, and there were times when he missed her terribly. Sometimes he found himself thinking, 'I must tell Mother about that,' in response to some event, or some observation he wished to share with her. While he had not seen his mother more than four or five times a year in the past, he had telephoned her often.

As to his writing, that seemed to have been put on hold indefinitely. His most recent novel had been published more than two years ago, and he had attempted no creative writing since his return to Africa. If Michael had had to rely solely on his writing to support himself, he might by now have been in financial difficulties. Fortunately, his father had left him a substantial legacy, to which would now be added his mother's estate. Money was not a problem for Michael. He did sometimes find himself missing his life in London, and his acquaintances there. He wondered whether he ought to write to Maurice Grainger, the closest he had to a real friend in England.

By September of that year (1962), Michael and Marjory between them were managing the estate with almost no input from Patrick, who was intoxicated to some degree almost all the time now, and who spent a great deal of his time alone in his study. What, if anything, he was doing in there, besides drinking, Michael had no idea. Karim would know; Karim saw more of Patrick than anyone else did during the day.

It was clear by now to Michael that his old friend had a serious drinking problem. His behaviour in public was increasingly erratic, veering between lengthy morose silences, occasional angry outbursts, and periods of manic high spirits. But much of the time, with Patrick holed up in his study, it was possible to forget his presence altogether. However, Patrick usually made the effort to accompany Michael, Karim, and Keith Hepburn (who brought his servant with him) on their fortnightly trips to Jiljil, for had he not done so, he may not have been able to ensure that the one and a half dozen bottles of Scotch whiskey he appeared to require each fortnight were obtained from Hari Patel's shop. (Since international sanctions had been imposed, most of the whiskey had to be routed overland from South Africa, and it was now extremely costly).

Patrick had acquired an alcoholic's deviousness, and he would have Karim help him carry the two boxes containing the whiskey, and hide them among the other purchases in the back of the Chevrolet or in the Land Rover. Michael, however, was aware of the extent of these purchases. He could not believe that Patrick – even accounting for the couple of bottles of Scotch the family got through in the drawing room drinks cabinet every fortnight – could get through so much whiskey every fortnight. He must, Michael thought, be stockpiling the whiskey – against some imagined time of dearth in the future?

Michael had had no close experience of alcoholism up to now, and for a long time he had ignored what would have been clear to him had he previously known someone with a serious drinking problem. But now he began to wonder whether he should suggest to Marjory that something should be done for Patrick. But how could you introduce such a topic into your daily conversation; a subject so intensely personal to both Patrick and Marjory? What, in any case, could be done for Patrick? There were no clinics in Equatoria where one could send an alcoholic to recover. It would mean sending Patrick to London – or perhaps to South Africa, and Michael knew that the estate could not carry such a financial burden. (However, thought Michael: if we were to send Patrick to London, I have ample funds in Britain to pay for his stay at a clinic). Perhaps, he considered, he should be talking to Patrick himself about his problem, but he shied away from such an idea; it seemed a gross infringement of Patrick's privacy, and a horrible diminishment of his friend's dignity.

Michael felt enormous compassion for Marjory, who, after more than two years of marriage, was still childless, and who had discovered that she was married to a drunkard. Michael very rarely saw that gleam of wicked mischief and humour in her eyes anymore that he remembered from his early visits to *Mahali pa Kupumzika*. Michael's feelings for Marjory had not diminished. Her presence filled him with a desperate, yearning amalgam of joy and anguish. Marjory was however the wife of his best friend from his school days, and he dared not express his feelings to her. To have done so would have contravened the code whereby he lived.

It was only once André Myburgh was no longer there that Michael began to realise how hard the estate manager must have worked. Most of the harvest was eventually brought in, although it took longer to do so than it had done in the past, for not only was the estate very short of labour now, but fuel for the farm machinery was scarce – and enormously expensive when it could be obtained. The fuel shortage was beginning to bite. Oil tankers flying Panamanian flags of convenience were ignoring the international embargo, but they were too few to supply Equatoria with all her fuel needs. Although farmers were given priority for the acquisition of diesel, petrol and oil, the oil company sub depot at Jiljil was itself unable to supply *Mahali pa Kupumzika* with all its needs, for other farms also had a call on their fuel stocks. A new department of state, the ministry of strategic supplies, allocated fuel allowances (along with allowances for animal feed, and many other products) to every bulk purchaser in the country. Then there was also the problem of actual delivery: the oil company tankers and lorries, and the animal feed co-operative's lorries, would no longer make the journey to *Mahali pa Kupumzika*. Every drum of diesel and petrol and lubricating oil and paraffin used by the estate; every bale and sack of animal feed, now had to be loaded onto the back of one of the estate's lorries, and the trip to Jiljil and back, with the convoy moving no faster than the best speed of the lorry, was made no more frequently than once a fortnight. The drive there and back could take up to three hours each way during the wet season, to which were added the two hours or so spent in the town itself.

As for *Mahali pa Kupumzika's* prized dairy herd, it was only a memory now. It had been considered both too dangerous and too costly to continue hauling the estate's milk yield into Jiljil every morning. Therefore (although Marjory wept at the time) the dairy herd was slaughtered and butchered, the beef sold, and only half a dozen milk cows were kept on, for the much reduced manufacture of cheese on the estate, and for the estate's own dairy needs. Participating in the slaughter with Michael, Karim had said to him, '*Bwana*, this is *nchi ya kilio*.' (This is a weeping land).

Chapter Seventeen

Michael, as, alongside Karim, he shot the cattle one after another, heard the lowing and bellowing of the terrified beasts, which could scent the slaughter taking place, and he felt sick at heart, but he carried out his task with a grim, tight lipped fortitude. The cows were driven one by one through a gate, which, like the fence either side, had been covered on Michael's instructions in hessian cloth, and so they were shot out of direct sight of their fellows, and their carcasses were quickly dragged away by farm workers.

With the bulk of the dairy herd gone, a valuable source of revenue was also lost. There was in fact a nationwide shortage of dairy products, for dairy herds across the Highlands (the heart of Equatoria's dairy region) were being much reduced in size and numbers.

At the big house, the garden was marked by riotous, near unrestrained growth. Only the splendid flame trees and the Cedar of Lebanon, the hydrangeas banked below the veranda, and the bougainvillea growing up the front and sides of the veranda, still showed themselves to advantage. The flower beds were a mass of weeds tall and short, and the lawns were very rarely mown. The last of the gardeners had disappeared – either scared off by the *Wa Chui*, or gone willingly to join them. Michael and Karim (when either had the time, for increasingly, Karim too had begun to assume occasional duties on the estate, although this meant that the dusting, cleaning and polishing in the house were sadly neglected) ran mowers over the lawns, but neither of them could spare the time to weed the flower beds, which, despite Lady Fiona Pencaitland's rather feeble efforts to tackle the weeds, were reverting to jungle.

The house itself was showing signs of neglect: the gutters needed cleaning and repairing, but more seriously, the roofs over both the north and the south wings had developed leaks, and several of the bedrooms in these wings had had to be closed up, their ceilings beginning to sag from the damp. (When, in an effort to involve him, Marjory made Patrick aware of this problem, he responded, 'What does it matter? No one comes to stay anymore.') Lack of money to hire the workmen and buy the materials needed to repair the roofs, and lack of workmen themselves had the money been there, meant that these problems simply grew more serious.

The problems being experienced by *Mahali pa Kupumzika* were being faced by numerous farms and estates in the Equatorian Highlands, with dire consequences for the economy. The new republic, as the first anniversary of its declaration of independence drew near, was facing an uncertain and increasingly difficult future. But Michael stayed on, the sense of loyalty he had begun to feel towards the embattled ex-colony hardening, even as his concerns for Marjory became more intensely felt.

As for Patrick, he was no longer capable of helping Michael, Marjory – and increasingly, Karim – to keep things going (other than to sign the cheques which Marjory presented to him once a month for settlement of various accounts). Michael was shocked at how rapidly Patrick's condition had deteriorated. Michael guessed that when Patrick closed himself in his study, he spent his time there drinking. He also took most of his meals in there, which Karim would bring to him. Sometimes Michael wondered what had brought this about; what had prompted Patrick's desire to escape reality (for that, surely, was why he was drinking so much; to escape a reality he could no longer face?), and he intuited that some sort of despair was probably behind it. He tried not to entertain the thought that it was fear that drove Patrick to such heavy drinking, but when such a notion did enter his head, he would consider only that Patrick was afraid for the future in general, rather than that Patrick might be physically afraid for himself. He would not believe that his school friend was a coward. And yet, Patrick's drinking had certainly become so much worse after André Myburgh's murder . . .

Chapter Seventeen

Sometimes Patrick would emerge from the study and practice with a pistol or rifle, shooting at the target he had set up in the front garden. Once in a while he would join the company for dinner. He would usually arrive as the others were about to sit down, or indeed, soon after they had already sat down. Invariably on such occasions, he would be wearing a dinner jacket (which was now a little too tight for his increasing bulk), as if seeking to declare an adherence to standards of propriety which he had in reality abandoned.

How quickly, Michael thought, a family group grows accustomed to altered internal dynamics – and speedily normalises them, so that they no longer require any comment or discussion.

'Good evening, Mother, Good evening, Aunt Catherine,' Patrick would greet the two older women, on those rare occasions he joined the family for dinner, his words only slightly slurred. He would kiss Marjory on the cheek, and greet Michael, 'Old chap! How are you keeping?' he would ask him. 'I hardly see you anymore. Where have you been?'

Michael did not reply, 'Busy running the estate with Marjory, and for the rest, I'm at home.' Instead, he would smile, and say, 'Oh, around and about, you know, Patrick.' The truth was, when he did see Patrick, he now found his old school friend saddening. His florid features, puffed up by drink, saddened Michael; his increasing girth (he must be eating, thought Michael) saddened him; his growing tendency to boom when he spoke, both saddened and irritated Michael.

But what truly angered Michael was that Marjory was married to him, and Patrick was, he believed, utterly unworthy of her.

Sometimes Patrick would retain his somewhat manic good humour right through the course of the dinner, and join Michael and the ladies in the drawing room afterwards for a cigar and several whiskeys (as if Patrick, who had had his wine glass topped up frequently by Karim throughout the meal, and had been drinking steadily since at least the mid morning, needed another drink!). Equally however, his good mood might evaporate during the course of the dinner, and he would begin to glower around him, and snap at Karim, and then, suddenly, he would burst out angrily, something like, 'Macmillan enrages me! That smug, self righteous representative of perfidious Albion! Do you know, Ian Blackfell [the Equatorian Prime Minister] tells me that Macmillan is threatening to use the Royal Navy to blockade us now? The ba–!' and he would cut himself short, looking wildly around, having suddenly become aware in his alcoholic anger that his mother, his aunt and his wife were present, and so he declined to use the unpleasant word he had been about to express. (Patrick had been born and raised a gentleman, and even drunk, he remained so).

So, Michael thought; he is still in touch with some of the people he knew in the government. I suppose that's for the good. (Patrick was no longer a member of LegCo). Had Michael thought about it, he might have wondered at the complete lack of enmity shown him by Patrick. Patrick must have known that Michael was spending a great deal of his time alone in Marjory's company, but he did not appear to resent his old friend doing so. Patrick continued to regard Michael as a trusted friend, no matter that Michael in his turn was increasingly irritated by Patrick. Michael, his objectivity undermined by his growing irritation and resentment of Patrick, failed to give his old school friend credit for his generous spirit.

In October, as the short rains set in, Michael received a letter from Richard Carter, his solicitor in England, who informed him that his mother's will had been probated, and asking him what he wanted done with the capital, and with the investments that his mother had left him. Michael wrote back, asking the lawyer to look into reinvesting the capital if he could safely obtain a better return on it, and to arrange that the income from his investments would be paid into his bank account in England. Already (thanks to his father) well provided for, Michael was now very well off. He could do almost anything he desired; he could go live on a Greek island if that was what he wished, and write splendid, critically acclaimed novels – all without giving up his family home in the Cotswolds, nor his flat in London. But for Michael, there was never any doubt what he wished to do; spoiled for choice, he chose to remain in Equatoria, working the *Mahali pa Kupumzika* estate with Marjory, the mere sight of whom brought him happiness (although it was a happiness shot through with the pain of frustrated yearning, for Marjory was another man's – and that man was Michael's best friend from school days, and had powerful claims upon his loyalty). When out riding with Marjory, her sustained company over several hours filled Michael with a desperate joy.

Michael had begun thinking of *Mahali pa Kupumzika* as "home." 'Right, let's head for home,' he would say, as they finished stocking up on supplies after a fortnightly trip to Jiljil. Michael felt a powerful emotional commitment to *Mahali pa Kupumzika* and to Equatoria, and there was now nowhere else he wished rather to be. Michael had found the purpose in his life whose absence he had been aware of at the time of his first visit to Equatoria. He would have liked to invest some of his wealth in the estate, putting the house to rights, and updating and improving the farm machinery, but when he wrote to Richard Carter, asking him to comment on the feasibility of doing so, the lawyer had told him that the British government had placed an embargo on the investment of funds from Britain in Equatoria. Even transferring funds from Britain to his Johannesburg bank account would be of only limited value, for the South African government severely restricted the amount of currency that could exit the Republic.

The estate would have to survive largely on its own merits, with only minimal financial help from Michael.

Chapter Eighteen

In December, Patrick had to attend another two week Equatorian Army Reserve training camp at Naburu. This was the second such camp that year. Michael did not believe that Patrick was up to it this time. He persuaded Marjory to agree that Patrick needed to obtain a medical exemption from Doctor Anstruther in Jiljil. 'Patrick is ill, Marjory,' Michael said. 'I don't see him managing to last out two weeks' military training.'

Michael and Marjory took Patrick to Doctor Anstruther's surgery during their next fortnightly trip to Jiljil. The doctor quickly realised that Patrick (who smelled of liquor, and who was sweating and trembling with desire for another drink) could not possibly attend a Reservist camp, and he furnished him with a medical certificate exempting him from the two weeks' training. Afterwards, Michael and Marjory spoke to the doctor. 'Lady Pencaitland and I would like to send her husband to a clinic in England, for drying out,' Michael told the doctor. 'I wonder if you would be able to recommend some suitable institutions, Doctor?'

'Lord Pencaitland needs more than mere drying out, Mr. Hood. He needs complete rehabilitation, a stay of at least three months. It would be very costly.'

'I'm able to afford whatever it takes, Doctor.'

'Very well.' The doctor looked at Marjory. 'I will see what I can find out, and I will write to you, Lady Pencaitland.'

Later, at the Standard Vacuum sub depot at Jiljil, only half their allocations for diesel fuel, petrol, paraffin and lubricating oil could be filled. Marjory, with Michael at her side, waved the allocation authorisation in front of the depot supervisor. 'This is ridiculous!' she exclaimed. 'How can I run the farm without fuel?'

'Lady Pencaitland, we've been turning away people all morning. Our tanks are almost empty. It's because of the Pencaitland name that I'm prepared to fill even half your order. The same goes for you, Mr. Hepburn,' the man said, looking at Keith Hepburn, who had accompanied them. 'If I were you, Lady Pencaitland, I would take it up with the Government.'

Perhaps for the first time, the full import of the international oil embargo hit home for Michael and Marjory. Never before had the sub depot failed at least to fill their official fuel allocations. By the time Michael and Marjory got home, it was already sunset, but the next morning, Patrick, with Marjory standing behind him, radio telephoned the Prime Minister's offices in Namuri.

'Good morning, Patrick. How are you? Over,' Ian Blackfell asked, when they were connected to him.

'Well, thank you, Ian, and yourself? Over.' It was only mid morning, and Patrick's words were not yet noticeably slurred.

'Busy. It's important that we put on a good show to celebrate our first anniversary of independence. I hope you are going to be here. Over.'

'Yes, I hope so. Look, Ian, we're having a problem with fuel supply. I wondered whether it might just be local. Yesterday the Jiljil Standard Vacuum sub depot would fill only half our allocation for fuel. I cannot run the farm without fuel, as you must appreciate. Oh – over.'

'It's the same for all of us right now, old boy,' the Prime

Minister responded. 'My farm manager is going short also. There just aren't enough tankers docking at Port Hardinge. I would like to help you, but in all fairness to others going short – or in many cases, without – I cannot make a special case for you. Over.'

'I understand, Ian. Say hullo to Joan for me. Over.'

'I shall, and my salaams to Marjory. Cheerio. Over and out.'

'You did your best, Pat,' Marjory told her husband. 'Thanks for trying.'

Patrick looked morose. 'Time was when the Pencaitland name counted for something in Equatoria,' he remarked. 'We don't seem to matter anymore.'

Later, Marjory asked Michael, 'How are we going to manage?'

'We'll find a way,' Michael replied. 'Should we have tried offering that chap at the depot a bribe?'

'Oh no,' Marjory answered him. 'That might work in England, or even in Namuri, but it wouldn't go down well here. He's already doing us a favour.'

'Well then, I think you should radio telephone the depot every day, and the next time they receive a delivery, we must drop everything and rush into town.' He smiled ruefully. 'Assuming we have sufficient fuel left to get there.'

Deirdre and Eleanor came home over Christmas, and Michael wondered at their reputation for wildness. They seemed to him to be perfectly well behaved young ladies. He got on particularly well with Eleanor, who was now sixteen years old. He smiled inwardly at her occasional flirting forays with him, her practice runs, as he thought of them, for more serious flirtations in years to come. She discerned that she was safe with Michael. His manner was old fashioned and courteous towards her, and he spoke to her as he would to an adult. The girls returned for three weeks in July the following year. They were both fit, sporting young women, and they would often join Michael and Marjory on their rides out on the estate.

'Surely there's a girl pining for you in England, Michael?'

Eleanor asked him during one of these rides, peering at him from beneath her lashes.

'No, there's no one in England yearning for my return,' Michael responded.

'I think you should find yourself an Equatorian girl, then. You're becoming an Equatorian yourself, aren't you Michael?'

Michael laughed. 'Perhaps I am. My ties to England seem to be growing rather loose. But no one comes visiting at *Mahali pa Kupumzika* anymore. How am I to meet this Equatorian girl?'

'Perhaps I should ask some of my older friends to stay,' Eleanor replied, smiling.

There were some outhouses alongside the stables that Michael had never looked into. One of these was an old coach house and barn. Michael decided to look inside these outbuildings. He was pleased to discover two wheeled iron horse drawn ploughs – somewhat rusted, but with undamaged ploughshares – in one of the outhouses. What brought him real delight was his find in the coach house of a pair of Cape carts (two wheeled, horse drawn carriages with folding canvas hoods), which must have dated from the early years of the century. There remained evidence that their woodwork had once been glossy with paint, but the paint was peeling now, although sufficient remained to have protected the woodwork from the white ants. The leather upholstered seats had been colonised by mice, but there still remained a man on the estate with leather-working skills, and Michael thought it should not be beyond him to make new seats for them. They would need new harnesses also. The folding canvas hoods were almost completely rotted away, but Michael thought that if he could beguile Weeping Moses, the Jiljil tailor, out to *Mahali pa Kupumzika* one day, he could make measurements for new hoods. Perhaps most usefully, Michael found a big farm wagon, of creosote soaked timbers so massive and sturdy that they had resisted the onslaught of time, and the wagon could almost have been put to use that day. It would, he guessed, originally have been hauled by a team of oxen.

Later, Michael showed Marjory his finds, almost boyish in his enthusiasm. 'We need to obtain heavy horses – like shire horses – for the wagon, if they can be had in Equatoria,' he said. He knew something about horses; he knew nothing about oxen. At the back of Michael's mind was the idea that they ought to prepare for a day when the fuel situation might become truly critical.

'I think my father might know where we can get some heavy horses,' Marjory said.

'Could you talk to him, Marjory?'

'OK. I'll do that.'

'How about I get two of the farm boys to clean up the Cape carts? They can scrape off the paint, and then sand and repaint the woodwork and metal parts. The *Fundi* [the native mechanic and handyman on the estate] and I will remove the wheels and grease the hubs and refit them. He can make new seats as well. I'll get Weeping Moses over some time to measure up for new canvas hoods. It's clear the woodwork of the wagon was treated with creosote as a preservative. That's why the white ants have left it alone. We'll give it another few coats.'

Marjory smiled, amused by Michael's enthusiasm. This was a good time of year to put some of the farm workers on the tasks; the harvest had been brought in, and the next year's planting season had yet to arrive, and the tail end of the short rains kept people from working outside.

'Yes, we can do that,' agreed Marjory. 'We'll see what we can pick up at Pierre Matteau's in Jiljil.' Pierre Matteau was the Mauritian Créole proprietor of the hardware store in Jiljil. 'You are serious about this, aren't you, Michael? You really believe there might come a day when we need these?'

'I hadn't really thought it through,' Michael replied, 'but yes, I think these might come in useful one day.' Michael grinned. 'Anyway, it'll be fun getting these on the road again!'

Chapter Eighteen

Marjory laughed, a light, unaffected laugh of pleasure. She touched Michael briefly on the arm. 'Boys never really grow up, do they, Michael?'

Thus far, *Mahali pa Kupumzika* had suffered just the one attack by the *Wa Chui*, and that had not been aimed at the big house, although the loss of André Myburgh made it a particularly tragic attack. The Equatoria Regiment special units which patrolled the Nyahurari Forest made it difficult for *Wa Chui* bands lurking in the western foothills of the Cairngorms Range to ravage the European farmlands of the Central Highlands, but as Michael knew, they managed to break out occasionally. There had been the ambush he and Patrick had been caught up in on the road between Jiljil and the estate, and the night attack in which André Myburgh had died, and there were other attacks across the Central Highlands, with European fatalities. As if to mark Equatoria's first anniversary of independence, such attacks now increased in numbers, and Michael wondered when it would be *Mahali pa Kupumzika's* turn again. But for the most part, the Equatoria Regiment "Simbas" – as they called themselves – had so far been able to force the *Wa Chui* groups that did break out to move fast, and if any of them had access to weapons heavier than automatic assault rifles, they chose not to slow themselves down with them. The exceptions to this were the *Wa Chui* groups carrying landmines with which to seed not only the main Namuri – Port Caroline road, but also minor roads in the Central Highlands.

Although it was the forest with the greatest extent, the Nyahurari Forest was not the only forested wilderness region in the Central Highlands. There were other forest regions, other wild hilly districts, and the Army lacked the manpower to maintain regular patrols in all of them. These forests and wild hilly regions served the *Wa Chui* as sanctuaries across the Central Highlands, which explained how farmsteads, railways and roads could be attacked far from the major sanctuary of the Nyahurari Forest itself. There was no "frontline" in this war, although the heavily forested western fringes of the Cairngorms Range constituted a region of stepped up Army activity. The long shoreline of Lake Louise, that vast inland sea via which the *Wa Chui* were able to supply themselves to the north-west of the Central Highlands, also required regular patrols.

No matter how determined the special units in the forested foothills of the Cairngorms, nor the patrols along the shores of Lake Louise, the numbers of *Wa Chui* groups continued to multiply, and it became more and more difficult for the Army patrols to prevent small guerrilla groups breaking through their cordons and striking at targets in the Central Highlands.

On the night of New Year's Eve, in the early hours of 1963, twin attacks against *Mahali pa Kupumzika* were carried out by one or more *Wa Chui* groups. What made these attacks so shocking was not only their symbolism – that 1963 was opened with a major attack by the insurgents – but that they marked a stepping up of the violence and destructiveness of the *Wa Chui* campaign in the Central Highlands, for they were carried out with mortars, supplied either across Lake Louise, or through the wild and arid Northern Frontier District. Michael, Patrick, Marjory and the two Hepburn girls had only been upstairs for about half an hour when the attacks commenced, for they had stayed up for midnight, wishing to see in the New Year.

Michael and Patrick both wore dinner jackets and black ties that evening. Their revolvers were of course close to hand. The ladies wore jewellery with their silk evening gowns, and the now seventeen years old Eleanor Hepburn, the older of Patrick's two nieces (home from school with her sister for the holidays), wore a silk cocktail dress. Her sister, younger by a year, wore a cocktail dress of lawn. Both girls wore pearl necklaces that had belonged to their mother.

Marjory's evening gown was of sky blue silk, which suited her fair hair and warm tan, and she wore a necklace of diamonds and sapphires – a Hepburn family heirloom. The Dowager Lady Pencaitland's evening gown was of shimmering grey silk, set off by another Hepburn family heirloom: a necklace of huge, lustrous pearls from which descended a pendant of diamonds and emeralds. Lady Catherine wore an evening gown of black silk, with a necklace of jet. None of the women had been to a hairdresser since the drive into Jiljil had become dangerous; they all three wore their long hair pinned up. Michael, a traditionalist, thought this suited them; in particular, he thought, it suited Marjory, emphasising her natural elegance and grace. How marked, Michael thought, was the contrast in Marjory with her general appearance during a working day, when she wore slacks of tough twill run up for her by Suffering Moses, the Indian tailor in Jiljil, and chukka boots, or sometimes, jodhpurs and riding boots. In the evenings she usually wore smart slacks with silk blouses.

That New Year's Eve, Marjory's mother-in-law (as always) had her Alsatian dog with her. The two Rhodesian ridgebacks were outside on the veranda. After dinner, with coffee served by Karim in the drawing room (excellent coffee was one shortage that Equatoria would not have to experience), the two men danced to some big band music from the gramophone player with both the Ladies Pencaitland, and with the two schoolgirls. Old Lady Catherine, seated, looked on benignly, a small glass of liqueur on the table alongside her. How graceful Marjory and the two girls were, Michael thought. How delightful it was to be dancing with such lovely young women.

At about a quarter past one that morning the 1st January 1963, the big house was quiet. Michael, Patrick, Marjory and the girls had gone upstairs to bed about half an hour earlier, having welcomed the New Year with Champagne. Patrick had been in one of his manic phases, which Michael preferred to one of his morose, silent moods, for in those he was quite likely to break out suddenly in a rush of bitter, angry words. He was of course drunk (there was never a time he was not drunk anymore), but during his manic periods he hardly displayed his inebriation (excepting only via his extraordinary high spirits and loquacity), and his speech was only a little slurred. With the strokes of midnight from the Regency longcase clock which stood against the wall, the chimes striking tunefully, Patrick had seized Marjory and kissed her on the mouth, and made her waltz a few steps with him. 'Pum-pum-pum, pum-pum!' he sang loudly. 'Darling girl! Nineteen sixty-three will be a better year for all of us!' Releasing Marjory, Patrick had grabbed hold of Michael's hand and pumped it up and down, declaring, 'Old man, you're a good egg. Couldn't manage without you.' Then Patrick turned to Karim, who was standing a little distance away, his back against the wall, and said, 'Karim – *heri ya Mwaka Mpya!*' [Karim – happy New Year!] Karim had relaxed his normally rather austere expression and almost smiled, perhaps a little embarrassed.

    Michael kissed both the young Hepburn girls chastely on the cheek, wishing them a happy New Year, then he embraced Marjory around the waist (Michael was only a little drunk) and kissed her too on the cheek, and Marjory, briefly returning his embrace, kissed his cheek in return, before withdrawing from his clasp. Michael let her go, yearning to give her a long, passionate kiss on the mouth. Proximity to Marjory was a torment of frustrated desire for Michael; prolonged absence from her was a torment of longing for her presence. Marjory was aware of Michael's yearning for her; she was not blind to the situation between them. By now, Patrick having proven himself so inadequate, such a weak and useless man, she had begun wishing that it were possible for she and Michael to be together, but it was not possible. Just occasionally she fantasized about commencing an affair with Michael, who was a real man, strong and sober, responsible and honourable, but those very qualities – above all that he was an honourable man – meant that such thoughts would remain no more than a fantasy, for although Marjory thought she could probably initiate such an affair, she was afraid that she would not forgive herself afterwards for compromising Michael's own decency and sense of honour. Failing which, Marjory believed it would have been best had they parted, made a clean break of it, but the estate needed Michael, for she and Michael were doing all the work that would have been done in the past by both Patrick and André. Marjory did not think she could have undertaken this work alone, not in these troubled and dangerous times.

Karim had been in attendance on the *Bwanas* and *Memsaabs* all evening, but he had stayed downstairs after the Europeans had left, tidying up in the big room. He had then closed the steel shutters across the French windows to the veranda, and went around the other downstairs rooms, checking that the shutters to their windows were also closed. He also checked that the front, back and side doors were secured by their heavy metal grills. All this took him some time, and he had not quite begun his ascent of the servants' staircase at the rear of the north wing before the *Wa Chui* attack commenced. Lady Catherine Hepburn, who had left the party at ten o' clock, unable to stay awake any longer, was long asleep, and the Dowager Lady Pencaitland, who had left the group in the drawing room at about eleven o' clock, was also asleep.

Chapter Nineteen

When the first explosion was heard, Michael was still dressed, although he had removed his evening jacket, black bow tie, cummerbund and gunbelt (the latter worn beneath the cummerbund), and undone the top two buttons of his dress shirt. Patrick had managed to remove his evening jacket, tie, cummerbund and gunbelt, dropping them where he stood, before collapsing, comatose, on the bed, stupefied by a day's drinking, and suddenly bereft of the manic energy that had carried him this far. Marjory was in the bathroom, having removed her beautiful silk gown and changed into her nightgown. Back in the bedroom she bent and picked up the gunbelt, and eased the revolver beneath her husband's pillows. She then removed his shoes. The two elderly Hepburn ladies were asleep. Karim was about to make his way up the back staircase in the north wing, heading for his room on the first floor at the rear of the north wing.

For a split second, Michael found himself transported back in time to his War years. He leapt to his feet, and reached for his gunbelt and revolver which were draped over the back of a chair, and strapped them around his waist. About twenty seconds later, the first shattering explosion, which had rocked the house and set the window in his bedroom vibrating, was followed by a second explosion, although this one was not quite as close. 'Mortars,' Michael thought. 'And we've been hit.' Then Michael heard a third, but much more distant, explosion. The military post at the native compound, he deduced. He began running along the corridor towards Patrick's and Marjory's suite of rooms. He heard a further explosion from the direction of the military post, and then another explosion much closer to hand again, but he did not think the house had been hit.

With the first explosion, Karim was thrown off his feet at the foot of the back staircase, and landed hard on the ground. The air was thick with heavy dust, which made him cough. He had at first no idea what had happened. He had no wartime experience to draw upon, but as he began to pick himself up, he saw that the back staircase he had been about to climb had disappeared some four feet above him, as had the wall it had been built against, and – he could hardly believe his eyes – he could see the night sky above him! There was no roof left. He realised that this must signal an attack by those dogs the *Wa Chui*. Once on his feet again, he began running for the front of the house, making for the *Bwana Mkubwa's* study. He had the keys to all the locks in the house on a large key ring fastened to his sash. In the study he unlocked the glass fronted gun cabinet, taking two .30-06 sporting rifles from it, and from one of the drawers below the cabinet, he took a box of ammunition. He locked the gun cabinet again, then turned around and made for the main staircase, one rifle slung over his shoulder, the other in his hand.

In their bedroom, Marjory was shaking Patrick, who moaned and refused to open his eyes. 'Oh – you useless bloody man!' Marjory exclaimed. She had pulled on a dressing gown and had strapped on her gunbelt with the holstered revolver. Then there was a loud knocking at the door, and she heard Michael calling from the other side of the door. 'Come in Michael!' she cried.

Michael entered the room. 'It sounds like mortar rounds,' he said to Marjory. 'I'm certain the house has been hit.' He looked at Patrick, out for the count on the bed. 'Leave him,' he said. 'He wouldn't be much use anyway. And we must turn the lights off.' He went to the door and did so, and Marjory turned the bedside lamps off. Then they heard Karim calling through the open door, silhouetted against the light in the corridor.

'Come in Karim,' Marjory responded. 'Michael, I must go and fetch Aunt Catherine and Fiona.'

'Yes, that's right, Marjory. We should all be together,' Michael said. Marjory left to fetch the two old ladies. Michael took one of the rifles from Karim and worked the bolt. The magazine was empty.

'Karim, have you got some ammunition?' Michael was speaking English. He had by now picked up quite a lot of *Kiswahili*, but his command of the language was not up to the present crisis.

'*Ndiyo Bwana,*' Karim replied, and handed him the box of .30-06 ammunition. '*Bwana*, the house is falling down behind.'

'Yes, we were hit.'

Michael could see well enough by the light in the corridor as he loaded the rifle, one sharp nosed round at a time. He handed the loaded rifle to Karim.

Michael then loaded the second rifle, which he kept hold of for himself. 'Which wing was hit?' he asked Karim. 'The north or the south?'

'*Bwana?*' Karim responded, a puzzled note to his voice.

'Never mind. Karim, you stay in the corridor. Make sure the *Memsaabs* are safe. The *Wa Chui* may try to break into the house. Do you understand me?'

'*Ndiyo, Bwana,* I understand. I will do that.' And he began to set off along the corridor towards the head of the main staircase, the rifle in his hand. Michael went to the large bay window looking out across the front garden, just as another explosion shook the house. Michael did not think the main range of the house had been hit. He was almost certain that the north wing had now been hit a second time. 'They're overshooting, and their aim is off,' he thought. He peered through the open window, but he could barely make out the lawns and the trees beyond them, for the night was very dark. The *Wa Chui* had chosen a new moon in which to launch their attacks, and there was very little light. Michael could hear rapid bursts of automatic gunfire from the Equatoria Regiment post at the native compound. He hoped the troops would succeed in driving off their attackers soon and coming to the rescue of those in the house. A soon as Marjory returned with the two old ladies, he would go downstairs and try to radio for the Police in Jiljil. He heard a dog barking from the corridor, and Lady Catherine's plaintive voice, sounding very old indeed.

'What are you doing, Marjory?' asked Lady Catherine in a querulous tone. 'I do not understand at all.'

'It's alright Aunty. Just come along and you can sit with us in our bedroom,' Marjory answered her.

Marjory shepherded the two old ladies into the bedroom. Both the old women had their hair down. Lady Catherine's white hair reached far down her back. The Dowager Lady Pencaitland was accompanied by her Alsatian dog, which was barking. 'Oh hush, Gretel,' Lady Fiona Pencaitland admonished the dog. 'Hush now.' The dog calmed down once the two older women had sat down. Lady Catherine had begun crying, and her sobs sounded like the weeping of a small child. Along with Marjory and the two old ladies, were Patrick's nieces, not at all nervous or anxious, but rather, excited. The eldest, Eleanor, looked at her uncle lying comatose on the big bed, then she turned to Michael. 'Let me have a revolver please, Michael.'

'I haven't one to spare right now, Eleanor,' Michael responded. 'Oh! You can have Patrick's. He's not going to be using it.' Michael turned to Marjory. 'May Eleanor use Patrick's revolver?'

'Yes – it's beneath his pillow.'

Michael found Patrick's revolver under the pillows, checked that it was loaded, and handed it to Eleanor. Then he said, 'Marjory, I'm going to join Karim in the corridor. Please keep watch through the window.'

'Right-O.'

The sound of automatic and single shot gunfire from the direction of the military post increased in intensity for a minute or so – perhaps the group that had been attacking the house had joined their comrades attacking the military post at the native compound? – then there was silence. It was Marjory who, about ten or fifteen minutes later, during which there had been only a few single shots of gunfire, and no further explosions, heard a voice from outside in the darkness, a voice calling, 'Hullo the house! It's Lieutenant Anderson here!' (Lieutenant Anthony MacDonald had been reassigned, replaced by an equally young Lieutenant Christopher Anderson).

'Oh, Christopher! Are your men alright? Let me fetch Michael.'

On hearing Marjory's shout, Michael had left his post with Karim at the head of the main staircase, and he joined her at the bedroom window. He leant across the windowsill. 'Lieutenant! What's the situation?'

'It looks like we've driven them off, Sir,' the young man replied.

'Have you taken any casualties?'

'Two dead and three injured, Sir. Are you OK in the house?'

'No casualties here. Do you need any help with your wounded, Lieutenant?'

'If we can bring the three men inside the house, perhaps one of the ladies can help my men treat their wounds, Sir.'

'Just a minute,' Michael called. He went to the bedroom door and called down the corridor. 'Karim, unbar the front door, please.'

'*Ndiyo Bwana.*' Karim made his way down stairs.

Chapter Nineteen

Returning to the bedroom window, Michael called to the Lieutenant, 'Bring your wounded inside. I'm having the front door unbarred. Then please would you detail some men to take up position round the back of the house, where we took some mortar hits. The rest of you can take station on the veranda.'

'Very good, Sir.' The young Lieutenant snapped some orders to his sergeant, who took two men with him and set off around the corner for the rear of the house.

Michael said to Marjory, 'I'm going to see what the damage from those mortar hits looks like. Then I'll try to raise the Jiljil Police on the radio telephone. If you think the ladies will be alright, would you go take a look at the wounded men downstairs?'

'I think I'll ask Fiona and Lady Catherine to stay here for now.'

'Yes – until we're sure things have calmed down. I'll see you soon.' Michael left the women and headed for the staircase. Downstairs, the three wounded men were being brought inside. Although supported either side, they were managing to stand upright.

Michael turned to Karim. 'Karim, we could all do with some coffee, I think. Would you mind making us some – presuming the kitchen is still standing? Make some for the Lieutenant also.'

'*Ndiyo Bwana.*'

'I'm taking a look at the rear of the house, Lieutenant. Then I'll try to raise the Police at Jiljil. Karim will bring you some coffee.'

'Sir, during the attack we radioed all security units in the vicinity. Our call was picked up by the Police in Jiljil – they're sending three units – and by a *Simba* base camp in the Nyahurari Forest. They will send out a couple of patrols to try to prevent the *shiftas* from regaining the safety of the forest.'

'That's very good,' Michael responded. 'If you need anything, tell Karim when he returns with the coffee.'

Hearing his voice, the two Rhodesian ridgeback dogs, who

slept on the veranda at night, had slunk back from the shrubbery in the garden in which they had taken shelter, terrified by the explosions. They crept through the open door, and stayed close to Michael.

The Police arrived about an hour before dawn. Michael had not gone to bed. Instead, both he and Karim, armed with their rifles (and in Michael's case, with a revolver also), had dozed in armchairs in the drawing room. Once the sun had risen, the soldiers found six *Wa Chui* casualties: five dead, and one man badly injured, but conscious. The Police patched him up sufficiently to prevent him from dying (although they did not waste any morphine on him), and when they left in the late morning, they took him with them in the back of the Police lorry, along with the three wounded troopers in the ambulance that had accompanied them. If the wounded *Wa Chui* man lived, he would land up in one of the prison camps dotted around the Central Highlands, where he would be rigorously interrogated.

To the distress of Marjory and Lady Fiona Pencaitland, they discovered a casualty in the house soon after seven o' clock in the morning. Lady Catherine Hepburn had died at some point after Marjory (having first seen to the wounded men, whom the young lieutenant had done his best to treat from the first aid kit one of his men had been carrying) had eventually led her back to her bed. Doctor Anstruther, who had accompanied the Police, said it was a heart attack.

'Poor Aunty,' Marjory said. 'Poor old lady. She shouldn't have had to go through all this. It isn't fair.' Marjory looked stricken, on the edge of tears – as much a belated reaction to the night's events as to Lady Catherine's death. Both the Hepburn girls were weeping.

Patrick had awoken from his alcoholic coma by nine o' clock that morning, and after giving him a brief summary of the night's events, Michael told him about Lady Catherine's death. Patrick shed some tears, as much for his own shame and guilt as for his aunt. Michael showed him the damage to the house: the end of the north wing at the rear of the house had been demolished, having taken (Michael thought) two mortar hits, but the fallen stones and bricks and roof beams had piled up just beyond the staircase Karim had been about to ascend, blocking the corridor beyond. Michael now understood why, in the dark, the *Wa Chui* had not managed to gain access to the house via the damaged wing.

'We were damned lucky,' Michael said to Patrick. 'Imagine if the *Wa Chui* had broken into the house. Nothing like this has happened before. A mortar attack! This represents a step up in the *Wa Chui's* activities. We truly are living amidst a war zone.'

Patrick was so ashamed of himself, he could not meet Michael's eye. He hardly knew where to look. He had slept (if that was the word for his unconscious condition during the night) right through the attack and beyond. He made for his study as soon as Michael let him go, and found a bottle of Scotch there, and drank greedily from it. Afterwards, he felt a little better, and he went through to the dining room, where his mother and Marjory, along with his two nieces, were eating a late breakfast. No one offered him a greeting. The two girls looked embarrassed. Only Patrick's mother responded with a 'Good morning Patrick,' when, shamefacedly, he greeted the group.

Later that morning, Marjory said to Michael, 'I must telephone Dr. Anstruther and ask him whether he's come up with the names of some places we can send Patrick for treatment.'

'Yes. I think that's a good idea. If Patrick is ever to learn to live with himself again, he needs help now,' Michael responded.

Soon after the Police had left in the late morning (taking the body of Lady Catherine with them, as a favour to the Pencaitlands, who would otherwise have had to transport her body to the undertakers in Jiljil themselves, for the undertakers would not have made the trip to *Mahali pa Kupumzika* anymore), a reporter for the *Naburu Chronicle*, the weekly newspaper for the district, arrived to conduct an interview. (The Police it seemed had tipped off the newspaper). He found himself interviewing not Lord Pencaitland, as he had expected, but Lady Pencaitland, on the veranda.

'My husband is somewhere on the estate,' Marjory lied to the reporter. Patrick was in fact closeted in his study. The reporter had a photographer with him, who took some photographs of Lady Pencaitland, the two Rhodesian ridgebacks at her side, standing in front of the damaged wing, wearing her rather mannish cavalry twill trousers, with a revolver on her hip.

PART THREE

Chapter Twenty

The Dowager Lady Pencaitland spent the afternoon working in the garden, the two Rhodesian ridgebacks and her Alsatian dog close by her. She sought, through the determined exercise of normality, to put aside the horrors of the previous night, but she found it difficult to concentrate on her task, and she kept breaking off from what she was doing, to stare unseeing at her surroundings. The short rains had ended not long before Christmas, and the garden (neglected now but for occasional ineffectual weeding forays by Lady Pencaitland, and those rare occasions when Michael or Karim could find the time to mow the lawns) was fast reverting to jungle. Fiona Pencaitland would miss Lady Catherine more than anyone else in the family would. So she sought escape from the previous night's traumas and the loss of her sister in law, through gardening, which had so often in the past afforded her pleasure and peace of mind.

Michael and Marjory had a pair of horses saddled for them (there was still one *syce* left at the stables), and spent much of the afternoon out on the estate. Now more than ever, the estate workers (those that were left) needed to know that one of the *Bwanas* and the *Memsaab* were keeping an eye on things. Both of them were back at the house by tea time.

'I shall contact Patrick's lawyer in Namuri,' Marjory told

Michael, as they sipped at their tea on the veranda. Michael was enjoying a fresh scone, with raspberry jam topped by estate cream, which *Mpishi Moja* had provided for them. 'There might have been insurance on the house, though I doubt it, and anyway, if there was, perhaps it would not apply in the case of war and insurrection.'

'Yes, it's a long shot, I agree.'

Patrick's absence at dinner that night went unremarked. He had not shown his face since he had been seen at breakfast. At about a quarter to eight that evening, as Marjory, Michael, Lady Pencaitland, and Patrick's nieces, were seated at the dining table, all five heard a gunshot from the vicinity of the library or the study.

'Oh my God,' Marjory exclaimed, standing up hurriedly. 'What has he done now?'

'No, wait here, Marjory,' Michael said to her. 'Let me go see.' Michael was overtaken by an intense foreboding of horror. Lady Fiona Pencaitland had dropped her knife and fork with a clatter on her plate, and Marjory went to her and said, 'It will be alright, Fiona,' and put a hand on her mother in law's shoulder. But Marjory knew that it would not be alright. Something terrible had happened. Michael closed the dining room door behind him, so that the two ridgeback dogs should not follow him, and he looked into the library as he passed the open door; there was no one inside the room. The door to the study was closed, but Michael could smell the acrid powder scent from beneath the door, and as he opened the door, the scent of the revolver's discharge was heavy in the air. So too was the slaughter house smell of blood and faeces. Michael, battle inured though he was from his wartime experiences, felt his gorge rise as he saw Patrick's body. Michael had seen more dead men during the War than he ever wished to see again. Patrick had fallen back in his big leather chair, his head flung back, and most of the back and top of his head was missing. The revolver lay on the carpeted floor to his right.

'Oh Patrick, you silly fool,' Michael said softly.

From the doorway came a short, piercing scream. Michael swung around. Marjory was standing there, a hand raised to her mouth, her eyes wide. Michael took three rapid paces across the floor and gathered Marjory in his arms and turned her around. 'Come with me, Marjory,' he said. 'Lady Pencaitland will need you. Do you understand?'

A convulsive tremble shook Marjory's body. 'Yes, of course,' she responded. 'I'm alright, Michael. He's shot himself in the head, hasn't he?'

'Yes, in the mouth.'

'Oh God, will this dreadful day never end?' Marjory asked.

'I think you should take Lady Pencaitland upstairs,' Michael told her. 'I will radio telephone for the Police once again.'

Karim, who had been serving at dinner, appeared in the corridor, his features anxious. 'Karim,' Michael said to him, 'the *Bwana Mkubwa* has shot himself. Do not go in there. We must not touch anything until the Police have been.'

Michael had never seen an African turn pale, but Karim's face turned grey.

'The *Bwana Mkubwa* is dead?'

'Yes, Karim, he is dead. Now come with us back to the dining room.'

His arm around Marjory's shoulders, Michael led the way back to the dining room. When Lady Fiona Pencaitland saw them she raised both her hands to her mouth. Her face had turned white. 'My son, what has happened to him?' she asked.

Marjory pulled up a chair alongside Lady Pencaitland, sat down, and put her arm around the elderly lady. 'Fiona,' Marjory said, 'I'm afraid Patrick is dead.'

Lady Pencaitland's eyes widened with shock. Freeing herself

from Marjory's grasp, she stood up, then swayed, and Marjory, who had also stood, grabbed hold of her. 'I want to see my son!' Lady Pencaitland cried.

'No, Fiona, not yet. That would not be a good idea.' Marjory called to Karim. '*Niletee brandy mbili*, Karim!'

Karim, whose face was still rather grey, so far forgot himself as to present the two *memsaabs* the glasses of brandy he had poured without bringing them on a tray. He placed the brandy glasses on the table in front of the two *mems*. Deirdre and Eleanor, their pretty features set in horrified looks, stared from their side of the table.

'Marjory – I must go raise the Police. I will ask them to bring a doctor for Lady Pencaitland. Please take her upstairs. Will you excuse me, my dear.'

Michael headed back to the study, that slaughterhouse, for that was where the radio telephone was located. Marjory gulped her brandy down and made her mother-in-law drink hers, then she took Lady Pencaitland into the hallway and, an arm around the older woman, headed for the staircase. The Alsatian dog, visibly anxious and troubled, its tail almost between its legs, followed close on its mistress' heels, nuzzling her legs and whining as they climbed the stairs.

It was eleven o' clock before the Police arrived, their second visit to *Mahali pa Kupumzika* that day. With them once again was Doctor Anstruther, who gave Lady Pencaitland a sedative so that she would sleep. He left a small bottle of Valium tablets with Marjory, a tablet to be taken by Lady Pencaitland as necessary. It took the Police little time to satisfy themselves that Patrick's death was indeed a suicide. When they left, they took the body with them. Afterwards, Michael, Marjory (who had left Lady Pencaitland sleeping upstrairs), and the two Hepburn girls, sat in the drawing room and drank respectively a whiskey, a brandy, and coffees laced with a dash of brandy.

Chapter Twenty

'What does one say?' Marjory asked suddenly. 'What does one do now?'

'I don't know,' Michael responded. 'We carry on.'

The next day Marjory stayed at home to keep Lady Pencaitland company, and Michael rode out alone on horseback to let himself be seen by the estate workers. For some time, because of the fuel shortage, he and Marjory had set out on horseback every morning, rather than – as they had in the past – using the Land Rover some mornings. Marjory would be notifying the family's lawyer in Namuri of Patrick's death, calling him on the radio telephone. As Michael made his rounds on horseback, he found himself experiencing guilt. His guilt was twofold: one, that he ought to be grieving more for Patrick than he was; two, that he ought to have done more for Patrick. But Patrick, through his relentless drinking and his abdication of his responsibilities to the estate, had long ago estranged Michael's affections, and Michael had felt that he had already lost the friend he had known and valued, long before Patrick had finally shot himself. But perhaps he had been tardy in recognising that Patrick needed help, yet he had at last come to this recognition, and he had begun making enquiries about sending Patrick to a clinic in England. But, oh God, Michael thought to himself; what a terrible waste of the friend he had been so fond of at school, the friend who had welcomed him into his home as if he were a member of the family! Michael let go of the reins and dug in his pocket for his handkerchief and blew his nose.

Just under a week later, joint funerals were held for Patrick, the last Earl of Pencaitland in the direct line (for Marjory's father, Keith Hepburn, a cousin of old Lord Pencaitland, was now the Earl of Pencaitland), and Lady Catherine, his aunt, at Saint John's Church of England church in Jiljil. Despite the difficulties with travel, Patrick's funeral in particular (which was held first) was well attended. The Equatorian Prime Minister, Ian Blackfell, was present, as were the South African, Nicaraguan, Panamanian and Taiwanese Ambassadors. An Equatoria Regiment company stood guard in the churchyard. Many of the mourners present were there not so much to honour the memory of Patrick himself, but that of the Pencaitland name, for old Lord Pencaitland had been the most prominent of Equatoria's founding fathers. This was certainly why the foreign ambassadors were present at the joint funerals. In recollection of Patrick's wartime service, an honour guard of Equatoria Regiment troopers in dress uniform formed up and fired a rifle volley into the air, and a bugler sounded the Last Post as the coffin was lowered into the freshly dug red soil. The Dowager Lady Pencaitland broke down at this point, and the widowed Lady Pencaitland, Marjory, had to lead her away, sobbing quietly herself. Next followed Lady Catherine's funeral. Many of the funeral goers from further afield disappeared at this juncture, keen to make a start for home before the night should catch them still on their journeys, but the surviving Hepburns (including the present Lord Pencaitland, Keith Hepburn, and his wife and son) were still there when Lady Catherine's remains were lowered into the ground alongside those of old Lord Pencaitland, her brother, and those of her nephew, Patrick Pencaitland. Afterwards a buffet lunch was held in a private room at the Jiljil Hotel. Three or four of the mourners returned to *Mahali pa Kupumzika* with the family after the lunch, unwilling to commence their journeys home so late in the day. Despite the damage done to several of the first floor bedrooms by the damp, and the ruins which terminated the north wing, enough viable bedrooms were found to accommodate the guests overnight. Karim was very busy indeed.

 Over a guineafowl dinner (the birds provided by Marjory's younger brother Andrew, who had shot them a day or two earlier, then hung them), a dinner at which nine or ten people sat down, and at which Karim had excelled himself, laying the big table with the Spode chinaware and the best silver, which gleamed and shone in the light from the two big candelabras, the reminiscences were more often of Patrick's father than of Patrick himself. As for Lady Catherine Hepburn, few people of her generation – the first generation of settlers in Equatoria – were still alive. After breakfast in the early morning the guests were gone, and the family had no one to distract them from their grief and anxieties, until the two young Equatoria Regiment officers boarding with them awoke later in the day, and came downstairs.

Alone in his bedroom that night, Michael thought, 'It looks as if I am going to be living in Equatoria for the indefinite future.' More than ever before, he felt he could not now leave Marjory alone to shoulder the burden of running the estate. And then, to his shame, the thought crossed his mind again (It had crossed his mind several times already since Patrick's death): 'Is my way clear now to pay my suit to Marjory?' He tried hard to push such an unworthy thought away from him.

As the months progressed, fuel, and other essential items, such as machinery spares, continued in short supply. Michael had only moderate mechanical aptitude, and he would have struggled to maintain the vehicles, and aged and worn farm machinery, had he had no one to turn to for help. Fortunately the estate *Fundi*, a late middle aged Sikuyu tribesman, was gifted in this direction, but his task was at times made extremely difficult by the absence of some or other essential spare part.

Equatoria's northern province – an arid, near desert region only thinly populated – witnessed the passage of arms from the lawless regions north of the border, destined for the *Wa Chui* in the Central Highlands. For every consignment of weapons seized on this route by Equatorian Army patrols, two more consignments got through. Across the Central Highlands especially there were almost daily attacks by the *Wa Chui*: attacks on isolated farmsteads or their native compounds, ambushes on country roads, and, despite the military patrols, the laying of mines at night on the major roads. In March 1963 the mainline passenger train from Namuri to Port Caroline was crossing a steel girder bridge over a river far below when the bridge was blown, and not only were there nine fatalities and almost two dozen injuries as a result of the collapse of the bridge itself, but the *Wa Chui* shot and killed eight of the surviving passengers as the Army detachments before and behind the train struggled to form up and come to their defence.

At *Mahali pa Kupumzika*, even had the craftsmen been located to rebuild the ruined north wing (and Michael supposed that they could in time have been found – in Naburu or Namuri or Port Harding – and brought to the estate), the estate could not have raised the money for the project. Michael felt an enormous frustration at being unable to use any significant part of his British-based wealth to help *Mahali pa Kupumzika*. He had however transferred the maximum annual allowances permitted him by the South African government, from his Johannesburg bank account to the account he had opened in Jiljil; this he had done both during the previous year, following his visit to South Africa, and again for the year 1963. Thus he had a far from negligible balance in his Jiljil account, which he could use if he wished for the estate.

Nor were the leaks in the roofs of the north and the south wings repaired. Michael and Marjory were staring up at the roof one morning towards the end of the long rains in May, for the ceiling had collapsed in one more of the north wing bedrooms.

'The house is going to ruin!' Marjory exclaimed, and Michael saw that she was close to tears, worn down by the magnitude of the task of keeping both the house itself, and the estate in general, from collapse. He took her hand tentatively, saying, 'We'll manage somehow, Marjory,' but she responded in angry tones, 'Oh for God's sake, Michael, must you always be so bloody positive!'

Chapter Twenty

Michael let go Marjory's hand and stepped back a pace, hurt and confused by her response.

'I'm sorry, Michael,' Marjory said. 'I didn't mean . . . it's just that it all seems too damn much.'

'I understand, Marjory,' Michael replied. 'I'll help you the best I can.'

Marjory smiled at him and patted him on the arm. 'Yes, I know you will.'

Chapter Twenty-One

Michael felt that the gradual collapse of *Mahali pa Kupumzika* – both the house itself, and the estate – was a metaphor for the slow disintegration of the Republic of Equatoria. In late May 1963 the British government had threatened a move that many in Equatoria feared might be the death knell of the Republic if implemented: unless the Equatorian government agreed to hold talks in London with a view to extending the franchise to blacks and Asians in Equatoria, and unless it accepted the inevitable establishment of a black majority government, the Royal Navy would blockade the Equatorian coast.

Equatoria had no navy; the republic possessed precisely four fisheries protection vessels, armed with only small calibre quick firing cannon. These vessels could put up no resistance to Royal Navy warships. It would be particularly easy for Royal Navy warships to prevent oil tankers – large, cumbersome vessels – from reaching the safety of Port Hardinge. On hearing the news, Michael's reactions were mixed, as was the response on the part of many others in Equatoria. On the one hand Michael felt a profound anger at Britain, whom he saw as having adopted a bully's role. On the other hand, Michael (and a growing number of Europeans in Equatoria) were grudgingly beginning to believe that an exclusively European governed Equatorian republic was an experiment that had gone wrong, and needed to be remedied.

Various solutions were proposed and debated in the *Namuri Times*. There were the so called Bitter-Enders, determined to hold out against all odds, and their number included the Prime Minister, Ian Blackfell, and many senior government figures. There were those who hoped that a qualified enfranchisement of the Indian and black populations (with the right to vote conditional upon either business or property ownership, or educational qualifications), and the inclusion of Indians and blacks in the government, would be acceptable to Britain. Finally, there were those Europeans weary of the chronic shortages, and of the suppression of economic activity that international sanctions had brought about, who argued in favour of talks with Britain with a view to enfranchising the black and Indian populations, and the creation of a black majority government. At a stroke, this group argued, the *Wa Chui* would lose much of their popular support, and when international sanctions were lifted, Equatoria would experience an economic boom. This view tended to be held by those in trade and commerce. Only a minority of European farmers held to this view. A Royal Navy blockade, however, would surely increase the number of Europeans who believed in what was essentially complete capitulation. The idea of such a complete and total surrender to British and international demands stuck in Michael's craw, but he could see its economic merit – in the short term, at least.

'Patrick was always afraid that under a black government, big European owned estates such as *Mahali pa Kupumzika* would be broken up,' said Marjory to Michael during breakfast one morning. They had been listening to the news on the wireless. 'I think that is very likely – if not straight away, then in due course.'

'The plain fact of the matter,' Michael responded, 'is that we're not surviving financially. The estate itself is in growing financial difficulties; the country's economy is being strangled. Another few years of this – or even earlier, with a Royal Navy blockade – and we will all be facing utter ruin.'

Marjory placed her hand over that of Michael, which was resting on the table, then withdrew it again. 'What will happen to us – to Fiona and I?' she asked. 'You can go home, but what about us? This is our home.' Michael was shocked to see tears forming in Marjory's eyes. He reached for her hand. Marjory did not withdraw it.

'You know I would always take care of both of you.'

'But how could we be happy in England? And what about my family here?'

'I would try to help your family. And anyway, it need not be England,' Michael responded. 'We could buy a farm in South Africa. Have you ever thought of that?'

'Perhaps you could – but I certainly couldn't. *Mahali pa Kupumzika* wont be worth much under a black government. Who would want to buy it, with the threat of the estate being broken up hanging over them?'

'Oh – Marjory! I said "We." You, I, and Lady Fiona. Although she might prefer to return to Britain, come to think of it. That could be arranged. But you and I, we could farm together in South Africa.'

Marjory freed her hand. 'I must call the depot in Jiljil today. We're almost out of diesel and petrol. And we need other supplies. If the depot has some fuel in stock, then I will call my father. It's time we made the run to Jiljil.'

Why, thought Michael, does Marjory not understand that I would marry her like a shot? But Michael failed to appreciate that perhaps Marjory was waiting to be asked. Michael was neither timid nor indecisive – his wartime record made that clear – but with Marjory, he was unduly reticent, hobbled by the guilt he felt

Chapter Twenty-One

at his failure to have helped his friend. Marjory in her turn could not help feeling some culpability for Patrick's death. She ought, she thought, to have tried harder to understand her husband's problem with alcohol, and to have made an effort to help him. With such thoughts ranging in her mind, she hesitated to allow what was thus far only a close friendship with Michael to develop into something more. Yet she knew that marriage to Michael would see the birth of a new future; perhaps not the future she would have wished for (and in this, she was only one of thousands in Equatoria who were seeing the destruction of the futures they had always imagined for themselves), but Michael was offering her a new life in South Africa. She would not after all have to leave Africa. She would be delivered from the prospect of dissolution and collapse that faced her now. Had Michael only made an outright proposal of marriage now, she would have accepted his offer. Must I put the words in his mouth, she wondered? Are all men cowards when it comes to things like this?

Marjory did not understand, however, that Michael's hesitation was as much the consequence of his uncertainty of her feelings towards him from one moment to the next, as it was a residue of the guilt he felt in Patrick's death. Had Michael felt certain of Marjory's feelings towards him, perhaps he would not have hesitated to propose marriage to her. He was suffering an agony of conflicting signals from Marjory. Sometimes he felt that the sensible thing to do would be to return to England. But Michael lived by a strict code of honour, and he could not have done such a thing. He owed a duty to Patrick's memory; whether Marjory knew it or not, Michael thought, she needed him, and he could not leave her in the lurch.

And Michael was in love with her. He could not bear to think of living a life in which he lacked Marjory's presence.

Marjory had spoken to her father about obtaining a pair of heavy horses for *Mahali pa Kupumzika*; horses that could pull a plough, and which could be hitched to the wagon Michael had found in the coach house. In July, the executors for Patrick's estate (for which probate had not yet been granted, nor would it be for some time, as the estate contained assets that were located both in the United Kingdom and in Equatoria) authorised the purchase of a pair of Clydesdale mares which Marjory's father had tracked down. These horses arrived late one afternoon in a large horse transporter, together with the breeder who was selling them. He had brought several armed companions with him, travelling in two separate vehicles, preceding and following the transporter. The threat of *Wa Chui* ambushes meant that few people were willing anymore to make solitary road journeys.

Michael's excitement communicated itself to Marjory, herself an admirer of a fine horse. They were beautiful animals, bays, seventeen and a half hands, and strongly muscled, with dense white feathering on the lower legs. At only five years old, they had many years of working life ahead of them. Their breeder was selling the necessary harness for hitching the two Clydesdales to the wagon, and he had also brought the harness for one of the horses already on the estate to pull a Cape cart.

The Cape carts had been cleaned, sanded, repainted and varnished (a task in which Michael had been personally involved), and new hoods had been made for them by Weeping Moses. The wagon had merely been treated with a wood preservative, and the axles greased. Tom Grant (who was selling the two horses), and his three companions, would be spending the night at *Mahali pa Kupumzika*, before setting off on their return journey early the next morning. Before the day's end, with the sun descending rapidly towards the horizon, already casting long shadows across the stable yard from a double row of eucalyptus trees, Tom Grant harnessed the pair of Clydesdales to the wagon, and Michael and Marjory watched him carefully, for neither of them had ever hitched up a horse to a wagon or a carriage. The arrangement of

Chapter Twenty-One

the reins merited close attention, for the inside reins crossed over, so that both left hand reins led to the driver's left hand, and both right hand reins led to the driver's right hand. The driver could thus easily control a pair of horses.

'Who would like to drive them?' Mr. Grant asked.

Michael and Marjory looked at one another. 'We'll both get up together,' Marjory replied. They clambered up onto the wooden seat at the front of the wagon, and Marjory said, 'It was your idea, Michael. You take the reins.'

Michael took the reins in his hands and said, 'Move on!' and the pair of Clydesdales took up the strain for a moment, then moved off effortlessly, the empty but still heavy wagon (which looked very fine beneath its coats of dark creosote wood preservative) following them. Michael found himself grinning with pleasure. The horses' big hooves striking loudly on the cobblestones, Michael directed the team across the stable yard, and out onto the track which led past one side of the house. Then he turned the rig down the driveway leading to the front of the house. 'Whoa!' he said loudly, pulling on the reins, as they reached the front of the house, and the team halted. Lady Pencaitland, who was sitting on the veranda, stood and came to the top of the stairs, Karim behind her.

'Oh! How lovely!' Lady Pencaitland exclaimed. 'I have not seen such a brave sight on the farm since before the War.' Michael grinned at her, and Marjory, sitting at his side, smiled.

'They are a fine sight, aren't they?' Michael responded. 'I'll use them for heavy work on the farm from now on, to keep them exercised and to save diesel fuel. They can plough, and transport heavy loads. Njeroge will enjoy looking after them.' Njeroge, who had followed the team, was *Mahali pa Kupumzika's* remaining *syce*, or stable hand. He too was grinning broadly.

The sun, behind the eucalyptus trees, was balanced on the western horizon as Michael drove the team into the stable yard again. He and Njeroge, observed by Marjory and Tom Grant, unhitched the horses from the wagon, completing the task just before it grew too dark to see. Then, leaving the Clydesdales in Njeroge's care, the Europeans made their way to the house for sundowners on the veranda. Michael served the two women, then the four guests, from the drinks cabinet in the drawing room, for Karim was preparing the four extra bedrooms that would be needed for Tom Grant and his companions that night. Even with the four or five bedrooms closed off due to collapsing, or collapsed, ceilings, there were still plenty of bedrooms Karim could choose from.

For the most part, as time went by, it was found that there was little work for the Clydesdales to do, and then Njeroge would hitch them up to the empty wagon and take them as far along the farm road as the native trading store at Ol Kamau (where very basic groceries and other supplies could sometimes be obtained) and back again, to keep the horses in trim. But once in a while the big horses would be very busy, being used for work almost every day. In September, when the maize harvest was brought in, they were out every day. Michael had plans too the next year for hitching each horse to one of the wheeled iron ploughs he had discovered, in preparation for the planting season in March.

The arrival of the two Clydesdales, whom Marjory rather whimsically renamed Artemis and Atalanta (Atalanta was the less forward of the two), was a happy development in a period otherwise beset by anxiety for the future of the estate. In August (the Equatorian government under Ian Blackfell having made no move to engage in talks with Britain), Britain announced the commencement of a Royal Navy blockade of the Equatorian coast. Over time, the occasional Panamanian or Nicaraguan registered oil tanker would succeed in evading the Royal Navy frigate keeping station off the Equatorian coast, and make it through to Port Hardinge, where her precious cargo of oil could be pumped to the big refinery located at one end of the harbour, but Equatoria's thirst for oil far exceeded such infrequent and unreliable supplies.

Ian Blackfell's government had been in secret talks with the newly independent black republic which lay immediately to the south of Equatoria, and also with the Portuguese colonial government of Moçambique (which anyway was sympathetic to Equatoria's plight), which controlled the region lying between that black republic and South Africa. Convoys of road tankers began to haul fuel north to Equatoria from South Africa. Other supplies were also transported north through these territories. On their return journeys, the lorries that had hauled supplies and goods north, took Equatorian produce south, for relabeling as South African produce, and eventual export. However, the fuel shortage in Equatoria was critical now, as was the shortage of a wide range of general goods. The service of mechanics able to keep old, worn out vehicles and machinery going was much sought after. By far the greater part of what fuel did reach Equatoria was allocated for military and government use, with farmers' needs being prioritised after those. Private citizens were low down on the list of priorities, and so a black market in petrol and diesel was soon flourishing.

Michael had been giving some thought to ensuring that his future included Marjory. During his visit to South Africa, he had been strongly drawn to the bushveld country; that open country, blessed with a benign climate; sparsely populated by humanity, but teeming with game: it had answered some need within him of which he had been unaware until his tour of the Kruger National Park. It was the need for a terrain that had not yet been spoiled by a concentration of Humanity; a craving for a land where Man was incidental, not central, to Creation. Michael's spirit was exhausted by the constant struggle of trying to run *Mahali pa Kupumzika* in a climate of chronic shortages, and of financial insecurity brought about by the sanctions; a struggle which at times, due to *Wa Chui* activity, took on the quality of a nightmare. The struggle had killed his school friend Patrick; it had killed Patrick's elderly aunt also. And this struggle – defined as it was by hopelessness – was aging Marjory before her time, and souring her outlook.

Michael, as he paged through some of the tourist magazines he had found in the hotel in Johannesburg last year, had become aware of the existence of a large number of privately owned game reserves lying to the west of the Kruger National Park. Lately, he had begun thinking about buying one of the game reserves in this region; somewhere he, Marjory, and (if they wished) the Hepburns, could live. It was possible, he thought, that he could make such a game reserve pay for itself by marketing it as a choice destination for visitors, who would stay a night or two.

Michael's ties with England had grown weaker since his mother's death. There was no one there whom he would mind very much never seeing again. Africa had got into his blood. He had found a purpose in Africa that had been lacking in his life in England. He realised now that it had been his mother's presence above all that had rooted him in England. He did not think that he would miss a great deal in England now – and if he found that he was missing England, he and Marjory could always visit on holidays. He and Marjory! Marjory was very much part of the reason Michael was contemplating settling in South Africa. He knew that she could not be happy living in Britain. He suspected that if he were to present Marjory with the option of remaining in Africa, she would almost certainly say "Yes" when he asked her to marry him.

South Africa, from what he had seen during his visit last year, was a well run, stable, wealthy country. South Africa was fighting no bush wars. There was no British government imposed ban against his investing some of his wealth in South Africa. Michael had a feeling that international tourism to South Africa's game regions was set to become a fast growing industry. He had an idea that well appointed accommodation and top-notch cuisine would

Chapter Twenty-One

be especially sought after by foreign visitors keen to experience big game country in some degree of comfort. He had no idea how much a game reserve would cost him; he ought really to make another short visit to South Africa to find out. Michael did not, however, wish to leave *Mahali pa Kupumzika* right now. How could he learn more about prospects in South Africa?

At the end of September, with the maize harvest in (how hard Artemis and Atalanta, and those loyal workers who had remained on the estate, had worked!), Michael decided that a visit to Namuri and the South African Consulate was necessary. He would ask the Consul to obtain the information he required. He would make the drive to Namuri and back alone. There was always a risk in travelling alone now, but at this time of the year, in what was still the dry season, he could reach Namuri by mid to late afternoon in the Chevrolet. Michael knew now that he could trust Marjory and Karim (with Keith Hepburn living within easy call by radio telephone) to deal with any emergency that might arise, during what he planned would be an absence of only two, or at the most, three days.

Chapter Twenty-Two

Staying as usual at the New Cedric Hotel in Namuri, Michael visited the South African Consulate the next morning. He introduced himself to the Vice Consul as a family friend of the Pencaitlands of *Mahali pa Kupumzika*. 'Lord Pencaitland and I were at school together. Since Lord Pencaitland's death, I have been helping Lady Pencaitland run the estate.'

'Yes, I was sorry to learn of Lord Pencaitland's death,' Mr. Charles Du Plessis, the Vice Consul, remarked, his South African accent barely discernible. 'Can I offer you some tea or coffee?'

'Coffee please,' Michael replied. 'I have never tasted better coffee than that of Equatoria.' The Vice Consul smiled and called through the open door, 'Miss Philips! Two coffees please.'

A few minutes later, during which the two men talked about the campaign against the *Wa Chui*, the tanned, long legged young woman who had greeted Michael once he had got past reception, entered the room bearing a tray with a coffee pot, a milk jug, a sugar basin and two coffee cups. Miss Philips was wearing rather a short skirt, and she had a tousled, brunette hairdo like that of Sophia Loren in *"Legend of the Lost"* (which Michael remembered watching in about 1958 at the Odeon in

Chapter Twenty-Two

Leicester Square). Michael's eyes followed the young woman as she left the room.

'Milk, Mr. Hood?' the Vice Consul asked.

'No thanks.' Mr. Du Plessis poured the coffee and placed the cup on the table in front of Michael. The china all bore the South African coat of arms in blue beneath the glaze.

As they drank their coffees, Michael explained that he was interested in buying a game farm – or rather, a game reserve – in the Transvaal Lowveld, preferably adjacent to the Kruger National Park's western boundary. 'I have no idea how much land is worth in that region,' he told the Vice Consul. 'If I find it's affordable, I would like to buy a going concern, a well stocked game reserve already equipped to take in paying guests. Although I expect I will wish to improve and upgrade the guest facilities.'

'We can find out what is on the market, Mr. Hood,' the Vice Consul told Michael. 'I shall make enquiries for you, and send you details of whatever I can find.'

'I would be very grateful.'

The two men chatted about South Africa for a while. Michael had mentioned his visit to South Africa the previous year, and his tour of the Kruger National Park. When he had finished a second cup of coffee, he stood, shook hands, and left the room. Michael would leave for *Mahali pa Kupumzika* after an early breakfast tomorrow morning. He had the rest of the day to search the shops for the sort of things that were either unavailable in Jiljil, or, if stocked, were not to his taste. He could not leave for *Mahali pa Kupumzika* now: he would still be travelling when first, nightfall, and next, the curfew, caught him out. He needed some socks, shirts and underwear, and Marjory had asked him to see if he could find some of the toiletries she favoured. Michael made for Cohen's (Marjory had advised him that they might have what he needed), a department store on three floors. After visiting their menswear department and the ladies' toiletries counter (behind which the shelves had large gaps in them), he had lunch in their restaurant – a vegetable consommé, followed by a surprisingly good veal Schnitzel, with a Tusker lager. He had a slice of cheesecake for dessert (he wondered whether the cheese might have come from *Mahali pa Kupumzika*), and of course, a cup of the superb Equatorian coffee, which he accompanied with a cigarette.

Michael had a strong feeling that in having approached the South African Consulate, he had altered what had been the mere possibility of settling in South Africa to an almost certain probability. He knew too that Marjory was part of this vision. He felt almost euphoric.

After lunch he asked directions to a tobacconist at the enquiries desk downstairs. As Michael walked to the tobacconist, two blocks from Cohen's, he noticed how few goods there were in the shop windows. At the tobacconist he bought the last three boxes they had of Montecristo Coronas.

'You are lucky, Sir,' the shopkeeper, an Indian, said. 'I do not know when we will be able to get some more.'

Michael would give one of the boxes to Marjory's father.

During the second week of October, the South African Consulate sent Michael a thick folder of information on game farms and game reserves for sale in the Transvaal Lowveld. These ranged from three or four only rudimentarily developed properties in the game region fringing the western boundary of the Kruger National Park, to a couple of game reserves well stocked with a rich variety of game, and possessing the infrastructure to cater for local and foreign visitors. It was these latter that interested Michael most. He was looking for a game reserve that would be able to generate an income.

In late February the following year, 1964, the South African Consulate sent Michael another folder of information on game reserves for sale. The Consulate continued to send Michael information through the course of the year. Michael gathered that this was a slow market, but while the prices for game properties may have been steep for a South African investor, they seemed very reasonable to Michael, translating the cost of various properties into Sterling. At that time, the Pound bought two Rand. Michael and Marjory spent much time poring over the information sent them by the Consulate, familiarising themselves with the market. Michael was delighted that Marjory had come to accept that she would be part of this venture. She might even (if she could find a buyer for *Mahali pa Kupumzika* when the time came to quit Equatoria) be a co-investor, although in a lesser capacity.

But finding a buyer for *Mahali pa Kupumzika* might not be at all easy: who in their right mind would wish to invest in a major farming estate in Equatoria at this time? With each passing month the *Wa Chui* gained in strength, and their weaponry was growing more sophisticated and their use of it more effective. Ensuring the safety of one's family and one's farm workers became an ever more fundamental priority. In light of the risk of ambushes by the *Wa Chui*, obtaining regular supplies from the nearest town (suppliers would only rarely make rural deliveries), and transporting one's produce to the nearest purchasing co-operative, became ever more challenging. Earning a decent living from farming (particularly in the Highlands, where the *Wa Chui* was most active) had become extremely challenging. The shortages, most noticeably of diesel and petrol, but which included a shortage of vital machinery parts and lubricants for machinery, created new challenges. Many farmers had reverted to the practice of their fathers and grandfathers before them, and had begun using oxen on their farms in place of powered machinery. A few, like Michael and Marjory, had turned to draught horses, although the use of these latter was not as common. They were expensive to obtain, and expensive to maintain. Necessarily, reliance on animals in place of machinery meant that harvest yields were down. Large estates like *Mahali pa Kupumzika* no longer benefitted from economies of scale; it was the small three hundred acre farms that could most economically use animals in place of machinery.

'We're slowly turning the clock back,' Marjory commented to Michael one day. 'Already, Patrick's father would have found little that was different in farming when he first arrived in the Highlands in the early years of the century.'

The situation was not yet quite that bad: farm machinery was still in use, although (due to the extreme fuel shortages) much less frequently than before the imposition of international sanctions and the Royal Navy blockade. Cars, pickup trucks and lorries were still in use, when fuel could be obtained for them. Without the private arrangement Michael had come to with the Indian assistant manager of the oil company's sub depot in Jiljil (whereby, to make up their government allocation, Michael bought fuel being sold on the black market), he would not have had enough fuel to run the Chevrolet and the estate's two Land Rovers and its big Austin lorry. Michael hated to enter this world of under-the-counter payments, of back door deals, but circumstances forced him to do so.

In early 1964 Michael arranged for the further transfer of funds from the bank account he had set up in Johannesburg during his visit to South Africa, and with these funds he covered some of the routine costs that the estate was now unable to afford. Farming overheads were now very high (due to a combination of *Wa Chui* activity and international sanctions), and Equatorian farmers battled to achieve a profit on their produce in the only foreign market now open to them – the South African market. And this market could only be accessed at the end of a very long, very expensive road journey, first through the new black republic to the south (a passage that was illegal in theory, and could only be made due to the payment of substantial bribes to government officials), and then through the Portuguese colony further south. This latter stage of the journey was only possible because the colony's officials were inclined to sympathise with Equatoria's plight, but the cash considerations they received helped ensure that they turned a blind eye to the road convoys.

Michael had paid for a security fence to be erected around the house soon after the New Year's Day *Wa Chui* attack. This was a nine foot tall wire mesh fence topped with barbed wire, and backed on the inside by rolls of barbed wire, so that even if the fence was cut, intruders would have to find a way through the barbed wire. The fence was placed at a distance of three hundred yards from the house, for the Chinese-made mortars used by the *Wa Chui* had a range of between two hundred to three hundred yards (and at three hundred yards, they were wildly inaccurate). In places, a way had had to be cleared for the fence through well established woodland. The project had been hugely expensive, and it had almost exhausted Michael's South African Rand allowance for the year (although he made sure that he had sufficient funds left in his Jiljil bank account to help with routine day to day expenses on the estate). But funding the installation of the fence meant that Michael could not offer to help pay for the repair of the mortar damage to the north wing of the house, and the end of that wing remained in ruins. In fact, much of the north wing (the first floor in particular) was now uninhabitable; what had not been destroyed by mortars had largely been closed off due to the damp.

As to the security fence, Michael was far from certain that it would pose much of a hindrance to the *Wa Chui*, but the house could not be left naked to further attacks. They were not alone in having had a security fence installed; across the Highlands, farmers were erecting security fences. Increasingly, Michael felt that they were fighting a rearguard action, not only for the future of the estate, but for that of Equatoria itself. He did not foresee a happy outcome to Equatoria's fight for survival. His concern for Equatoria's future was bound up in his love for Marjory, and in his concern for her future. He knew that he could provide for her future – if she would allow him to do so. Marjory however – her feelings for him in particular – remained an enigma to Michael, and he needed to be rather more sure of himself before he found the courage to propose marriage to her. At times he felt hugely frustrated, and not a little despondent, then he would throw himself with even greater energy into his work on the estate. He did however take a break sometimes during the rainy season, and retreat for an hour or two to the library, where he would not have to talk to anyone (for only Lady Pencaitland, accompanied by her Alsatian dog, ever visited the library, and she was no conversationalist).

Late October 1964, and it was a wet day. It had been raining since dawn. There was little to be done on the estate at this time of year, and neither Michael nor Marjory had left the house. At tea time that afternoon, the two of them, together with Lady Pencaitland and Deirdre Hepburn (who was now staying at *Mahali pa Kupumzika*), gathered in the drawing room. Karim brought in a large ebony tray with brass fittings, on which a silver tea pot, together with bone china tea cups and side plates, a silver sugar basin, a silver milk jug, and a freshly baked fruit cake, were arranged. He placed the tray on the small table alongside Lady Pencaitland. He had earlier lighted a fire, which hissed and crackled in the grate, and there was a rich, aromatic scent of burning juniper wood filling the room. After tea, the radio telephone would have to be manned for an hour, for between four-thirty and five-thirty, incoming transmissions were usually monitored. (At other times, it was hit or miss whether incoming transmissions would be picked up). Sometimes Karim would sit and listen for incoming calls, but as was now usually the case during the wet season (for in that cool damp weather, sundowners on the veranda were far from appealing), both Marjory and Michael would sit together in the study. The study was still imbued with Patrick's presence, Michael thought. He did not miss Patrick very much, not the Patrick he had known during the last year or so of his life, but he missed his school friend, the Patrick who had first invited him to *Mahali pa Kupumzika*.

'We should be thinking hard about moving to South Africa, Marjory,' Michael said, as they sat together in the study. Sometimes Michael felt that Marjory would rather not think about having to leave Equatoria.

'I wish we had somewhere to go to, though, when we got there,' said Marjory. 'There could be seven of us, after all.'

Marjory's parents were thinking about accompanying Michael, Marjory and Lady Pencaitland if they left for South Africa. Michael thought for a moment. 'How do you get seven of us, Marjory?' he asked.

'Well, there's you and I, and Fiona; my mother and father, and Andrew, and Deirdre.'

Michael took his cigarette case from his pocket (engraved with Michael's initials – which he had shared with his grandfather, to whom the cigarette case had originally belonged – it was of heavy silver), and extracted a cigarette and lighted it. Marjory was still a non smoker. 'Of course,' he said. 'I had forgotten about Deirdre.'

Eleanor, the older of the two Hepburn girls, was already at university in Cape Town; Deirdre had left school in December the previous year (in Equatoria, as in South Africa, the academic year followed the calendar year), and she had not at the start of 1964 joined her older sister in South Africa.

'Marjory,' Michael continued, 'I need an agent in South Africa, to facilitate my purchase of a game reserve there – and perhaps other matters as well. Do you think Gordon Fleming would know of someone reliable and trustworthy who could represent my interests in South Africa?' (Gordon Fleming had been Patrick's lawyer and agent in Namuri, and he now represented Marjory).

'I expect so,' Marjory replied. 'Shall I ask him? You could meet him in Namuri and talk about it, if he thinks he can help you.'

'Yes, please ask him. If he needs to see me, I'll drive down.'

They sat in silence for a short while, then Michael said, 'Tomorrow, if it's not too wet, I would like to ride out to the north-eastern sector and see if the elephants that Mwangi reported this morning are still in the vicinity. Would you like to come with me?'

'Yes – of course! It's been quite a while since elephants last visited us.'

The north-eastern sector of the estate was uncultivated, a mix of grassland and woodland. To the east it was bounded by the outliers of the Nyahurari Forest.

'You must bring the Rigby, Michael,' Marjory continued. 'I wouldn't want to shoot an elephant – glorious beasts! – but it does not pay to take them for granted. They can move with surprising speed.'

The next morning (Michael with the heavy calibre Rigby rifle slung across his back) they found the elephants, close to the edge of the forest; a family group of four adults – three females and a bull – with two adolescents, and a baby. One of the females was suckling the baby, which stood beneath her, reaching up with its prehensile lips. The bull was a little way upwind from the group. Michael and Marjory were able to draw quite near to the animals, for the elephants seemed to regard the horses with no fear, but Marjory led Michael in a half circle, until they were able to approach the group from downwind. As yet, Michael had little bushlore (although the day would come when he would be well versed in bushcraft), and these were the first elephants he had seen at *Mahali pa Kupumzika*. Two of the adults and both adolescents were browsing off a stand of white stinkwood, reaching up with their trunks for the clusters of small, berry-like fruit. Michael and Marjory, astride their horses, sat watching these magnificent animals in silence for a long time. Later, Michael considered that while watching the elephants, his mind had been entirely free of anxieties and doubts; indeed, he had existed wholly within the present.

Chapter Twenty-Two

No one at *Mahali pa Kupumzika* had wished to celebrate New Year's Eve at the end of 1964. Equatoria's third anniversary of independence, too, had been a muted affair. There was little official celebration. At *Mahali pa Kupumzika,* Equatoria's independence day had passed unacknowledged, although both Michael and Marjory were aware of the date. Michael did not believe that he and Marjory would still be here in a year's time. They remembered Patrick's suicide two years ago on New Year's Day. Lady Pencaitland, who had aged terribly since the *Wa Chui* attack on the house, and her sister-in-law's and son's deaths two years ago, and who was increasingly prone to periods of bewilderment and confusion, went upstairs to bed at ten o' clock, the faithful Alsatian dog at her heels, and Michael and Marjory were in their respective beds by eleven o' clock.

Marjory had contacted her lawyer in Namuri in November. He thought he might indeed know of a lawyer in South Africa – a friend he had been to university with – who could represent Michael in his purchase of a game reserve in the Transvaal Lowveld. Michael drove down to Namuri in early January of 1965. On the way he came across two military checkpoints, but he was waved on immediately, his white skin a *laissez-faire*. Gordon Fleming took him to lunch at the Suffolk Hotel. Over lunch, Michael showed him some of the material he had been sent by the South African Consulate.

'This is the sort of thing I'm after,' Michael told the lawyer. 'There's a property in the Klaserie block I am particularly interested in. Here – let me show you.'

Gordon Fleming looked at the pages Michael showed him. He made a note of the property's name and location, and of the seller's contact details.

'I will explain what you're after to John Stephanos, my friend in Johannesburg – in particular, your interest in this property,' said Gordon Fleming. 'I shall be sending you some documents to sign and return to me, Michael,' the lawyer continued, 'if he agrees to represent you. You will need to give him power of attorney in this matter. Lady Pencaitland can witness your signature.'

'What I really need is someone on the spot who can actually inspect the property, and report back to me,' Michael told the lawyer. 'Do you think your friend could arrange that?'

'I'm sure John has someone in his office who can do that,' the other man responded. 'Tell me, what exactly would Lady Pencaitland's interest in your purchase of a property in South Africa be?'

'I believe she is thinking of selling *Mahali pa Kupumzika*,' Michael replied. 'Whether Lady Pencaitland invests in the property I'm after in South Africa, is uncertain at this time. I have hopes that she would join me in South Africa, and we could run the game reserve together.'

The lawyer looked thoughtful. Lady Pencaitland was, after all, his client.

'If Lady Pencaitland decides to sell *Mahali pa Kupumzika*,' Michael continued, as he poured himself some more of the rather good South African wine, 'would it perhaps be better to put the estate up for auction – as one, or perhaps several, lots – rather than to put it on the open market?'

'Yes, it would probably be better to auction the estate,' Gordon Fleming replied, 'and as several lots. You would probably get a better price that way. There's a reputable auction house in Naburu,' the lawyer continued. 'I would of course represent Lady Pencaitland's interests in the matter.'

'Of course,' Michael agreed.

After the meal, over the usual excellent Equatorian coffees, both men having lighted a cigarette, Gordon Fleming asked Michael, 'This is just curiosity on my part: do you happen to know whether Keith Hepburn – or Lord Pencaitland, as I should call him now – will be staying on in Equatoria?'

'I'm not sure. He may follow us to South Africa,' Michael answered.

'It will be a sad thing when there are no more Pencaitlands left in Equatoria,' Gordon Fleming remarked. 'More than anything else, to my mind, that would signal the end of Equatoria as we know it.'

Chapter Twenty-Three

Michael sometimes thought of his family home in the Cotswolds – that old house of grey stone in its gentle combe – and of his flat in Frith Street in Soho. There was no one living in the house now but the cook-housekeeper, Mrs. Hughes, and his mother's dog, now grown very old indeed. Michael's family solicitor in Chipping Norton, Richard Carter, argued that the house was a wasted asset; that it could at least be let out, but Michael liked to feel that it would be there, ready for him, anytime he wished to return to England. His flat in London he had let on a six monthly roll over basis to his friend, Maurice Grainger. (As time went by, Michael's sense of fair play – it was surely no fun for Maurice not knowing beyond six months whether he would keep his home – caused him to increase the rental period to five years at a time). It seemed almost inconceivable to Michael now that he could ever enjoy living in a city the size of London again. Even his occasional forays into Namuri caused him unrest, and unsettled his mind, leaving him yearning within hours to return to *Mahali pa Kupumzika* and its wide skies and open countryside. Michael no longer missed his friends in London (Maurice Grainger perhaps excepted); for the most part, they had been pub friends only. He thought that if ever he had to return to live in England, he would be happier in the old house in the countryside, with its memories of childhood and his mother.

A large part of Michael's mind was now focused on the purchase of a game reserve in the Transvaal Lowveld, somewhere he could bring Marjory and her mother in law – and the Hepburns also, if they wished to come. In June 1965, with the long rains set in, and the sky over the Central Highlands a lowering, rain sodden grey, Michael received news which raised his spirits considerably: John Stephanos, his representative in South Africa (using the power of attorney Michael had granted him in the matter), had signed the papers for the purchase of a two thousand hectares game reserve in the Klaserie block (two thousand hectares equated to almost five thousand acres), located forty-two miles from the village of Hoedspruit in the Transvaal Lowveld.

Keith Pencaitland and his family had decided that they would, for now at least, be staying on in Equatoria. Their farm, of not much more than a thousand acres in extent, generated little profit at present, but Keith Pencaitland was cautiously optimistic for the future.

'I think there will be room for medium sized farmers, no matter our colour, in the new Equatoria,' Keith Pencaitland told Michael. 'Equatoria will still need to earn foreign exchange, and she will rely on agricultural and mining exports to obtain it. Once international sanctions are lifted, there will be money to be made again.'

Michael feared that ideology and race hatred would trump sound economic common sense. Furthermore, he did not believe that the granting of majority rule in Equatoria would necessarily bring *Wa Chui* depredations to an end. The *Wa Chui* movement sought the creation of a Marxist state, but the figures likely to assume dominance in any black government that would take over when European rule ended, were on the whole committed to a capitalist and free market economic philosophy. Whatever the outcome, neither Michael nor Marjory intended to remain in Equatoria to find out.

By June that year, *Mahali pa Kupumzika's* struggle to keep going financially had assumed mammoth proportions. With the shortages and scarcities, the economies of scale that a large estate like *Mahali pa Kupumzika* could once have applied, were no longer possible, and the estate was no longer breaking even. The truth was that *Mahali pa Kupumzika* was on the brink of bankruptcy. If it had not been for the periodic injection of cash from Michael's funds in South Africa (and this cash infusion was severely curtailed by the South African government's limit to the amount of currency that could be sent abroad each year), the estate would by now have been in serious difficulties. Fuel (diesel, petrol, and even paraffin for the lamps), and machinery lubricants, had become so scarce that the work on the farm that had once been done with machinery was now being done almost entirely by the two draught horses – at a fraction of the pace. Only a small part of the acreage that was normally planted out had been planted with maize, barley and lucerne in March.

Diesel was so precious that it was used only for running the electricity generator (and that, sparingly). The two Land Rovers, and sometimes the lorry, burning up scarce petrol, adding more wear to already worn tyres, would make the journey to Jiljil every fortnight. The shrunken dairy operation, which still produced a limited range of quality cheeses and yoghurts, saw its much diminished output transported to Jiljil on a fortnightly basis in the backs of the two Land Rovers, which would make the return journey laden with ever more expensive supplies. Even basic commodities, such as sugar, salt, tea and coffee (that superb coffee of Equatoria) and tobacco for the farm workers, had become scarce. This was despite these commodities themselves being produced in Equatoria. The Equatorian government, in its desperate need for foreign exchange, was enforcing the export of the bulk of these commodities, via the tenuous land link to South Africa, and the occasional freighter that had successfully run the Royal Navy blockade (and hoped to run it again on the way out). Other than these fortnightly journeys to Jiljil, the Land Rovers sat idle. Where once Patrick and André Myburgh had driven around the estate in their Land Rovers, Michael and Marjory now used horses almost exclusively (either as riding animals, or once in a while, as a treat, pulling one of Michael's Cape carts). Only in the wet season were the Land Rovers occasionally still used on the estate.

Every journey by road was now potentially dangerous, for despite the ever expanding size of the Equatorian Army, the *Wa Chui* ranged the Highlands with what seemed to many of the European farmers to be near impunity. Most of their activities were carried out between sundown and sunrise, but there were occasional daytime attacks on isolated roads, such as that which Michael, Patrick and Karim had endured as early as mid 1961. Perhaps the majority of black workers in the Central Highlands had by now taken the *kiapo* – the *Wa Chui* oath – if only through fear of *Wa Chui* retribution had they not done so. (The administration of the *kiapo* was a loathsome ceremony, consciously devised by the *Wa Chui* to break fundamental sexual and dietary tribal taboos, using alienation and shock to render the participants feeling bereft of their clan and tribal support networks, and with no choice in the future but to look to the *Wa Chui* for the support they had once obtained from the clan and the tribe).

Wa Chui insurgents and their weapons were hidden during the day, and provided with food, by these oath-sworn native farm workers. Without their weapons, there was nothing to tell an active member of a *Wa Chui* guerrilla group from a farm worker in appearance. Through good fortune, Michael, and Keith Pencaitland (for the two of them made the journeys to Jiljil together), had so far not run into further trouble on the road to

Jiljil, but reports of attacks in the district were commonplace. Farm houses had been converted into fortresses, most of them surrounded, as was *Mahali pa Kupumzika*, by security fences.

But following the purchase of his South African game reserve in June 1965, Michael had in his own mind already abandoned *Mahali pa Kupumzika*. However, Michael had by no means abandoned Marjory also: she would, he was certain, be with him in South Africa. He was excited at the prospect of taking possession of the property he had bought. Situated deep within the Klaserie block, down more than thirty miles of dirt road, the fenced reserve was, he would find, well stocked with game. There were impala beyond counting, those pretty, graceful, triple-toned antelopes with lyre shaped horns; there were a score or more of waterbuck, a score of blue wildebeest, and an unknown number of common duiker – such pretty, petite antelopes, barely twenty inches in height. There were large numbers of warthogs, a sizeable herd of zebra, one and a half dozen giraffes, and fourteen much prized white rhinos. The reserve had a small herd of Cape buffalo, and an unknown number of leopards (as nocturnal, shy animals, their numbers were difficult to tally). There were two prides of lions, comprising two older mature males, two younger mature males, an adolescent male, seven adult females and (at the time of the purchase of the game reserve) eight cubs. And – surely a draw card equal to that of the lions – there was a family group of ten elephants, made up of five mature animals, three adolescents and two infants. There were several hyena clans, and numerous species of smaller mammals, including porcupines, honey badgers (or as they were known locally in Afrikaans, *"ratels"*), tree squirrels, banded mongoose, bushbabies, vervet monkeys and chacma baboons.

The bushveld bird species, Michael would come to appreciate, were so much more profuse and colourful than the birds of Northern Europe, and many of the birds were larger than the

Chapter Twenty-Three

birds he saw in England. (Yet there was nothing, Michael always thought, lovelier than the song of a blackbird in the springtime in an English country garden). Almost the first bird Michael learned to identify in the bushveld (because of its distinctive acrobatic flight and its brilliant colouring – lilac and sky blue dominated) was the lilacbreasted roller. Often seen (and heard) was the woodland kingfisher, another very pretty bird. One of Michael's favourites among the smaller birds was the little bee-eater, with its green back, its cinnamon coloured throat, and its salmon pink breast; once you knew where they perched, you would see them using the same perch day after day. One of the loveliest sounds, heard early every morning, was the call of the blackheaded oriole. Another bird call woven into daily life in the bushveld was that of the grey lourie, the "go away bird" (for its call sounded somewhat like the words "go away" being repeated). Also heard in the mornings was the loud, resounding booming of the ground hornbill. Its cousin, the yellowbilled hornbill, a large, predominantly pale grey and dappled dirty white bird, with a fantastically large, curved yellow bill, was ubiquitous in the bushveld.

Michael and Marjory, out walking together on their land, would stop and stare at the sky periodically, to see whether they could spot vultures, or large raptors, far above them. The whitebacked vulture was the most commonly seen vulture in the bushveld, and after that the lappetfaced vulture, the largest of the vultures. Yellowbilled kites were very common throughout the summer months, and easy to identify high in the sky, due to the concave silhouette of their tail. An equally conspicuous silhouette in the sky was that of the bateleur eagle, with its very short tail. But should Michael happen to see the mightiest of the raptors, a martial eagle – the largest eagle in Africa – perched nearby, often high up in a dead tree, he would experience a particular pleasure.

In the gardens near the house at *Kupumzika* (this was the name that Michael and Marjory were to give their wilderness

Paradise, in memory of *Mahali pa Kupumzika*; the word standing alone meaning simply "to rest" in *Kiswahili*), the gentle cooing of Cape turtle doves in the trees imbued the surroundings with an atmosphere of serenity.

The terrain was mixed mopane and bushwillow woodland, with scattered large trees, among which the acacias were common. These latter included the iconic umbrella thorn, the brack thorn, the knob thorn – and on low lying ground, fever trees, with their greenish-yellow bark. Marula (whose ripe fruit was beloved of elephants) and leadwood (the latter growing very tall indeed) were far from uncommon. A narrow strip of dense riverine woodland (comprising wild date palm, lala palm, giant sycamore figs, Natal mahogany, and jackal berry) grew on the banks of the Nhlaralumi River, a largely seasonal watercourse marking *Kupumzika's* western boundary.

There were two resident European rangers: the chief ranger, who was in his forties, and his young assistant, in his twenties. There was also a black anti-poaching patrol of four armed rangers. In addition to the main house (a square box with a green painted corrugated iron roof, built of plastered and painted brick sometime in the late nineteen-forties, whose one redeeming feature was a deep covered veranda along its front and sides), there were a variety of garages and outhouses, stabling for four horses, including feed and tack rooms (for neither Michael nor Marjory would contemplate a life without horses in it), accommodation for the rangers and the domestic staff, and six guest chalets – also built of plastered and painted brick. In time, Michael and Marjory were to tear down the house and the chalets, and replace them with far more environmentally conscious structures built of river stones and timber, with thatched roofs. There was a large black domestic staff, and Michael located and hired a black cook who had previously worked in the kitchens of one of Johannesburg's five star hotels. Almost from the word go, *Kupumzika* would be welcoming paying guests, clawing back some of Michael's huge financial outgoings. Without Michael's considerable fortune, he would have been unable to pursue the venture without outside investment – and this latter, he did not want. *Kupumzika* would remain always a family owned business.

But for the present, leaving *Mahali pa Kupumzika*, and quitting Equatoria, still lay some months ahead. In July, the long rains a month past, Michael and Marjory were riding one morning at *Mahali pa Kupumzika*. Michael, who had barely expressed any greater degree of intimacy with Marjory than could be conveyed by a chaste kiss (for Michael was one of those Englishmen not uncommon of his generation and class; bold as lions in warfare, but somewhat sexually repressed), drew his horse to a halt. Marjory drew up alongside him, and looked at him enquiringly.

His face solemn, and without preamble, Michael said, 'Marjory, will you do me the honour of marrying me?'

Marjory's features, with their golden tan and an attractive flush from the exertions of riding, had never, Michael thought, been more beautiful. In finding the courage at last to propose marriage to Marjory, Michael was showing greater bravery than he had had to show in many years. Marjory looked at him, then smiled.

'It took you long enough to ask, Michael,' she responded. 'Yes, of course I'll marry you.'

Exultation overcame Michael. He had hardly dared to hope that Marjory would say "Yes."

'My dearest darling,' he declared, and leaning across he took her hand and kissed her, missing her mouth and landing the kiss on her check, for the horses were shifting beneath their riders, tugging at their reins in order to reach the sweet new grass at their hooves. 'You have made me so very happy! Let's get married before we leave *Mahali pa Kupumzika*. Where would you like to get married? Here – or at Saint John's in Jiljil?'

Michael would have liked to kiss Marjory properly, but her horse had suddenly advanced two paces. How often was a marriage proposal made where both the would-be groom and the bride-to-be were mounted on horseback? Marjory caused her horse to step back a couple of paces. 'It will be easier for the guests to attend the wedding if we marry in Jiljil,' she answered.

'Yes, of course, you're right.'

And so in late September 1965, the harvest (such as it was these days) having been brought in across the Central Highlands, Michael finally married the woman he had fallen in love with over five years earlier. The wedding was not very large, for few people wished to travel any distance in Equatoria anymore, but it was a pretty wedding, the weather perfect, with masses of flowers in the church. Very few guests from further away than Naburu were present, although a very few had driven up from Namuri. Other than these, only family members were present: The Dowager Lady Pencaitland, and Marjory's mother, father and brother were there, along with a scattering of distant Hepburn cousins on Marjory's side of the family. There were no guests for the groom: Michael had no family left in England, and none of his few friends in England, now much neglected, was inclined to make the long journey to Equatoria. Andrew, Marjory's brother, looking very smart in his Equatoria Regiment uniform, was Michael's Best Man. Deirdre, the younger of Patrick's nieces, served as a bridesmaid for Marjory.

Standing at the altar with Marjory (who was wearing a hat and a simple dress of pale ivory silk which reached to her calves), Michael was suffused with a heady mix of joy and jitters; his hand trembled slightly as he placed the ring on Marjory's finger; he felt almost as he had sometimes felt when he was about to go into battle. He thought for a moment of his mother: how he wished she had been able to see him getting married. The newlyweds did not go away on honeymoon – they did not feel it would be safe to leave Lady Pencaitland alone at *Mahali pa Kupumzika*, with only Karim to look after her – but Michael moved into Marjory's big bedroom (the same bedroom she had shared with Patrick), and (Michael should not have been surprised, but he was) Karim now began addressing him as *"Bwana Mkubwa."*

Of outward passion in this marriage there was little. Marjory had contracted the marriage as a practical measure; as a means of providing for her future (and perhaps that of her family also), after *Mahali pa Kupumzika* and Equatoria were both gone, but her calculations were not entirely mercenary; she did feel a genuine fondness for Michael, and as the years passed, that warm affection was to grow into an abiding love. Michael however was passionately in love with Marjory, and he had been for more than five years, but constrained both by his temperament and by his upbringing, he was incapable of freely expressing this passion.

Less than a month after the wedding, *Mahali pa Kupumzika* was auctioned off in two major lots, along with almost all its goods and chattels, these latter in individual lots. The auctioneers and Gordon Fleming, Marjory's lawyer in Namuri, had suggested that a higher return could be gained if the estate were broken up in two. Marjory agreed. Neither Michael nor Marjory attended the auction, which took place over the space of two days. They spent three nights in Namuri, taking Lady Pencaitland with them, and driving down (well armed) in the Chevrolet. In a sense, this visit to Namuri served Michael and Marjory as a belated honeymoon, although a sad one, for both were hurting at the thought of leaving *Mahali pa Kupumzika*, although Michael would find the move easier to make than would Marjory, who had known *Mahali pa Kupumzika* all her life, and who had, for some years, been its mistress.

When, after three days and nights in Namuri they returned to *Mahali pa Kupumzika*, it was to find the house stripped of many of its possessions. But *Mpishi Moja* was still there, as was Karim. The newlyweds were to spend little more time in the house before the day came when they quit *Mahali pa Kupumzika* for good, and began the first stage of the long journey by sea to Durban.

Michael wished he were bringing the horses with them to South Africa (he had a particular affection for Artemis and Atalanta, the Clydesdales), but it would have been prohibitively expensive to have done so. He did however arrange that one of the Cape carts (for he was extremely attached to these pretty carriages) would be transported by lorry to Jiljil Station (this was expensive enough, for road haulage was now extremely costly). The newest of the two Land Rovers, together with the Chevrolet, would be driven to the station on the day of departure, and along with the Cape cart, would be loaded onto the train for Port Hardinge. These three vehicles would accompany them on the Lloyd Triestino liner to South Africa. Some of the Pencaitland heirloom pieces of furniture, silver, chinaware and oil paintings, and of course the three dogs, would also accompany them to South Africa.

It would be hard saying goodbye to Karim, but the South African government would not permit him entry to the country. The Apartheid regime felt it had more than enough people of colour already present within South Africa's borders.

Keith Pencaitland accompanied Michael to Jiljil Station in the Land Rover the Hoods were to take with them to South Africa. Andrew, who had been granted a two day pass, followed in his father's Land Rover, with his mother by his side. Marjory was driving the Chevrolet, and had Lady Pencaitland by her side, with Karim in the back seat. At the station, the Chevrolet and the Land Rover was loaded onto a flat bed wagon and lashed down. (The Cape cart, which had arrived at the station a few days earlier, was already loaded onto a flat bed wagon). The two flat beds were coupled to the train when it came in. The three dogs, in a pair of Equatoria Railways dog kennels, were placed in the guard's van. None of these operations was conducted very smoothly, the Equatoria Railways staff tripping over each other's feet and shouting at each other, and several native idlers had gathered to enjoy the spectacle of the Chevrolet and the Land Rover being driven up an embanked loading platform, and from there onto the flat bed wagon. The two flat bed wagons were attached to the end of the train, just after the guard's van (and just before the Army machine gun detachment in their open wagon at the very end of the train). The operation entailed much shunting back and forth, and would set back the train's schedule appreciably, but the Pencaitland name still counted for something in Equatoria.

'If things get too bad, come and join us, Keith,' Michael said.

'Maybe I'm wrong,' Keith Pencaitland replied, 'but I think there's a future for us here still.'

'Oh, Mum and Dad – I wish we weren't saying goodbye,' Marjory addressed her parents.

'I know, Darling, I hate goodbyes,' her mother responded. 'But we will be seeing each other again, Marjory. This is not goodbye for good.'

Marjory embraced and kissed her mother and father, and did the same with Andrew, her brother. Michael shook hands with Marjory's family. Then both he and Marjory turned to Karim, who was standing to one side of the group. Marjory, speaking *Kiswahili*, said, 'I will miss you, Karim. I will think of you often.'

'*Memsaab*. Is this a good land to which you go?' Karim responded, also speaking *Kiswahili*.

'*Ndiyo*. It is a good land.' Marjory took Karim's hand and held it for a moment. '*Kwaheri* Karim. *Kaa vizuri.*'

Michael gave Karim an envelope in which was two hundred Equatorian Dollars, then worth about seventy Pounds – a fortune for a native in Equatoria. Karim had earlier received his final wages. He would almost certainly be returning now, after these many years, to Somalia, there to buy camels and find a wife. Michael took his hand. '*Asante sana*, Karim. *Kwaheri.*'

'*Bwana Mkubwa. Nenda vizuri. Kwaheri.*'

'You must say goodbye to Karim, now, Fiona,' said Marjory.

Lady Pencaitland looked somewhat confused for a moment,

then her face cleared, and she reached for Karim's hand and held it for fully thirty seconds. *'Asante sana,* Karim. *Kwaheri, kaa vizuri.'*

'Msaba!' Karim's voice had a catch in it. The uniformed train conductor, a Sikh wearing a large maroon turban, who had been hovering near the group, said at that moment, 'You must please board now, Ladies and Sir. We must be on our way.'

The three Europeans boarded the train and made their way to Michael's compartment, where the two women sat down. (Come night time, the women would retire to the sleeping compartment they were to share). Michael leant out the open window. The conductor blew his whistle once, before hopping aboard, and from the rear of the train, the guard blew his whistle twice, loud and long, and waved a green flag up and down, up and down. Up ahead, the engine whistled piercingly, the train jerked, then began to move off, the deep booming of exhausted steam from the cylinders very loud. Karim, who had a runnel of tears down each dark cheek, called from the platform, *'Kwaheri Mamemsaba! Kwaheri Bwana Mkubwa!'*

'God bless you!' Keith Pencaitland shouted, as the train drew away. *'Kwaheri! Safari salama!'*

In the compartment, Marjory's eyes were moist. Lady Pencaitland began weeping. Michael sat, grim faced, white around the mouth. It had all been a bit too much.

EPILOGUE

In November 1965 (despite the widespread economic hardship all too evident in Equatoria due to international trade sanctions, exacerbated by the internal security problem), Rhodesia, under a European government, declared her independence from Britain. But the following year an agreement was brokered in London between the British Government, moderate black nationalists from Equatoria, and Ian Blackfell's government. In August 1966, multiracial elections were held, and Equatoria found itself with a black government, a black Prime Minister, and (once the caretaker British Governor had left, almost as quickly as he had arrived) a black President.

But the *Wa Chui* fought on. A moderate, pro-free market government in Namuri was no part of their plan. They desired the imposition of a Marxist proletarian dictatorship, and the seizure and nationalisation of all farms of any size. The Equatorian Armed Forces, still predominantly officered by European settlers' sons, did not stand down. But now, British Army contingents campaigned alongside them, and money was pumped into the country from abroad. This injection of capital, taken together with the ending of international trade sanctions, saw a moderate economic boom occurring in Equatoria. Keith Pencaitland and his family felt justified in having remained in Equatoria, and in South Africa, Michael and Marjory sometimes wondered whether perhaps they ought to have stayed and made a go of it at *Mahali pa Kupumzika*.

But five years later, in 1971, Michael and Marjory were shown to have had the greater foresight, when in Namuri the moderate black government collapsed, mired in corruption scandals, and accused of numerous unfulfilled promises to the majority of black Equatorians. In the elections which followed, the *Wa Chui* at last came to power in Equatoria. The bush war was over. The new regime immediately nationalised the gold and copper mines in the republic, and seized all European owned farmland. Keith Pencaitland and his family were left almost destitute. Had it not been for the welcome that Michael and Marjory gave the family at *Kupumzika* in South Africa, they would have had nowhere to go.

(In time, Keith Hepburn – he had foregone the use of his title and the name that went with it, finding it more of a hindrance in South Africa than not – was to find a position as a farm manager in Natal. Andrew, Marjory's brother, would study conservation and game management at Natal University, and would in due course work for the South African National Parks, based no very great distance from *Kupumzika*, in the Kruger National Park).

Michael's and Marjory's wilderness venture in the Transvaal Lowveld flourished, and after a few years it began to generate a profit. Within less than ten years it had gained an international reputation for excellence. In 1992, the game fence between Timbavati and Klaserie was removed, and the block comprising Klaserie, Timbavati and Umbabat (along with Umbabat's immediate neighbour, Kupumzika Game Reserve) saw the fence with the Kruger National Park removed in 1994 – in the same year that South Africa obtained a black majority government. The major private game reserves were at last part of a vast region incorporating the entire Kruger National Park, a region in which

Epilogue

game could range freely, unimpeded by man-made barriers.

In the South African spring of 1994 (that watershed year in South Africa's history), with the land rapidly greening up under the fresh new rains, Michael and Marjory were out riding. Michael had a rifle slung across his back. He reined in his horse and Marjory did likewise. Michael turned to his wife.

'We've been blessed, haven't we, Darling?' he asked her. 'We live in one of the last few unspoiled regions of Africa, and we have a grandson!'

Michael's and Marjory's son, James Keith Hood, who was twenty-eight years old, had (together with his wife, a South African girl) just had a son of his own, Michael's and Marjory's first grandchild. James was managing the game reserve now, as his father was in his seventies. Marjory, however, who had recently turned sixty, was still managing the domestic staff and the hospitality side of the business (with her daughter-in-law's help).

'Did you believe, when we left Equatoria, and that poor wrecked house, that we would succeed in a new land?' Michael asked Marjory.

'Yes, I knew we would. But sometimes I can still remember *Mahali pa Kupumzika*, and the life we used to know.'

'So can I,' Michael responded. 'I still remember Patrick sometimes, too.'

'I try to remember Patrick before things began to go wrong.'

'So do I. The Patrick I knew at school. My friend Patrick, who invited me to *Mahali pa Kupumzika* – where I met you, my Darling. And look at what we've built. And we have a son, and now, a grandson also, to whom to leave it someday.'

A NOTE TO THE READER

In 1913, my paternal grandfather, aged ten, left Scotland with his two brothers, his two sisters, and his mother, to join his father in the recently declared East Africa Protectorate, the forerunner of what became, in 1920, the Colony of Kenya. His father, my great-grandfather (who had been a tea planter in India), was a pioneer coffee planter in the Protectorate.

Three generations of settler stock, reaching back to the earliest pioneers, were to create legends, a culture, a mindset, which would indelibly mark those of us for whom the colony was home.

For those readers who are familiar with the region, it will immediately be apparent upon which country the geographical framework of this novel is based. But this novel is entirely a work of fiction, and you would seek in vain in the region once known as British East Africa for any recollections of the aristocratic Hepburns who feature in this story, or for any memories among its oldest residents of the central character, Michael Hood.

In telling this story, I have not updated the vocabulary and attitudes that were commonplace in late colonial East African settler society during this period, and the story reflects the cultural assumptions and racial prejudices that were generally held by the European settlers of that time.

Robert Dewar, Lochaber, February 2023.

This book is printed on paper from sustainable sources managed under the Forest Stewardship Council (FSC) scheme.

It has been printed in the UK to reduce transportation miles and their impact upon the environment.

For every new title that Matador publishes, we plant a tree to offset CO_2, partnering with the More Trees scheme.

For more about how Matador offsets its environmental impact, see www.troubador.co.uk/about/